Wolves and Assassins

The Mercenary Trilogy
Book 3

J.W. Webb

Copyright 2019 J.W. Webb. J.W. Webb asserts the moral right to be identified as the author to this work.

All rights reserved. No part of this publication may be reproduced, stored in a retrieval system or transmitted in any form or by any means, electronic, mechanical, photocopying, recording or otherwise without the prior permission of the author:

Acknowledgement for:

John Jarrold for editing

Roger Garland the late Tolkien Artist for the illustrations and map

Ravven for the cover design

Kristen Forbes for Proofreading

Kari Holloway for Book Design

This one's for Sue Bentley, who knows Corin an Fol better than most.

Would you trade your soul to save your life?

The Crimson Lady knows that's the only way to find the man she wants to kill—the mercenary known as Corin an Fol.

Sign up to the JW Webb VIP Lounge newsletter and receive this exciting tale at the door! More details at the back of this book.

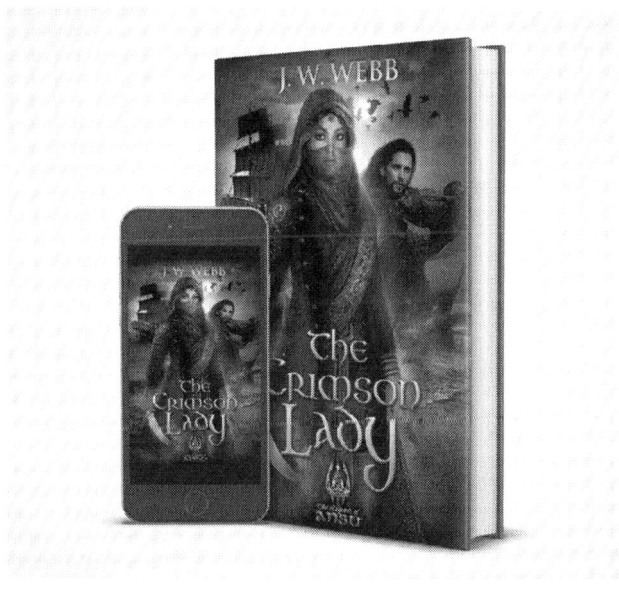

Part One
Outlaws and Rogues

Chapter 1 | The Green-Eyed Killer

Rain lashed the walls as Keel climbed, gloved hand over hand, up toward the tiled roof. The ground below was barely visible. A quick glance revealed the fuzz of thorn bushes, a lane puddling off into the murk, the distant lanterns flickering. Not much purchase here—one slip and he'd be gone, extinguished like those lantern flames in morning. All his grand plans and schemes lost to the void. The thought excited him. Without risk, what was the point? Life without danger and glory was a drab affair. Keel the Killer reveled in both.

He was a good climber, lithe and quick, well balanced. Confident, with twin blades hanging from his back, and three daggers secreted in the sleeves of his sable woolen shirt. He ignored the rain, the gusty wind, instead focusing on heaving his wire-strong body up the wall until he reached the roof tiles and rolled over.

Keel lay still for several minutes, regaining his breath and getting his bearings. The rain washed over him, soaking his clothes. His cheeks stung, nose was running. Cold tonight. Slippery on this rooftop. Crossing it could prove as hazardous as climbing up there; the tiles were weak and crumbly, most covered with moss—he cursed the climate. Port Wind pulled in storms from the sea almost every day, a shithole with one important citizen. The reason why he was here, to pay a visit to the man who owned this roof.

Keel rose carefully, balancing, arms wide, the wind lashing his face and the hood flapping around his legs. He braced, took a furtive step forward, another, then commenced clambering over the tiles. Spider quick, his soft shoes scarcely touching, lest he break one and fall. A long way down, and if he survived the fall, those dogs would be on him. Not a good way to go.

He reached the gable, swung over and dropped to a second roof, which angled down to a balcony overlooking a flagstone courtyard fifty feet below. Keel dropped into the balcony. He smiled, defying the rain, the gusting wind and the chill on his hands and face.

Keel wiped his nose and rubbed his legs, banishing the numbness caused by the long, wet climb. He slipped a dagger from his sleeve and gripped its leather sheath between his teeth. Keel approached the door at the far end of the balcony, latched and boarded against the weather. He carefully pulled back the shutters and worked the latch with deft fingers until it clicked open.

He inched forward, leaned against the door, and pulled it towards him until a crack hinted the room beyond. Curtains. He saw a thick rug strewn across the floor and the smell of lavender candles burning somewhere close. Keel crinkled his nose, pulled the door wider. It creaked, and he froze. Keel stood there in silence, ignored the rain lashing his back until satisfied no one had heard him.

He slipped inside the room and glanced around. A boudoir or office, a bed in the corner but no occupant, a lone oil lamp flickering on a table by the bedside—the candle half burnt through. Keel eased across and slid his gloved fingers over the flame, grinning as the light danced across the walls, casting shadows. His eyes shot to a door at the far end of the room. He approached warily and then leaned against the oak panel, ears listening until he heard the sound of snores rising and falling away again, somewhere in the room beyond.

Keel opened the door slowly. It didn't creak, but the glaring light from candles within made him blink and shield his eyes.

He waited until his vision adjusted, smiling slightly as he saw the shapes beneath huddled in blankets. A woman lay there, her bare arms slung across a bigger shape—her lover. Terini Dal, the governor of this forsaken city, and the man Keel sought.

He spat the dagger into a fist and crept toward the bed. He made no noise, but the woman opened her eyes. She made a soft mewling sound but Keel sliced her throat before that scream could resonate. He watched her shudder, the eyes glaze over, her naked body twitch and then settle. *Too bad . . .*

The dead girl's lover stirred, opened his eyes and then froze as Keel's dagger pricked his neck. "Recognize me?" Keel smiled slightly—vanity had always been his weakness.

The governor shook his head. Then he noticed his lover, her blood seeping beside him, and his eyes widened. "Sorry about that," Keel whispered in his ear. "Needs must—she was about to scream, and I don't want to wake your guards. They would prove a distraction and I need your full cooperation." The man blinked, so Keel poked the steel point deeper into his neck.

"I want some answers, then I'll let you be," he said. "Though if you so much as grunt for help, I'll slice off your manhood. I've done worse, believe me." Keel saw the horror on the man's face and nodded slowly. "Good—*that's good.* You're a sensible man" Keel's eyes hovered over the blood staining the blankets, seeping crimson, pooling on the floor, the dead girl's face already ashen gray. He removed the dripping dagger and it held above the governor's head.

"I heard the king is in town?" Keel smiled again. "Is that true?" The man stared at him in glazed horror, so Keel slapped his face hard and then reached down and squeezed his groin. He spun the dagger through his finger's deftly as Port Wind's most important citizen coughed and buckled over in pain.

"I'm waiting for an answer," Keel said.

"He is here—yes!"

"And you are his foremost adviser in this town—Terni Dal?"

"*Terini* Dal. Yes, the governor—the king trusts my word."

"Excellent." Keel smiled. "That means you know where he can be found, where he stays during visits to the coast. Heh, Turnip Dal?"

"Cragowan Castle—ten miles north." Terini Dal blinked. "He has many guards, you'll never reach him."

"Of course, I'll reach him." Keel, irritated, slapped that face again. "Can you not guess who I am?"

Terini's face paled and he nodded. "Keel the Knife."

"Some folk call me that." Keel glanced down at the blood and mess staining the floor. Shame, the girl had been pretty. A wasted opportunity. "Cragowan Castle." Keel pinned the governor with his gaze. "Why haven't I heard of such a place? Castles are scarce is this region."

"It's more of a manor house," Terini Dal said. "A hunting lodge—there's a large forest nearby."

"The Wood between the Waters," Keel said, nodding. "This castle's on the coast road then?"

"The Reln Highway, yes." Terini Dal nodded again, his bloodshot eyes flicked to the girl at his side and blinked back tears.

Keel smiled seeing that. "I doubt you loved that servant wench, Governor—so don't look so glum. Your lady wife was in Calprissa last week. I saw her in the market. Ugly as a sow, so I guess while she's away you get to play." He lowered the dagger again.

"Please!"

"Sorry, I was distracted," Keel said. "To work! Do I need to heat this blade?"

"I told you where King Nogel is . . . please, no!" Dal Terini gasped as Keel rested the flat of the blade against the governor's inner thigh.

"This king likes to hunt?"

"Of course, what king doesn't?"

"How many attendants?" Keel cut into the flesh, making a shallow slice.

"A score . . . maybe more." Dal Terini blinked again. "Please . . . I . . ." Keel turned sharply, hearing the sound of boots shuffling somewhere outside the room.

"Guards must have—"

"—Guess so." Keel buried the dagger in Terini's throat, twisted the blade and then slid it free. "Sorry about that, Governor. Time I made myself scarce."

Keel fastidiously wiped the weapon clean on a handkerchief retrieved from his pocket. Once satisfied, he stowed the dagger in his belt and crept toward the door as the footsteps became louder outside.

A knock. "My lord, is all well?"

"What's up?" Keel held the bloodstained handkerchief to his mouth, muffling his voice. "Why have you woken me?"

"An intruder's been spotted outside the gates."

Keel pulled a face. Another assassin—what were the chances of that?

"Well, *you idiot*—deal with the rogue and then report back!"

"My lord . . . ?"

Keel feigned a coughing fit until the guard got the hint and excused himself, saying he'd return in a moment with news of what had happened. Keel waited for the sound of retreating footsteps and then pushed the door wide and leaped after the guard, plunging his dagger into the man's back while gripping his mouth with his free hand. He stabbed three times and lowered the corpse to the floor.

Past time I wasn't here.

Keel stowed the dagger and reached back, easing a sword into both of his hands. He heard voices below—the other guards coming to check on their master. A man stepped into the corridor, blinked. Keel's sword sliced across his chest and he tumbled forward. Keel skipped past and dispatched the guard with a backwards twist of the blade.

A second man appeared, saw his comrades' bodies and yelled. Keel stabbed into his guts and left him screaming and rolling. "Noisy bastard!" Keel kicked the body as his face flushed hot with anger. He didn't like mistakes, hadn't wanted to wake the entire fucking household.

Ten minutes later, and with another six corpses dripping blood in hallways and doors, Keel found the scullery—and after scampering among pots, an exit to the walled gardens beyond. There were shouts and the sounds of steel everywhere in the house above. They'd be on him in seconds if he lingered here. Keel hovered for a moment, caught between the dread of being apprehended and the excitement of the chase.

Then, as he heard the scullery door kicked open and saw the first face appear, Keel flitted through the soaking plants and shrubs and vaulted the wall, dropping silently into the foggy street beyond. He laughed deliriously as he heard the dogs growl and snap and the angry voices yelling behind them.

"You're no match for Keel the Knife," he shouted before sprinting off beyond the shadows and lanterns.

Keel guided his stolen horse into a small hamlet, comprising several low-roofed houses, a smithy and a coaching inn the following evening. He rode towards the inn, its torchlight welcoming as dusk stole the light and the woods closed in upon the lane.

Keel dismounted, tied the horse to a rail, and then dusted down his hands and made for the door. He glanced through the smoky windows, seeing people hunched inside. The door swung open and a hard-faced man glared at him.

"Where the fuck have you been?" Hagan Delmorier said.

***

King Nogel of Kelwyn sat his horse and smiled at the rain, ignoring the words of warning issued from his oldest friend. Rowen was such a worrier.

"I have to advise against this, Highness," Lord Rowen Staveport sat his horse, cloak drenched and helmet squeezing his narrow face into an expression of abject misery.

The king smiled. *Poor Rowen.* The loyal old retainer would much rather be back at the hearthside, a large flagon of mead in his fists. Not for him the hunt in this weather. The other men were younger, keen as their king—all anxious to make a name for themselves. Twenty riders, each soaked to the skin, but their smiles warm as summer sunshine.

"Stop being an old fart, Lord Rowen," young Tamersane said, as his brother Yail cuffed his ear. Lord Staveport glared at the pair of them. Rascals, and cheeky little sods at that. The king loved them. They reminded him of his youth, those carefree sunny days lost so long ago.

"It's not the weather that concerns me," Lord Staveport said to his king, after rewarding the younger men with another frosty glance. "Highness, we are too close to the border. Reln is scarce thirty miles from here."

King Nogel's smile ran away from his face. "And why should that be a concern, Rowen? Are we not all loyal vassals to our High King, up there?"

Lord Staveport chewed his moustache, unwilling to say what he was thinking.

"Ugh, man—you worry overmuch," King Nogel said. He smiled at the other riders. "You lot—it will be dark inside an hour; I suggest you round up some quarry so we can have a healthy feast tonight. Lord Staveport here is missing his place by the hearth."

"Missing his tipple, you mean." Fair-haired Tamersane grinned and urged his mount to follow his companions deeper into the gloom of the forest.

"You indulge that pup," Lord Staveport said.

"True," King Nogel said, wiping the rain from his gloves. "But Tam reminds of myself when I was that age. A joker, whereas his brother is more of a brooder, as was mine."

"Yail Tolranna is the better man," Lord Staveport said, watching the riders fade beneath the trees. "That pretty boy Tamersane will waste himself on drink and loose women. Calls himself a poet, the fool."

"Maybe so," King Nogel said, "but there are worse perils in this life, are there not, Rowen? Let's allow those boys their fun while you and I get back to Cragowan before this fading light fails us."

An hour later, as rain beaded and streamed against the opaque windows, King Nogel and his most-trusted retainer shared a flask of brandy by the fire, the king's favorite hounds stretched out at his feet. Nogel smiled as he stroked the nearest one's shaggy head.

"This feels good, old friend," the king said, warming his hands. Early summer and yet so chilly in these north-western parts. Damp and cold. Too close to Kelthaine. That land was famous for its gloomy weather, not to mention its rulers who resembled the climate. "I've been saddled to that bloody throne for months," Nogel said. "I needed this excursion."

"There are other hunting lodges, Highness."

"I like this one," King Nogel said. "Besides, it's a long time since last we rode this country. A neglected corner—my subjects deserve better."

"That dreadful little man Dal Terini would prefer you stay away," Lord Staveport said. "That one likes to pretend he's the ruler in this region."

"Terini's a turd—so what?" Nogel stroked the other hound until it rolled over and he scratched its belly. "Petty baron, would-be despot and trade highwayman. But it's hard finding good administrators out here. The man handles taxes and tariffs well enough. I see no need to replace him."

Lord Staveport shrugged and wrapped his bony fingers around his flask. He took a sip and sighed. "I just don't think we should be here, Highness. Not after what you said to that conniver up in Kella City."

"I don't fear Caswallon," Nogel snapped, irritated by the subject.

"Well, you should." Lord Staveport gave him look for look. "The man's dangerous as a viper, and no friend of yours."

"True enough. He is a snake in the grass," Nogel said. "Needs a heavy boot stamping down on his scrawny neck. Caswallon's a disgrace."

"Caswallon's an accomplished player," Lord Staveport said, knotting is brows. "A careful schemer with a black soul. He doesn't like you, Highness. Never did—but now he fears you too. That makes him more dangerous than ever."

"Because I alone chose to accuse him of hoodwinking Kelsalion?" King Nogel tipped his beacon and slurped a large gulp of ale, slamming the mug down next to the brandy flask on the table. "The High King's lost, Rowen. Kelsalion fell apart when his queen died in that storm off Fol."

"Not everyone is a strong as you, Highness," Lord Staveport said.

A cloud passed over Nogel's vision. He thought of his own beloved queen—Cailine, and the last time he'd seen her smile, before the goddess took her from him.

"Kelsalion lost his heir as well as the queen," Nogel said. "Hard for any ruler—let alone a descendant of Kell whose line has remained unbroken for a thousand years until now. But the Four Kingdoms need a strong ruler, else worms like Caswallon become too prominent. Kelsalion fails his people."

"You too, are also descended from Kell through Wynna's line, Highness."

"I don't need to be reminded of that, Rowen." King Nogel downed a shot of brandy and wiped his mouth. "Enough, old friend. I tire of this conversation. You're like a dog with a favorite bone—you never quit chewing."

"Nor will I until you come to your senses and ride back to Wynais," Lord Rowen Staveport said. "You insulted and scared Kelsalion's high councilor—the only man with any power in Kelthaine now that the High King's mind is crumbling. Caswallon has spies in this part of the world. And assassins, I dare say—a stray arrow while hunting can be easily fobbed off as an accident."

"You're a paranoid old fool, Rowen." The king folded his hands behind his neck and yawned. "And you worry too much, it'll be the death of you. I am King of Kelwyn, and this damp forgotten corner is part of my domain. I rule here! I'll not creep in the dark like a whipped cur at nightfall. Enough of this nonsense, else my patience fades."

The king looked up as sudden shouting and a clash of hoof on flagstones announced the company returning from the hunt.

"Not before time," Lord Staveport grumbled. "Let's hope they caught more than rabbits."

***

Hagan watched Keel take a seat across the table, the hood pulled down over his face. The hunter had blood stains on his hands, Hagan noted. He narrowed his gaze and stared hard at the other man until Keel caught his glance.

"I asked you a question," Hagan said. "We've been waiting here for hours—not very sensible with all these king's men infesting this area."

"And you are . . .?" Keel's green eyes flashed at Hagan like jade daggers. A handsome face, yet disturbing—this villain Keel had something of the night about him.

"You know who I am. We met last week. Name's Hagan."

"The renegade Morwellan Caswallon mentioned." Keel yawned as though bored. "Yes, I remember, but so what? You're just another dog-turd mercenary." Keel yawned again, theatrically this time, his green gaze on Hagan who refused to be goaded, despite the shiver along his spine. Hagan knew this man's reputation.

"I need a drink," Keel said. "Get me ale." He turned and shouted to the proprietor, currently busy serving locals in the common room. Hagan and company were seated in the snug, a low fire burning and trapping smoke in the room, the thick aroma of peat stinging nostrils and eyes.

"Who's he think he is?" Hagan muttered, his eyes still pinned on Keel. A struggle to hold his temper, but why tempt the fates? Postin the Giant shuffled uneasily beside him, as did Kulvin the Bowyer, both uncomfortable now Keel was back amongst them.

Once supplied with ale, Keel turned to survey the others. He smiled briefly at Hagan. "The contact said you were part of an outlaw band in Permio—a common brigand but useful with a blade. A peasant from the slums of Vangaris."

"You want to find out how useful?" Hagan rose from his seat, his face flushed hot, the cup spilling ale. His temper had gotten the best of him. "I'm of noble stock!" Keel's green eyes showed wry humor. The smaller man remained seated, arms folded neatly.

Confident bastard.

"You are not in my class, Morwellan," Keel said. "So sit down and shut the fuck up." His cold green eyes pinned Hagan's until the taller man shrugged and slumped back in his chair, this not being the time nor place to draw attention to themselves.

"We are nine," Hagan said. "Against how many—over a hundred? It would help if we communicated and shared our thoughts."

"Let Keel talk," Postin belched the words out. Hagan glanced at the brute seated beside him. Over seven feet tall and ugly as a cow's behind. The missing right ear and purple rope scar on his neck only added to the smoldering glare from those bloodshot eyes. A local thug and bully, Hagan suspected. Rumored lethal with that poll-axe resting against the wall. Nasty looking weapon.

Half hammer, half axe, and longer than its owner. The rest of the crew were almost as bad. Fair to say that Hagan didn't rate any of his new companions much.

"So . . . talk." Hagan smiled at Keel and imagined a blade twisting into that handsome face.

Keel ignored his glance and shrugged. "Nine against the king—they should make a song about us," he said. "A tale of murder, villainy and derring do."

"Quite the joker, aren't you?" Hagan said.

"I find this existence of ours humorous at times," Keel said. "But while you simpleton fools were cozy inside this den sipping ale, I was out gleaning information. I know where Nogel's staying."

"And how did you find that out?" Hagan asked. They'd been watching the roads either side of Port Wind to no avail—seen soldiers riding past at regular intervals but no sign of Kelwyn's robust ruler.

"The district governor told me."

"What?" Hagan stood up again, spilling more ale.

"Before I cut his throat."

"Are you insane? You'll bring the hornets' nest down on our heads." Keel ignored his gaze again so Hagan took to his seat, his face flushed by hearth and rage. This madman would prove the death of him.

"Cragowan Castle," Keel said, sipping a second ale hastily delivered by the sweating innkeep. "Close by—a hunting lodge of sorts."

"I know of it," whip-lean Kulvin the Bowyer said. "'Tis scarce five miles north east of here, hidden by the woods—I used to poach game on the grounds, that and fish."

"How *quaint*," Keel said, his sharp green gaze flicking to where the innkeep hovered outside.

"I have supper for you," the man said, his brown eyes twitchy.

"Bring it in here," Keel told him, and then started blinking rapidly to mock the innkeep.

"The dining area is by the kitchens," the patron said, rubbing his hands together, his round face red and awkward. "That's where we serve the food."

"We'll have ours in here," Keel said, blinking again. "And more of your shite ale." The innkeep stared at him, blinked, and then nodded and closed the snug door behind him.

"Charming," Hagan said. "Now the roads will be filled with soldiers looking for the governor's murderer."

"So they won't be looking in the forest—will they?" Keel said as though addressing an infant. "And, I prefer the term *assassin*," Keel said. "Has a certain elegance."

"You sure he's there?" Kulvin asked, chewing at his meat.

"Him and his people—a score of idle nobles, no more," Keel said. "The governor's soldiers are all garrisoned around Port Wind. King Nogel won't get word from them any time soon. The guard captains will let the king be, hoping he returns to Wynais soon so they can smooth over the incident, then report it when he's far away. What I'd do."

"Well, what do we do?" Big Postin yawned and stretched his huge arms behind his back. "All this talking makes a man thirsty, but it don't get us any richer. The *Big Man* in Kella wants results—a head in a sack. I've heard he's tight with his coffers."

"Shut up, fat boy," Keel said, his green eyes fixed on Postin until the huge man looked away. "No one's cutting off the king's head and sending it anywhere—what, are you even stupider than you look?"

Hagan glanced at Postin, whose face was red and fit to burst. But the man said nothing, Keel having a hold over all these brigands. Hagan would have to watch Keel closer than ever. The man was a psychopath.

"An accident then," Hagan said, sipping his brew. "Hunting can prove hazardous."

Keel smiled. "The folly of kings." He stood up and dusted down his tunic. Outside, the rain lashed against the windows and tree branches cast shadows like creeping fingers over the lane. The lantern creaked on its chain, swaying in the wind. "Foul out there," Keel said. "Time we got moving."

Chapter 2 | Krugan's Gang

It could have been worse, though not much. Corin squinted. Hot sun, stinking street, and half a dozen thugs standing over him. His swords were gone, and his hands lashed cruelly behind his back. They were kicking him without much interest. Just another day in the desert.

Why was he here? Trussed up like a hog on market day in this shit-pot of a town. *Town* was generous—more like a shitty little sprawl of hovels wedged deep in a rock-strewn valley renowned for its biting flies. Some of these damned insects had turned up for the occasion and were taking chunks out of Corin's face. Amazing how one small mistake can mess up your day.

"I'm not swinging from that," Corin had told Ugami, who had his legs, while Shemala's grubby fingers tugged his ears. They'd ignored him, stripped Corin down to his breeches and lashed his wrists together on one end of the rope. Then Ugami cheerfully tossed the other end over a transom and hoisted Corin up until his kicking bare feet swung over their heads.

Shemala found a sharp stave and commenced poking the soles of his feet. This awarded a lot of smiles and general appreciation. Not much entertainment down here. Simple pleasures for simple folk.

A tall figure strode into view through the swelter and haze of a deep desert afternoon in Permio, Corin's favorite place.

You must be Krugan the Cruel.

The men parted to let the tall one approach. The stick stabbed his feet, and Corin kept lifting his legs to avoid the worst of it. The flies settled around his face, one entered his mouth. He spat it out with what little spittle he still retained.

In between turns, Corin watched Krugan, now grinning up at him. Robes and shemagh, crimson sash which meant he'd bribed the boys in Sedinadola to turn a blind eye. Crimson was the sultan's color, used by his elite guard. The sash ensured they'd leave him be. Krugan was a bandit through and through. Hook-nosed and raffish, a blue silk patch covering his left eye, two curved blades swinging from his studded belt, and a jeweled dagger thrust between. Krugan also wore a thick gold chain around his neck, with a pendant resembling some horned beast Corin had never seen. The bandit's teeth were good, flashing white in the sun as Krugan grinned up at his catch.

"You work for the wrong person," the bandit said, as Shemala and Ugami parted to let him through. "You could have approached me any time, Longsword—I pay better than most and don't begrudge mercenaries having their share. We've all a job to do. Besides, I sided with the sultan during the war—so we were allies then."

"Happy for you," Corin spat the words out, and winced as the stave poked his instep again.

This Krugan raided a village now and then, butchered a few unfortunates, fondled the odd lass and stole stuff. Nothing untoward; business as usual in the arid wilderness surrounding the sultan's cities. Corin had served down here during the Second Permian War. He knew the drill, steel being the only currency bar gold. But the stabbing stick wasn't welcome, nor was the rough hemp cutting deeper into his wrists, as he hung and swung half-naked and filthy in the marketplace, a score of grubby traders watching on and placing bets behind Krugan's team.

"Silon paid you to murder me—yes?" Krugan's one eye was baleful and sharp as an eagle's. Corin wondered how long this charade would continue before the brigand cut his throat. Krugan wasn't known for his patience. "I'm right, aren't I?"

Corin swung about a bit and feigned a yawn. He hoisted his knees, making it harder for Shemala to get him with that bloody stick. It was hotter than a camel's hump this afternoon and he really needed a beer, but the ale was crap down here, as was everything else.

"Just do for me and move on," Corin croaked, and then swung wide as the stick found his feet again. This was getting tedious. Krugan showed his dazzling smile again, and slid the ornate dagger from his belt. He motioned Shemala to lower Corin until his sore bleeding feet impacted the cobbled street of the market square with a thud.

"As you wish," Krugan nodded his men to hold their captive steady. "You are clearly too stupid to know anything useful." Krugan handed his jeweled dagger over to the big oaf behind Corin. "Ugami, cut this bastard's throat and leave him for the dogs. It's time we got moving, lest Barakani's people find us."

Ugami grinned and readied the knife. Corin winked at him. "On reflection"—he feigned that yawn again— "I probably should have hidden that stolen gold better."

"Nice try." Krugan smiled but Ugami's knife hand froze. "Desperate ploy, and somewhat unimaginative."

"What if he's telling the truth?" Ugami said. "Perhaps I can carve it out of him?"

"No, he's bluffing," Krugan said. "If there was gold around here, I would know about it."

"Silon's secret stash." Corin coughed up blood. "He had me help him hide it in the desert right after the war. I took a pony, two saddle bags, and stowed the gold in a cave near here. *Insurance*, Silon told me, in case things turn wobbly."

Krugan shook his head. "Feeble lies. Past time I cut out your liver and fed it to the vultures."

"I could lead you there," Corin said, his eyes on the dagger inching toward his throat. "Show you the stash, and then you can cut out my liver—if not satisfied with the gold. Or I can help you kill that merchant up in 'Sarfe."

"Betray your master?" Krugan shook his head slowly, but at least he'd lowered the knife, a small hint of curiosity gleaming in his single eye. *Greed will win through. Hold your nerve.*

"Silon ditched me in it," Corin said. "And not for the first time. Five months I've worked for that bastard, with little to show. I even saved his daughter's life, and for a reward he sends me down here to protect his investments. Happy to see me gutted while he sits up there counting his coffers."

"You're expendable." Krugan shrugged. "As are all your kind. But I do see your point, and I've heard you've a rare skill with that oversized blade."

"I've two swords," Corin said. "Where are they?"

"Safely bestowed in my camp up in the hills." Krugan pointed south to a dark line of ridges.

"The cave is close by." Corin smiled his winning smile and got a kick in the balls from Ugami for a reward. "Not far from your camp—a brief detour, no more." He clenched his teeth and swallowed the pain. *Can't show weakness here.*

"We should check it out and kill him afterwards," Ugami said. "Nothing to lose."

"Nothing to lose," Corin repeated, nodding sagely. The men stared at him as though he'd lost his mind. Perhaps he had, hard to tell in this desert sun.

"So you say." Krugan rubbed his chin.

"I get you that gold," Corin said, carefully, "and after you've seen it and you're satisfied, then you let me go, and I kill Silon for you."

"You hate him that much?"

"I'm a mercenary—as soon gut him open as anyone."

"It's a reasonable suggestion," Krugan said. "Free him, Ugami. We'll let this longsword lead us to his hide. If there's nothing there, I'll drill a hole in his belly and pull his guts out, leave him for the jackals and buzzards."

"Sounds fair enough." Corin nodded as Ugami unlashed him from the rope.

"How far?" Krugan yelled from behind.

"A mile—no more," said Corin. "It's just up this ridge." *And just beyond that...*

His feet dragged over the dirt as the donkey clumped up the climb. Krugan and his men had horses. Their plan was the donkey would be used to carry back the gold, Corin not needing a second ride. He'd either be hurrying about his next task or sitting in the sun with a hole drilled in his belly, the buzzards circling above.

Ugami held the donkey's reins as well as his own beast's. The big brigand grinned at Corin whenever he looked that way. Corin smiled back. *Not long now, big fellow.*

The hill flattened out, revealing a long ridge of crumbled stone, here and there were splits and chasms with deep drops to the valley below. "I'll need to dismount," Corin yelled back to Krugan. Ugami yanked the donkey's reins and the smaller mount hee-hawed and kicked, almost pitching Corin from the whicker saddle.

"You're staying put," Ugami said.

"I wasn't addressing you, turd-face" Corin said, and ducked low as Ugami switched the beast with his riding crop, narrowly missing Corin's face. The donkey brayed again. Krugan rode up alongside them, the other four men close behind.

"What you say?" Krugan spat in the dust.

"The cave is up there, so I need to climb those rocks." Corin hinted the closest cluster of boulders arranged in a haphazard pile. "Can't do that while lashed to this fucking nag." They stared at him for a moment, and then Krugan nodded.

"Untie him from the saddle," the leader said. Ugami complied with a scowl. "Follow him close, Ugami. You too Shemala, any nonsense, gut him from behind."

"Be my pleasure," Ugami said.

Corin slid from the donkey and almost fell flat on his face. He wobbled and straitened, head throbbing, and crutch burning from the constant rubbing. Small details to help focus the mind. Survival then vengeance. He hobbled toward the rocks and then reached up, pulling himself higher. A short climb. Ugami and Shemala pulled themselves up behind. Corin waited for them at the top.

"Come on, fat boys." Corin grinned as they grumbled and sweated into view. "Just around this corner." He watched as Shemala crested the top, and Ugami turned quickly to help him.

It's all about timing in this life. Good timing.

The moment Ugami's attention was distracted, Corin barreled his bones into the huge man's midriff, knocking him forward into Shemala, who in turn was buffeted off the rock, falling with a crash below. Judging by the short scream, he didn't land well. One less to worry about.

Corin kicked Ugami's rump before he could turn about, knocking him off balance, and ran like a mad fool, jumping from boulder to boulder, a sideways glance revealing Ugami struggling behind. Corin smiled; it helped to do your homework. Research was seldom wasted time. He rounded the corner and jumped . . .

A long fall—perhaps forty foot—and then crashing into the river, his body jarring on the slippery rocks, bruising bones and twisting his ankle, half drowning as the tepid water engulfed him. He surfaced and spat water, swam over to the far bank, rose and hobbled up, staggering and aching from head to toe. From somewhere behind and above, Corin heard shouts, and looking back up that ridge he could see Ugami's silhouette, the hands grasped by his sides.

Krugan won't be happy with you, lardy.

Now it was time to implement phase two of his plan. Corin hobbled along the river bank until he found the track he'd discovered last week leading further into the wilderness. Krugan would return with dogs, so he'd keep going until nightfall and then he'd change direction, making for the one place they wouldn't expect.

***

Krugan watched the campfire flames as he sucked at his pipe. High above, a white moon rode the night sky beside two stars. It was chilly, and the desert chief had his blanket wrapped close around his shoulders. Ugami and the others were still missing. They should have been back by now, and he should be hearing those dogs.

He was angry with himself—and Ugami—for letting the northerner trick them. He'd have Corin's eyes for that, then slice him lengthways from belly to throat with his heated knife. *But where were they?*

An hour passed, the night wore on. Cold, the stars and moon his only companions, and somewhere far away, the eerie cry of a desert fox. Krugan was tired, and about to doze off, when Ugami's bulk shuffled into camp, followed by the shapes of his other scouts.

"Where is he?" Krugan asked. "And where are my fucking dogs?"

"Gone, and lost," Ugami said. "The beasts took the scent, but disappeared somewhere beyond that wadi. We found footsteps by the bank, so maybe he took a track. Followed that for an hour or two, but it led back to that ridge where Shemala died."

"You should have died there too." Krugan spat tobacco on the ground. He rolled from his blanket and kicked the fire, sending sparks across the camp ground. Most of the men were huddled in blankets sleeping, or drowsy after their evening smokes.

"Don't fret." Ugami loomed close. "The dogs will come back soon enough, and we can resume the hunt at sun up. I mean, it's not like there's anywhere he can hide out here."

"True enough." Krugan coughed. He'd smoked too much tonight and that was Corin's fault too. "We'll catch up with him in the morning. Let me know when the dogs get back." He rolled over again and tried to rest.

***

Those dogs were yelping and growling like mad things. The pit had done its job. Hastily dug with grubby fingers, and just deep enough to ensure they stayed in there for several hours. It was amazing what you could get done with just bare hands when there was a pack of toothy hounds on your trail. The hole had already existed of course—he'd known it was there and had only to widen it and then block the top with an adjacent rock. They'd dig their way out by morning, but that was small concern.

Months of scouting had given him sound knowledge of almost every nook and cleft, lone tree, and river wadi in this godsforsaken corner of the vast Permio Desert. He'd scouted Krugan's camp several times over the last few weeks, taking note of their number, defenses and such. The hide lay at the far end of the same hills where his imaginary gold was hidden.

Corin clambered through those hills as best he could, exhausted, his ankle screaming at him, and his entire body aching and shivering with cold. How he loved the desert—roasts you during the day and then freezes you at night, and him still wet too.

Corin stopped for a moment, resting against a scrubby bush. He could see firelight in the distance, and the odd lantern flickering—half a mile south of his position. It would be dawn in an hour, so he needed to act fast. Pain was irrelevant. Corin needed his swords. A vest or shirt would be good too.

He staggered on across the ridge, hobbling, skipping—he found a stick and used it to aid his passage, half pole vaulting himself forward to pick up speed. The lights were nearer, a hundred yards or so. Corin glimpsed a stockade, saw the horses standing silent, the odd steam of breath and shuffle announcing their closeness. Beyond the horses stood a scatter of tents, small and pointed, a larger one nearest the fire. That would be Krugan's. Common sense—the leader has to have the biggest tent.

Corin approached the camp, stopping in a gap where the last boulders awarded some cover. His night vision allowed a reasonable study. Corin knew Krugan's gang numbered around twenty, and they weren't all here. The numbers didn't matter as long as they remained sleeping. He saw one guard, and half smiled as he recognized Ugami. Doubtless a punishment post for losing the northerner.

The big man leaned against a spear, using its base to poke the dying embers of the fire. He was preoccupied, either fighting sleep or lost in thought. Corin shuffled close. A horse stirred, another. Ugami looked across and Corin froze, the moon silhouetting his position helpfully. But Ugami turned away and yawned. Corin, after letting out a long, slow sigh of relief, crept closer.

He saw a fist-sized rock, picked it up, and smiled again. Ugami turned, and then grunted as the rock impacted his face. Corin struck again, and then a third time, and Ugami dropped to his knees. Corin kicked him in the face as hard as he could with a dodgy ankle.

Ugami sprawled face first. Corin almost fell on top of him, the kick having unbalanced him. He reached down for Ugami's belt. Ugami was stirring, so Corin retrieved the brute's curved dagger from his belt and sliced the steel across his throat. Ugami gurgled, thrashed, and lay still.

Corin glanced around the camp. The horses stirred again, uneasy. But there was no other sound, except the distant cry of an owl hunting beneath the desert moon. He glanced up at the sky, and for the briefest instant glimpsed a figure riding high above. A rider, a host of dogs running behind, and the sound of distant horns.

Corin blinked and the vision had gone. He cursed. He needed water and rest, lest he start to lose it altogether. Ghostly visions weren't a good sign. Knife in hand, Corin hobbled to the largest tent. He crouched low, untied the flap, and peeked within. He was right. Krugan lay snoring, an arm sprawled around a girl. Corin guessed she was a slave—when she opened her eyes and saw him, she froze but kept her mouth shut. Corin winked at her.

The girl nodded and started sliding out from the cot. Corin tore his glance from her naked limbs and instead focused on the lone table with Clouter leaning against it, and Biter lying on top. Both swords were sheathed.

"My swords," Corin whispered to the girl, who nodded. She stood before him naked, showing no sign of fear, her face half hidden by the dark.

"Let me kill him," the girl breathed the words, her voice deep and husky.

Corin nodded slowly. "Do it quietly." He tossed the dagger over and she snatched it deftly with her left hand. The girl kneeled next to the sleeping man. Her free hand shot out and covered his mouth. Krugan's eyes opened. He blinked once, then the knife came down, piercing his right eye and killing him instantly.

The girl rose gracefully, the knife dripping Krugan's blood on the rug at her feet. "That felt good," she said, as Corin strapped Clouter to his back. "Are you going to kill the others?"

"There are too many," Corin said, thrusting Biter, the one-edged short sword—"saex" they called it in the north—into the spare scabbard hanging from his belt. "Besides," Corin added, "I've no grudge with those men. Only the leader."

"Well, I do," she said, slipping into a shift that clung to her figure, leaving her dark legs and arms free. She found some boots and slipped them on. Corin lifted the flap. Still no movement outside.

"Be light soon," he said. "Best I get going."

"You're not leaving me here."

"I wasn't planning on company," Corin said. "I'm not feeling my best—need to lie low for a time, once I've stolen a nag and got the fuck away."

"I'll help you with that," she said, and without further word slipped beneath the tent flap and glided off toward the horses. Corin followed her, feeling lightheaded and giddy.

The girl whispered to the beasts as she approached, calming them. She flashed him a grin as she untied the reins and freed every beast save two.

"You look like shit," she said as Corin staggered toward her. "Drink this." She tossed him a gourd she'd purloined from a saddle bag. Corin pulled the cork and gulped down the brackish contents. Stale water had never tasted so good.

"Better?"

"Much." Corin grunted thanks and hoisted himself up onto the nearest horse's back. It snorted at him, and Corin laughed when he recognized Thunderhoof, his war stallion, a gift from his employer's daughter. Long story.

"I thought that bastard had sold you," Corin said, patting the big horse's mane.

"You two acquainted?" The girl flashed that grin again.

"He's a gift from someone I know. Raleenian war horse."

"Nice gift," she said, and then flicked her glance across to the nearest tent. A man stood there, his jaw dropping in alarm. "I think it's time we left," she said, as the man yelled and other figures shuffled into view.

Corin nodded and urged Thunderhoof to canter down from the camp, the other horse running alongside with the dark-eyed girl riding at ease. Her name was Kara, he learned later that day.

Chapter 3 | Forest and Tavern

Hagan watched as the man fumbled with his drawstrings in the rain. Clearly drunk, he seemed to take forever to attend to the business. He stood leaning against the door, lean frame draped in an expensive blue-dyed leather cloak of a young nobleman, his other hand gripping a tankard, the frothy contents spilling out.

Tosser.

Hagan despised men like this. Rich boys who'd inherited a cozy life of hunting and wenching, their fathers having doted on them. He recognized the blonde mop of hair as belonging to Lord Tamersane, once a petty noble of Port Wind but now one of the king's favorites together with his older brother, the more dependable Yail Tolranna.

So easy to just walk up and slit that idiot's throat. But that wasn't their task today. Keel had been explicit about what he'd do to anyone who gave away their position. This had to look like an accident, so corpses strewn around the manor house might make folk a tad suspicious.

The blonde noble finished his business and almost fell back through the door; the glow of warmth and firelight beyond made Hagan hate him all the more. Standing out here in the cold rain, almost he missed the desert—easy to forget that relentless heat, the filth, stench and squalor while you're cold and soaked to the bone. *Perhaps I should go back there.*

Keel wanted to watch and wait, assess their habits—these king's men. No immediate action to be taken. *This needs careful planning.*

Sly Keel liked things done in a certain way. Reputation seemed to matter more than it should to that one. Were it down to Hagan, he'd find a way inside, murder King Nogel, and vanish. Take the money and be gone. Who cared what people thought?

But Caswallon, that treacherous schemer way up in Kella City, had told Keel that on no count should any blame point his way. Keel had promised the High King's councilor their utmost discretion. Who was Hagan to argue with that?

But Hagan didn't like Keel. Worse than that was the dread he had of the man. Hagan had never feared anyone in his life, even as a boy he'd been a fighter. Tough and self-reliant—something that had always given him an edge. A survivor. That and the bitterness of his banishment from home. The resentment ran deep. Morwella had forsaken Hagan Delmorier. Only one man had bested Hagan, and that was something he would address when next they met. The world wasn't so big for men such as them. Hagan knew he'd encounter Corin an Fol again. He'd bide his time until then.

But the green-eyed killer leading this motley crew was different. Hagan knew very little about Keel. The middleman and broker acting out Caswallon's wishes. Trusted by the Big Man up there. The other rogues were shit scared of him; even big dumb Postin couldn't face the man without a flinch. Keel had a hold on everyone, and Hagan hated to admit to himself he felt the same way. The man was uncanny, crueler than most, and the gleam in those jade eyes hinted madness. Keel could creep up on you at any time, then disappear again, only to turn up later just when someone mentioned his name, and always in whispers, a knife in his hand.

So when Keel had said they were going to stake out the manor house and spend all night doing it, Hagan had just shrugged away his objections. It was almost dawn and as far as he could tell, they'd learned bugger all. Except those high-born shitheads inside were having a grand old time.

A soft sound behind him. Hagan turned, slowly. He chewed his lip as Keel blurred into view, a half smile on the killer's handsome face. "Your face is longer than my hounds, Morwellan," Keel said, his green gaze on the door where the revelers could be seen, shadowy shapes moving inside. "Enjoyed the night, did we?"

I'm sure you did, creeping around in the bushes is most likely your preferred pastime. He forced a shrug. "As long as it achieved something."

"Do you doubt me, Hagan?"

"No, I'm sure you have your reasons for spending an entire night out in the rain." He tried in vain not to sound bitter.

"You're not a simple as those other fools, Morwellan," Keel eyed him closely. Too closely, thought Hagan. That green gaze was lizard-cold. "This has to be done right. With precision and finesse. A good kill is an art, my gloomy friend."

"I prefer hearing the gold jingle in my purse," Hagan said. "Method doesn't much concern me."

"You're missing the point," Keel said, his tone hinting irritation. He yawned theatrically, feigned a studious expression, like some learned professor imparting knowledge to an obtuse student. "It's not about the money," Keel said after a moment. "Men like you wouldn't understand."

Men like me.

"What happens now?" Hagan was aware of his cloak dripping icy water into his boots. His back ached, and he was developing a cough from the infernal damp.

"We head back," Keel slapped him on the shoulder and grinned. "Breakfast time."

Later that morning, they were back at the tavern and mercifully dry. Hagan leaned against the chair and sucked on his pipe after finishing a large plate of cold gruel. Tasteless, but filled the hole in his belly. Better than nothing, and so happy to be out of that rain. Their gathering filled the snug again. Six hard-faced men seated around a table, their stools pulled close around the smallest one there. Keel had ordered the other three to keep watch in the woods.

Keel seemed in his element, his green eyes shining in the lamplight. Outside, the lane was deserted, washed clean by fresh rain. Hagan wiped snot from his nose. He wondered if it was ever dry in this region. For the second time that morning, Hagan thought about returning to the desert again, but on reflection things hadn't turned out too well down there. This was a new start for him, albeit a soggy one.

Hagan studied the men in the room. Big Postin barely balanced on the stool, his buttocks bulging either side, the massive poll-axe resting against the wall behind—such a formidable looking weapon. Beside him sat sour-faced Kulvin. The archer looked more miserable than Hagan, and apparently had done most of the scouting work during their long night.

Across the table were the friends Torke and Rasheffan, the first whip lean, the other broad as a tugboat. Torke was rumored clever with a knife. He didn't say much, his long face dominated by that drooping moustache. Hagan heard Torke the Knife came from a land far to the east; certainly the man had an accent. Rasheffan spoke enough for both of them. Nearly as big as Postin, but craftier with hard brown eyes, and a curved Permian scimitar strapped to his side, a small crossbow slung across his back.

That left pale Crall, seated in the corner with one eye open. In his forties and skinny, the wide-brimmed hat and loose coat gave him a scavenger look. But Crall's eyes were the color of blood, and his hair white as snowfall. The albino came from the midnight realms beyond Leeth and was rumored steeped in witchcraft. Next to Keel he was the most feared of the conspirators. Hagan kept his distance from Crall whenever he could. Something unsavory about the man. Not that any of them were merry company this morning.

Except Keel. The designated leader seemed in excellent spirits. He was hunched over a map of the grounds and woods surrounding Cragowan Castle, a flask of brandy in his fist despite the early hour. "The hard part will be separating the king," Keel said. "We'll need a diversion; it's where you boys come in."

"We should draw lots on who gets to kill Nogel," Rasheffan said, and Torke nodded beside him.

Keel shook his head. "That's my task alone," he said. "You men need to be content with the coin you'll receive—leave the wet work to me."

"Suits me," Hagan said, puffing at his pipe.

But some of the others looked uncomfortable, and Crall stared hard at Keel, holding his gaze for a moment before turning away.

"Are you really as good as they say?" Crall muttered, his voice crow-raw.

"Better," Keel said, eyes gauging the map again. "The woods are large and dense in places, and they hem those gardens tight. Shouldn't prove over difficult to lure the king off on a false trail."

"Does Postin get to play the pig, the one the king hunts down?" Rasheffan said, grinning at his joke. Some of the others laughed but Postin rose to his feet, face red with rage. He reached for his poll-axe and took out the lantern.

"Sit the fuck down," Keel said, and Hagan ducked low as the weapon almost impacted his right ear. "Wankers." Keel rolled his eyes as he caught Hagan's wild stare.

"I'll kill you for that, Sheff," Postin said, sinking back into his stool. "So don't go sleeping at night." Rasheffan grinned at him, and Hagan thought Postin was going to get up again, but then Crall, who'd been watching the window, hushed them with a wave.

"Riders," the albino said. "Coming this way." Hagan cursed as he heard the clatter of hoofs approaching from somewhere down the lane.

"Soldiers coming to tell the king about your handiwork," Hagan said to Keel, who shrugged indifference. "No doubt they'll drop by. Most of us are strangers here, but Postin here is well known in these parts, as is his pole."

"Yeah—you better hide, Postin," Keel yawned again. "Go on, bugger off before they reach the taproom, the fuckers are bound to be thirsty."

"There's nowhere big enough for him to hide," Hagan said, receiving a chilling glance from Postin. "Just saying," he added.

"Try the cellar," Keel said, his eyes on the window where at least a dozen well-armed cavalrymen were dismounting from their horses and making for the tavern door.

"And I was hoping they'd gallop past," Rasheffan said, reaching for his sword.

"You won't need that," Keel said. "I'll take care of this."

"Seems to me you're taking care of everything," Hagan said. Keel flashed him a sharp look and then turned away.

"Caswallon needs this done right," he said. "And I've my reputation to consider."

"No one knows anything about you," Hagan said. "I don't think you should worry over much on that score." Keel winked at him. A knock on the snug door turned their heads. The innkeep appeared.

"The soldiers are looking for someone," he said. "They'll be wanting to come in here."

"Then let them come in," Keel smiled. "We've nothing to hide. Just weary hunters discussing our quarry over breakfast." The innkeep looked uncomfortable but nodded and vanished behind the door again. Hagan heard sharp voices and gruff laughter. The soldiers were in the taproom.

Postin had retired to the cellar below, Keel having found the hatch outside the backdoor the day before.

The door creaked open. A man stood there. Immaculate in his polished breastplate, green cloak and leggings. He wore a sword scarcely longer than his scowl. An officer, and in a rare foul mode.

"It's customary to knock," Keel said. They'd stored their weapons below the table, hidden by the cloth covering. No need to provoke more than was necessary.

"Who are you?" The officer glared at Keel, then at Hagan and the others.

"Hunters," Hagan said. "After wild boar."

"You don't look like hunters."

"What's it to you?" Keel said. "Damp saddle soaked your arse, officer? Or maybe it's that time of month?"

The man's face whitened and he reached for his sword. Not near quickly enough. Keel's tossed dagger pierced his throat, and the officer pitched forward into the room.

"What the fuck did you do that for?" Hagan jumped up—and then dropped to his knees, scrambling for his sword, the others diving to join him. Keel laughed at their capering about.

"I wearied of the conversation," he said, opening the door wider and walking out to confront the other soldiers.

"He's insane," Hagan said, cursing his involvement. "Get us all killed."

"It's a game to that one," Crall said, his pale face even grimmer than usual.

The shouting in the taproom announced Keel's arrival. Hagan crashed through the door, sword in hand, and ducked as a young cavalryman swung a sabre at his neck. Hagan twisted, skewered sideways, his broadsword's tip piercing the man's side. The soldier screamed and slid to the floor.

Hagan jumped over him, trying to swing out without getting the blade stuck in a beam. Low ceiling, smoky. Hard to see.

A table flew into his leg. Hagan cursed as his shins absorbed the shock. Another soldier lunged at him. Off balance, all Hagan could do was fend that blow with his pommel, while jumping back. The soldier stabbed at him again, but Hagan blocked that with a stool he'd grabbed for a shield. A clumsy fight. Scant room to swing, and the cavalrymen were slowed by their heavy rain-soaked cloaks.

Hagan was vaguely aware of Keel stabbing and leaping around, the screams following him. Then the others crashed in shouting. A vicious melee followed, but within a few minutes the soldiers were all dead.

Hagan slunk to a stool and nursed his bruised leg. They'd killed a dozen of the king's finest troopers. *His royal fucking guards.* The only option was to depart this land soonest, else his head leave his shoulders. Hagan cursed Keel, currently leaning against the wall, grinning and wiping blood from his knives.

"I fail to see what's funny," Hagan said, then the innkeep surfaced from behind the counter and Keel turned to him.

The poor man gaped at the mess in his taproom, caught Keel's expression and paled. "I'll not say anything, but you had better leave."

"I know you won't say anything." Keel smiled at him, and then vaulted the counter and stabbed the innkeep through his eye. The man dropped out of sight. Keel wiped the dagger clean on an abandoned apron. He poured an ale into a tankard and swallowed, wiped his mouth and grinned at the others, all watching him from their various stations in the taproom.

"That was invigorating," Keel said. "But it does mean we have to step up our plan."

"What are you talking about?" Hagan saw Postin emerge from the back door, his bald head covered in dust. He shook it and glared at the carnage, seemed angry he'd missed the action.

"What happened?" the big man asked, but no one answered.

"Back to the forest," Keel said. "Time to kill the king before more of his finest arrive and see our handiwork."

"Your handiwork," Hagan said. "And you can count me out. I'm riding north to the border, I don't much like Kelthaine, but I think our welcome here has run its course."

Hagan made for the door, his face flushed with rage. He stopped when a knife flew past his head and quivered into the wood, inches above the handle. Hagan turned, saw Keel poised with a second blade in his fist.

"I'd sooner you stayed put," Keel raised the knife slowly. Hagan took the hint and slunk against the wall. "Wise choice, Morwellan." He showed that crooked smile and then addressed all of them with outstretched hands. "Unfortunate business," Keel said, gesturing at the corpses and mess surrounding them. "But they would have reported us whatever the outcome. Sometimes you have to be decisive."

Hagan said nothing. He looked at the others, but no one was going to challenge Keel. Crall stood in a corner with his arms folded, a cynical grin smearing his bloodless lips. To his right, Torke chewed nervously on a pipe, belching rings of smoke into the already cloying atmosphere. The inn stank of blood and shit and stale ale. Having eaten and dried off, the thought of returning to those woods was a pleasant option.

I have to survive this.

Keel's actions would see them all dead by nightfall. The man was unhinged, and clearly keeping most of his plan to himself, and Hagan suspected most of the forthcoming gold as well. He wouldn't be surprised if the green-eyed killer stabbed them all while sleeping and pocketed the reward for himself.

I'm going to be watching you, Keel. Hagan forced his muscles to relax and let the tension ease from his troubled mind. No point getting over-stressed. *Stay focused, watch your back, and then grab that gold and run. Oh—and kill the king too.*

"Looks like it's going to be an interesting afternoon," he said.

***

Lord Rowan Staveport watched the rain bead on the glass, a flask of brandy gripped in one hand and a half-filled cup of wine in the other. The king was seated to his left, his keen eyes studying some manuscript written by one of his ancestors. The old kings descended from Kell the Conqueror had left a rich legacy. King Nogel liked history, had a curious mind, and had ordered a young scribe to compose an accurate chronicle of his family going all the way back to Wynna, Kell's second son and Kelwyn's first ruler.

Lord Staveport had little interest in such leisurely material. He preferred to keep both eyes on the politics of today. Outside, the young nobles were playing murderball, a rough game that involved kicking, punching, gouging, and running past the other players with the ball, a vaguely round bag of leather stuffed with grain. A senseless waste of energy in Lord Staveport's opinion. But at least it kept the knuckleheads occupied and out of his hair.

Nogel looked up from his parchment. "You look uneasy, Rowan. Whatever is the matter, man?"

"I'm ready for the rain to stop," Lord Staveport said. "Tired of this drizzle. Saps my resolve."

"Nonsense. We've plenty of cheer with the fire, ale, wine and brandy. We've hardly dented the rack, and there are plenty of barrels still to tap."

"My lord, I lack your capacity to drink from dawn to dusk. Sometimes I need a break. A walk in the sunshine would be refreshing. I miss my roses, the vines growing back home."

"You are such a city man," Nogel said. "I like it here. Drinking and hunting. Good company—what's better in life?" The king put his parchment down and sighed. He was a good bluffer, but Staveport knew how lonely Nogel was. How devastated he'd been when his beloved queen had fallen to sickness and died several years back.

Nogel—always energetic and athletic—had thrown himself into provocative politics and hunting, the more dangerous the chase the better, whether on horse or in the council chamber goading Caswallon's sympathizers. This part of Kelwyn was overrun with boars. Staveport knew the king wouldn't quit until he'd gored a good half dozen. That meant this infernal rain needed to stop else they'd be holed up here for days.

"How's the princess?" Lord Staveport asked, changing the subject. He turned his gaze to the window. The game was over and the players laughing and quaffing ale, some of them with bloody noses.

Nogel followed his gaze and watched them for a moment. Eventually he answered. "She does well," he said. "I've high hopes for Ariane. The girl has a warrior's soul."

"That's because she spends more time with your captains than at court. She's developed a foul mouth lately, Highness. I worry for her."

"You worry for everyone, old friend." The king shrugged. "Ariane has a free spirit and fine temper. I'd not thrash that out of her. That girl will rule Kelwyn one day—far better she learns the rigors of everyday life rather than mixing with those dreamy ladies in the courtroom. You know the floozies that are always clustered around Tamersane."

"I do, and Ariane is worth ten of them. But she needs to learn statecraft, my lord. The girl has the manners of a troll. Besides, you're still young enough to remarry and have a male child."

Nogel scowled at him. "Ariane is a match for any man, Staveport. Have a care with that tongue, else you forget yourself."

Lord Staveport bowed stiffly. "It's only that I worry for her, Highness. You know I love that girl as though she was my daughter too." The door crashed open, and Yail Tolranna walked in.

"Rain's stopped," he said, his long black hair soaked and lips bloody.

"State of you, man," Lord Staveport said.

"Tam looks worse, as does Rallen. Poor Tostic got one in the balls," he laughed. "He's still spewing over by the water trough." Tolranna moved over, allowing his younger brother to enter.

Tamersane's pale hair was matted with blood, but a broad smile covered his lips.

"Good game," Tamersane said, punching his brother in the ribs. "I'm ready for a rematch."

Nogel laughed. "You pups are way too restless. Now the rain has stopped, I think we need some real entertainment. I trust you have those boar spears handy?"

"They are in the storeroom, as are all our weapons," Yail Tolranna said.

"Well fetch them and tell the boys to ready my mount and the other horses. We ride out within the hour." The brothers departed, leaving the door wide open, their young faces flushed with excitement. Lord Staveport lacked their enthusiasm. Nogel saw his expression and grinned.

"You stay put, Rowan," the king said. "Sip and cogitate, old friend. Enjoy the tranquility, and we'll return ere dark. We'll have a hearty feast tonight and then ride back to Wynais in the morning. You'll be sipping in the warm sun and clipping your roses before this week is over."

"Thank you, Highness," Lord Staveport said. "I shall do as you suggest. My bones ache with this infernal damp, I'd sooner not test them on some mad-cap chase through this forest. And I beg you take care also, Highness—hunting boar can be very hazardous."

"Enjoy your afternoon, Lord Staveport." The king stood and slapped him on the shoulder. "I'm off to wake the lazy hounds. Goodbye."

Lord Staveport watched the king stride out into the courtyard, a broad grin on his face. *You are a fine man, my lord. But not the most cautious.* The retainer folded his arms and leaned back in his chair. Nogel was right, he should stop worrying. Such a useless pastime. He determined to take Nogel's advice and enjoy the wine and solitude of the late spring afternoon.

Rowen watched the party ride out just as a thin line of blue sky promised more. The trees shivered slightly in a sudden breeze, and Lord Staveport saw an owl glide past and settle on an outbuilding at the far side of the stockade.

The owl turned its head towards him where he watched by the window. Lord Staveport felt a shiver run along his spine. The owl called out a warning, then lifted, disappearing into the canopy of green above. Lord Staveport realized something terrible was going to happen.

Chapter 4 | Summoned

"You can't stay here," Corin told Kara, as the dark-eyed girl slipped into her trousers, which he'd recently purchased at market. She scrubbed up well. Kara was small, comely if not particularly pretty. They'd shared a few nights together, back in the desert and here in Cappel Cormac. She liked it here, but Corin had no plans to stay. The fact that Silon's tavern was as safe a place as any in Cappel meant little. "You need to go home."

"Too far," she said. "Laregoza is beyond the great plains—a month's hard ride, or three times the distance by sail."

Corin grunted, he'd never heard of Laregoza. "Well you need to go somewhere—can't stay here. Too dangerous, especially as Krugan's leftovers are going to be mad as hornets and searching every nook for me. And you, sweetling."

"I can handle myself," Kara said. "I'll find work, I've lots of talents."

"That I do not doubt," Corin replied. "But the fact remains—you cannot stay here."

"You don't find me attractive?"

"What's that got to do with anything?"

"Do you?"

"Yes. But, I'm not staying in Permio, and nor should you."

She smiled. "You should have said so earlier. Where are we going?"

"*We* are not going anyplace," Corin said. "I am returning to Raleen, and you are going someplace else where you're not going to be the target of every cutthroat and rapist."

"You don't like me." She folded her arms and stared at him.

Corin winced. "Kara, I actually think you are lovely, but you can't accompany me. I work alone, if you came with me you'd be in more danger than staying here while wearing a sign that reads *Shag Me Slowly*. It's not you, it's me. Wherever I go, people want to stick something sharp in me. Occupational hazard."

They'd parted company after another hour of arguing. Against his counsel, Kara had opted for working in the tavern. They were always looking for people, so no problem there. But Corin doubted she'd survive a week once the word got out that Krugan was dead, killed by a mercenary and a runaway slave.

But that was her choice and she knew the risk. Corin had payment due for a task completed. *Find Krugan and kill him.* Nearly five months of meticulous reconnaissance work. That time had passed painstakingly slow until Corin knew every inch of that arid terrain. But now—at last—he was owed a large dividend. The big job completed and payment overdue. Past time he went home. If you could call a scruffy inn at the corner of Port Sarfe dockyard home. Served as good as any place. Once there, he'd stay drunk for a week at least. Something to look forward to. *You have to have clear goals in this life.*

Two days later, Corin smiled in the sunshine as the salty air and warmth drove away any reservations he might have. They hadn't discussed his wages, but Corin believed he'd get a good amount of coin. Months working under that spiteful sun. Certainly, enough to put some by, maybe buy his own gaff, or just get drunk in the 'Knife for a decade or two, or until some fucker stabbed him in his sleep. He wouldn't worry about that. Everyone died. Better steel than some lingering ague. Drinking and wenching, living for the day. It was the simple pleasures in this life that made it worthwhile.

Corin watched the wake trailing behind and wasn't surprised seeing the dolphins coming to greet them again. Dol Craile's fisher pitched north along the coast, a fuzzy haze of marsh and mist a mile or so to starboard.

The skipper was yelling up at one of his crew. Craile saw Corin standing by the stern rail and walked back to greet him.

"Dock in an hour or so," the ebony skinned captain said, rubbing the large gold hoop in his left ear. "My last trip for the week. You were lucky you caught us in time."

"I'd have found someone else," Corin said.

"I doubt that." Craile awarded Corin a shrewd look. "The passage across gets more treacherous every month. Pirates, slavers, galleys, and thieves at the docks—not to mention those fucking Crimson Guards, they're taking more interest in harbor affairs these days. Since that business away in Sedinadola a few months back."

"What business was that?"

Dol Craile laughed. "I heard a rumor you were there, Corin. And a certain renegade from Morwella—you tried to topple the sultan."

"We did no such thing," Corin said, rubbing his eyes and wondering how tales got twisted so easily.

"How is Hagan?"

"Probably dead," Corin said. "And if he's alive, he'll be wanting me dead. It wasn't a joyous parting." Corin gave the skipper a hard look. "How do you know him?"

Dol Craile shrugged. "I was in Vangaris when he was proclaimed outlaw. Apparently, he'd just escaped from that city and the harbor was crawling with guards. I assumed such an infamous brigand would make for Permio, so when Hagan's name cropped up a month later I wasn't surprised. He sailed with us a while back. Never mentioned you. You know Duke Tomais offered a reward of twenty thousand in silver?"

"What were you doing up there?"

"Business."

Corin smiled. That meant Silon had needed news from the north. He knew Dol Craile was the merchant's eyes and ears at ports and harbors. "Maybe I should go find Hagan and kill him myself," Corin said, amazed at that sum. "What did he do to earn such a price on his head?"

"They say he was involved in the murder of the duke's wife some years back. Nothing was proved, and Hagan denied it. Whatever the facts, Hagan's a dangerous man."

"Yeah, well. It's a dangerous world," Corin said, watching as gulls weaved and dived along that hazy shoreline. "But today I'm happy."

"Enjoy that feeling. It won't fucking last."

True to his word, Dol Craile docked the craft an hour later, and Corin waved thanks and vaulted ashore. He promised the skipper he'd settle up when Craile joined him for a drink after he'd seen to his stock.

Light was fading as Corin led Thunderhoof through the alleys, making for his favorite inn. The sign creaked as he walked up to the *Crooked Knife* and yanked the door ajar. A few faces turned his way. Traders mostly, the odd customs guard off duty. Rado the patron sat at a table playing dice with two fellows. He saw Corin and pulled a face.

"I hope you're not planning on staying the night?" Rado said.

"I am . . . *was*. What's up?"

"Silon was in here this morning, left a package for you."

"Good," Corin said. "I hope it rattles."

"If it does, I'll relieve you of some of the content. You owe me three weeks' rent."

"I've been away for over two months," Corin said.

"Then you owe the interest as well."

Corin waited as Rado went into the kitchens and returned with a bundle. He tossed the package at Corin, who caught it and shook the contents. It was light, hardly a jingle. Corin frowned as he tore into the package.

A leather bag; it contained a small purse and a rolled, sealed parchment. Corin tossed the letter on the table and opened the purse. Six silver pennies. Hardly a fortune.

"I'll take three of those." Rado leaned across and scooped his fingers inside the purse as Corin stared at the lack of contents in disbelief.

"He owes me four months' pay," Corin said, in a loud voice which had everyone staring at him. "My latest job in the desert—you know the one I bitched about. It's done, sorted. The perpetrators are dead."

"Happy for you." Rado brought him an ale. Corin gulped the contents down. "I'll take another," he said.

"Aren't you going to read that?"

"Nope," Corin said, sitting on a table and downing his second ale. "I'm going to get drunk and then ride to Vioyamis and stick something sharp up that merchant's arse." Rado left him to it, and his customers turned back to their own affairs. Corin stared at the letter as though it were a snake.

He sighed, reached down and tore open the seal. Silon's bold hand. The words read:

> *I need you in Kelwyn—yesterday. There's a worrisome development.*
>
> *That silver should tide you over, you'll be paid in full when we return south.*
>
> *Do not tarry on the road, Corin. I will expect you in Calprissa three days from now.*
>
> *I got word via bird from Dol Craile, so I know you're due to dock this afternoon.*

You will need to ride out before dusk—get some miles covered, and then push on at first light.

Corin read and reread the contents over, and then stuffed the letter up his sleeve. Rado wandered over with a pitcher of ale. He filled Corin's mug. "Bad news?"

"Not sure," Corin said. "He needs me in Kelwyn."

"Silon?"

"He's already up there," Corin said. "In Calprissa."

"That's a long ride, unless you can get a boat to take you sometime this week."

"He expects me up there in two days," Corin said. "A worrying development." He passed Rado the letter, and the innkeep studied the contents with a furrowed brow.

"What do you think?" Corin asked him.

Rado shrugged. "Whatever it is—it's big. Something's awry."

"Clearly," Corin said.

"You'll be wanting supper before you leave," Rado said. "I'll get Goshad to groom your horse, and see that he's fed and watered."

"Who?"

"My useless nephew," Rado said. "He works here now, as no one else will have him, and I'm still short staffed."

"My heart bleeds for you," Corin said.

Half an hour later, as dusk settled in the harbor, Corin led Thunderhoof through the cobbled alleys toward the barbican. The gate guards let him through without a word. Once outside the city, Corin mounted and bid Thunder canter north along the Atarios road. Once he reached that city, Corin would cut across country, striking north for Kelwyn and the coastal city, Calprissa.

A week's ride—and Silon expected him in three days. *Nothing changes.* "Come on Thunder, let's see what you're made of." Corin urged the big horse to pick up speed as dusk settled deep on the highway and a waxing moon flanked his passage.

It was the morning of the fourth day when Corin arrived at the land gates of Kelwyn's second city. He'd only been here once, years ago when he'd been a raw recruit in the Wolf Regiment, heading for Permio, and war. A trip that had scarred him for good.

The gates were open as carts wheeled in alongside beggars and traders, rich folk on expensive horses—though none of these beasts were a match for Thunderhoof. His worthy steed had maintained a steady trot throughout their arduous trek. Horse and rider had encountered no one, and Corin had slept in his blanket for less than four hours a night, using the moonlight to guide his stallion long before sun up.

"You did well boy, we'll locate your old master and then I'll see you're well fed and watered and get some good rest." Corin slid off the saddle and squeezed through the gates, leading the big horse between wagons and trailers, amid shouts and curses. Another busy morning in the city.

Calprissa was known as the City of Diamonds. A bit grand that title, in Corin's opinion, as he saw no evidence of the precious stones. But the walls and buildings were all carved from local stone, a white gleaming alabaster that gave the city a polished look.

The people were pretentious and self-opinionated. Corin received many a dismissive look from the well-heeled city folk. Another grubby courier, or fighting man from the south. Kelwynians were rumored friendlier than their grim cousins in the north, but Corin preferred Raleenians, who were more practical, honest folk in his opinion. And this city was far too grand for him.

Corin led Thunderhoof through orderly streets until he found the place he knew was where Silon stayed when he visited this city. An immaculate groom met him in the courtyard of what appeared to be an expensive hostelry. Corin saw statues, and a large ornate waterfall tumbled down from the roof. An intricate, useless construction that no doubt cost a fortune. But then Corin wasn't the aesthetic type.

"He needs a good rest," Corin told the groom, who nodded aloofly and led Thunderhoof away to the stable yard. Corin adjusted his swords and strolled up to the main doors. A man in a purple tabard opened the door with a curt nod.

"He's in the lounge," the doorman said. Evidently Silon had told them to expect him.

Corin walked through several atriums and corridors until he saw Silon seated in a large room with a flask of brandy, and a map strewn across a table. He didn't stir as Corin's boots scuffed the polished floor, announcing his presence.

"I'm here," Corin said.

"What kept you?" Silon glanced up from the map, his dark eyes pinning Corin, and his expression sour.

"My horse hasn't got fucking wings."

"How fares Akamates?" That was Thunderhoof's Raleenian name. A pompous way of saying "hoofs of thunder."

"He is an excellent horse," Corin said. "I've come to love him. Your daughter was most generous. Shame that trait isn't shared by her father."

"She had cause to be." Silon bid Corin take a seat at the table. He complied after unstrapping Clouter and leaning the longsword against the wall.

Silon stared at the sword. "I cannot get over the size of that thing," the merchant said.

"How is Nalissa these days?"

"Tolerable, and resting in Atarios with her uncle again. Rubaan is also much recovered from his ordeal the other month"

"That was a grim business." Silon nodded. Corin smiled, thinking of his recent coup with Krugan. "Here, I've some exciting news—I—"

"—You haven't come here to boast," Silon said, shoving the map across the table while Corin helped himself to a glass of brandy.

"Very nice," Corin said, holding the crystal glass up to catch the light. "Lots of culture here, think I'm going to like Calprissa. Now Krugan—"

"—The map," Silon said, his expression grim.

Corin studied the contents, shaking his head. "Port Wind and Reln—those cities are miles north of here. I trained in Port Wind. It's a shithole."

"You'll blend in well," Silon said.

"I don't understand." Corin refused to take the bait. Instead he sipped his brandy and waited until Silon chose the right moment to explain. "I'm not staying here then?"

"King Nogel of Kelwyn is in danger," Silon said eventually.

"What does that have to do with us?" Corin scratched his chin, the stubble over a week old.

"What do you know about Caswallon?" Silon said in a quiet voice.

Corin shrugged, wondering where this conversation was leading. "I know he's our enemy, the one who sent the Lynx who caused Nalissa so much distress." Silon didn't respond. "I've also heard he's rumored a magician," Corin said. "I saw him once when I was a lad. Made an impression on me. Not a good one. By the way—Krugan's dead."

"About bloody time," Silon said. "As for Caswallon. The rogue's hold on the High King strengthens every day. Kelsalion is ailing, his mind weak and wandering. I fear for the High King and his heir, the young Prince Tarin."

"Shame, perhaps it's not a good time to be a king. What has this to do with me?"

"Caswallon wants Kelsalion's crown—that's no secret. With the Tekara's power, he can coerce the puppet Tarin into usurping his father, or even killing him. I have no proof of this, but the logic is sound and I'm not the only one concerned. You listening?"

Corin scratched an ear and nodded.

"Both your Lord Halfdan and King Nogel have challenged Caswallon's ambitions," Silon said. "But Kelsalion's high councilor is a consummate liar and a clever politician. Neither of them have been able to pin the sorcerer down."

"So then—he is a magician?"

"Steeped in ancient lore," Silon said, arching his fingers and staring hard at Corin. "My people were getting close before they showed up dead. Ever since Caswallon sent that demon to haunt my dreams and torment poor Nalissa. Since then he's been watching my every move. I've had to take a step back from the main stage, as has your former general, Lord Halfdan, now banished to Point Keep, and holed up there."

"I heard a rumor Halfdan was dead."

"Almost. There was a failed coup up in Kella City, the generals against Caswallon. Perani betrayed the others and now his Tiger Regiment have put a curfew on that city. Belmarius's Bears are stationed down on the Liaho, and your old regiment have joined their leader in Point Keep. The Wolves suffered most from Perani's betrayal. Many of your old comrades were killed in that affray."

"You want me to take out this sorcerer?"

Silon laughed. Corin failed to see the joke. "You've got guts Corin an Fol, I'll not deny that. Damn it man—you are not in his league! No. I need you to watch the border between Kelthaine and this country. The king's visiting Port Keep, the hunting's good there, and Nogel likes to hunt. With both myself and Halfdan outmaneuvered, I've good cause to believe our enemy will make a move against Nogel, his only real challenger."

"Interesting," Corin hoped they'd discuss Krugan shortly, and his forthcoming payment. Here's to patience.

"I fear there'll be an attempt on King Nogel's life while he's away from court," Silon said. "Nogel's vulnerable up there."

"And you want me to protect this king? Doesn't he have guards, an army?"

"Shut up and listen," Silon said, waving an attendant to come in and replenish their brandy. "Your old friend is in Port Wind, as are other unsavory characters."

"I don't have any friends, especially old ones."

Silon smiled at some private joke. "Hagan Delmorier was spotted in the harbor by one of the dockers, a man I pay to keep watch up there."

Corin leaned forward. "You think Hagan's going to murder this king?"

"I don't know," Silon said, habitually rubbing his golden earring. "But nothing untoward ever happens in Port Wind, so why visit? The city's not on the way to anywhere, and as I said, there are reports of other rogues arriving over the last week. I'm smelling a fat rat here, Corin."

"I suspected Hagan was dead," Corin said. "We didn't part on good terms back in Permio."

"I need you to find him, and these others," Silon said. "Watch their movements and see what they are up to. Only for a few days, as I suspect Nogel will tire of that climate and head back to the Silver City."

"How do you know all this?"

"Lord Staveport wrote me last week."

"Lord who?"

"He's King Nogel's old retainer, a former knight, and a gentleman. A trusted contact I've had dealings with for years. Good fellow." The merchant seemed to have dealings with everyone of account across the Four Kingdoms. "Staveport was the one who warned me there might be an attempt on Nogel's life."

"Well aren't there people in Kelwyn who can deal with this?"

"I owe Staveport," Silon said. "He also told me that Caswallon was onto me. Besides, I think you're more suited to the task than any Kelwynian, as long as you stay in the background and use discretion. Find out what these impostors are up to. And then kill them if our suspicions prove valid."

"Including Hagan?"

"Especially Hagan. The man's wanted by the Duke of Morwella, only a matter of time before Caswallon recruits him as a spy or assassin, if he hasn't done so already. You have a problem with that?"

"Not really," Corin said. "I mean, he's not a friend, but . . ."

"This is serious business, Corin. I need you to take that in. Digest. If Nogel dies, then the Four Kingdoms are left without a capable ruler, worse still someone with the balls to stand up to Caswallon. Without Nogel, that conniver will have no one left to halt his ambition, and gods alone know what that will mean. We cannot let that happen."

"Do I need to leave right now?"

"Once your horse is rested, you'll be back on the road. Ride to Port Wind and find out what you can. If King Nogel returns to Wynais, then the emergency is over, you can make your way back to 'Sarfe at your leisure, and I'll have you fully compensated for your trouble."

"What about Krugan?"

Silon almost grinned. "We'll discuss that too."

"Sounds almost reasonable, though I could use more silver to tie me over in case I'm stuck up there."

Silon produced a purse. He placed six silver pennies on the table. Corin snatched them up. "Don't spend it all at once."

"Thanks," Corin said, wondering why the merchant was so chary with his coin. "I'll expect a hefty wad of gold when next we meet. Krugan the bandit is dead."

"Yes, so you keep saying," Silon said. Corin let it rest and decided he'd put his price up on his return.

Silon ordered lunch, and Corin tucked in to some delicious deli of hams, fish and vegetables. Two hours later, he was back in the saddle, following the coast road to Port Wind, a place he'd hoped he'd never see again.

Corin arrived at dusk and booked lodging at a wayside inn close to the harbor. He took a walk as drizzle filled the sky, and beyond the stone quayside the sea shone like polished silver. Behind him were cliffs looming stark above the town, and Corin could just make out the barracks where he'd trained to be a Wolf.

Happy days.

So long ago. He thought of Lord Halfdan, and that bastard Taskala. Then Corin remembered that first night with Yazrana, and a hollow feeling of loss found him returning to the tavern, his expression as gloomy as the leaden sky above.

Late that night, Corin questioned the innkeep casually, not wanting to appear over curious. "Many visitors this time of year?"

"More than usual," the man said, dusting down his apron. They were alone in the taproom, the hour past midnight. "And not the sort I care for."

"Problems?"

"You could say that—there was a killing in town two nights ago."

Corin feigned casual interest. "Who?" He thought of the king. *Perhaps I'm too late.*

"Dal Terini the district governor, found murdered with his lover in his bedchamber. Grim business—and done by someone who knew what he was doing."

"For what reason?"

The innkeep shrugged. "No one knows." Then he stared hard at Corin and his longsword resting against the table. "Why are you in town, warrior?"

"Just passing through."

"No one passes through Port Wind—it doesn't lead anywhere. Reln, up in Kelthaine, has much more to offer travelers such as yourself."

"Alright, if it satisfies you, I was stationed here years ago. Up there on the cliffs."

"You were a *Wolf*?" The innkeep eyed the golden broach on Corin's cloak with a smile.

Corin caught his gaze. "You recognize it."

"There aren't many gold ones around. Forgive me, but I thought you might have happened upon the item."

"Stolen it, you mean?"

"I'm sorry—I meant no offense, but you're a rough-looking character."

"Thanks, nice of you to say so. You obviously aren't acquainted with the Wolves then?" Corin smiled at the irony. His regiment were regarded by the others as thieves and murderers.

"No—I bought this tavern after Halfdan left," the innkeep said. "Those barracks have been deserted for years. Nothing up there save sea birds and wind."

Corin shrugged indifference and turned to his ale. It was late and he needed to formulate a plan. But the man seemed uneasy and grabbed his arm. "If I were you stranger, I would leave at first light. There's going to be trouble."

"What kind of trouble—another murder? Didn't catch the villain?"

"He's still at large, and that killing made no sense. The assassin would have had to scale the buildings, roof and walls, and evade a score of guards—not to mention those dogs. He took nothing—just murdered the governor, his leman, and left. An outrage, and a senseless one."

"Sounds like a contract killer."

"Terini was small fry. It's peculiar, but that's not what I'm talking about. There are other strangers here, and Postin was seen making for the forest."

"Who's he?"

"A local villain."

"Maybe he's your man."

"No way." The innkeep shook his head as though the suggestion was absurd. "You are right, Master Wolf; the murder was committed by a professional. Postin is a thug and a brigand. A clumsy, brutal giant. The odds are, he's got involved with a gang up here in the woods. The other thing is Nogel's here."

"The king?" Corin feigned surprise. "Why?"

"Hunting boar up in the Wood between the Waters. There's an old manor house deep inside that forest called Cragowan Castle. The king uses it sometimes." The innkeep looked up suddenly, as though someone might be eavesdropping. The lantern flickered on the wall and a strange hush filled the air.

"Something amiss?" Corin noted the concern on the man's face.

He rubbed his apron. "Past my bedtime," the innkeep said, face paler than before, and Corin knew something was wrong so didn't press the man. He'd leave before dawn, make for the woods and lie low.

The innkeep left him in the taproom alone. The fire dwindled to hazy faggots glowing crimson in the gloom. The lantern flickered again, and then a sudden gust extinguished the light. Corin sat up, the small hairs lifting on the nape of his neck. *I am not alone.*

A scraping sound at the window. Corin saw a bird outside perched silent on the sill. An owl, white as snow, watching him with deep dark eyes. They blinked once, the bird lifted its wings and glided off into the night. Moments later, an eerie call reached him from somewhere far off in the trees.

A warning.

Corin stood up and rubbed his eyes. He was tired and needed rest. Was it his imagination, or were there shadows creeping along the walls? He chuckled. That landlord had spooked him too. He studied the walls and ceiling until satisfied all was as should be. Then he shoved another log on the fire and riddled the grill until new flames mustered, bringing a modicum of cheer.

After that, he settled back in the chair and slept without dreams.

Chapter 5 | Deeper in the Woods

The next morning Corin led Thunderhoof through an avenue of trees dripping endlessly from the relentless rain. Corin remembered how wet this part of the country was—so unlike the rest of Kelwyn, a land famed for its warm sunny days and mild winters. Not hot and dry like Raleen, nor bitter cold and bleak like Kelthaine and the northlands.

He'd taken this road long ago. Part of a company riding from Kella City to Port Wind. Sixteen years old. It felt odd to be back here.

The woods closed in as Corin rode north toward the border, the sea sometimes flanking his left, a distant glimmer of steely gray. He reined in, seeing a thatched cottage half hidden in the trees. Some kind of inn or homestead he assumed. Strange the lack of smoke rising from the chimney.

Corin rode closer, eyes scanning the lane ahead. No one about. He approached the building, deep set windows hinted two long rooms, the front door half open. A tavern, but where were the customers? Corin tensed when he saw a fox run out the door.

"This doesn't look promising," Corin muttered to Thunderhoof and dismounted carefully, eyes not leaving that door. He tied Thunder's reins to a hitching post and unsheathed Biter. Opening the door wider he stopped, seeing the corpses sprawled inside.

Soldiers. Cavalrymen judging by their sabers and furry hats. The king's men murdered, but by whom, and why? Corin took stock of the mess, stale blood and severed limbs everywhere, here and there a kitchen knife buried in flesh. The men who'd done this had been efficient, making short work of the soldiers. Strange how he hadn't seen any horses on the road. Perhaps they'd stolen them—though that didn't make much sense. But then nothing here made sense. Who would risk attacking a well-armed troop inside a tavern?

Corin walked through the carnage into an adjacent snug. He saw signs of recent activity, an abandoned plate with a half-eaten piece of pork pie. Corin grabbed the pie and shoved it in his mouth, not having stopped for lunch. There were flagons of ale, some half-filled as though the drinkers had left in a hurry. And why wouldn't they after leaving a mess like this behind? A further search revealed the patron lying on his back with a bread knife protruding from his left eye. There were chew marks on his neck, and Corin guessed the fox had been at work here.

Nasty bastards whoever they were. This couldn't have anything to do with Hagan, who was a killer but not one to court trouble. Perhaps the villain the innkeep in Port Wind had mentioned. Postin? If so he must have had company. Even on a good day Corin would struggle to kill twelve soldiers by himself.

He found the kitchen, helped himself to a larger piece of pork pie, and then poured a flagon from the abandoned keg. Good ale. Corin gazed down at the butchered patron. Poor fellow. "Cheers," he said, downing the contents.

Once he'd satisfied his appetite and thirst, Corin left the inn behind. It was already late afternoon, and he needed to get close to Cragowan Castle, and take stock. Once he had an idea of the surroundings, he would lie low and keep watch.

He'd studied Silon's map in detail back in Calprissa and knew there was a fork in the road, a track that led off deeper into the woods. Corin reached that junction just as the sun set far out across the ocean, glimpsed like a flash, spraying gold on the leaves shading the road.

A mile or so—no more judging by that map. Corin rode for a time and then when he spied some distant roofs, he dismounted and led Thunderhoof to a large tree hedged by thick brush where he tied the horse to a sturdy branch. "Wait here, friend—I'll not be long." Thunderhoof looked at him mournfully.

Crouching low with Clouter bouncing on his back, Corin ducked and weaved his way through the dense undergrowth beneath the trees until he reached the outbuildings of what appeared to be a very large house. Some noble's country estate. It had to be Cragowan Castle, though there was no evidence of crenulations or portcullis.

A single lantern glowed from a room, and Corin could just make out someone seated in there. A lone figure, a flask of brandy in his hand, the head stooped as though he was asleep. Corin made for the door. No one else around, though he saw plenty evidence of boot scuffs and horses' hoofs, dog tracks too. He teased the latch and turned the large brass handle, stepping inside, Biter's steel glinting in his free hand.

A large hall opened to several rooms, the only light coming from the one on the left. Corin entered and stopped when he saw the figure seated there. Asleep?

Corin had that bad feeling again. He approached the man. He was richly clad in a warm coat and leggings, the coat trimmed with silver fox fur. He clutched an empty flask and wore an expression of surprise. The blood from his severed throat was still pooling on the floor, albeit slowly. An elderly man, noble looking and dignified. Corin felt sudden rage inside. There was evil at work here.

He heard a creak and turned. A man stood there. *Hagan Delmorier.*

"Hello Corin, I've a score to settle with you." The Morwellan leveled the longsword in his hand.

"Just the one?"

"Several."

"This your handiwork?" Corin clicked his tongue.

"You *think?*" Hagan spat. "No, I just got here like you. Saw you walking through the door. Quite a surprise, though not a pleasant one."

"So where does this leave us?" Corin watched Hagan's sword as it flicked towards his face. There wasn't much room in here. The fight could go either way. But Hagan smiled and sheathed the weapon.

"This is hardly the time," he said. "I suspect that Keel will return shortly."

"Keel?"

"You're going to like him, Corin. The man has a certain charisma."

"The killer?"

"Oh yes," Hagan said, "and more besides. He's special, Keel. Gifted you might say. The one who left those bodies in the inn back on the road. Sure you noticed them on your sojourn here. The rest of us had to intervene once he'd started of course, but it was mostly Keel's handiwork."

"So where is this Keel?"

"Out stalking the king with the others."

"How many?"

"Seven including Keel."

"Why aren't you with them?"

"Let's say I had a change of heart."

Corin shook his head, wondering if he should kill Hagan while he had the chance. But they had been companions for a time, and despite his telling himself otherwise, Corin had once abandoned Hagan and some others at tariff station back in Permio.

"Who is this?" Corin hinted the corpse clutching the flask.

"Lord Rowan Staveport of Wynais. As decent a man as ever lived, they do say." Hagan showed his lopsided smile.

"This man Keel works for Caswallon?"

"We all work for Caswallon," Hagan said. "Or rather I did—I'm abandoning my comrades, Corin. That sound familiar to you?"

"I had a job to do that day," Corin said. "A life to save."

"And others to sacrifice."

"I had no choice."

"Well, as I said, this is hardly the time to pursue the matter," Hagan said with a lopsided grin. "Here we are together again—call it an impasse. And we need to get moving in case the king or that bastard Keel wander back.

Corin nodded. "I presume the king and his men are still out hunting. It will be dark soon. They could return at any moment. I'll need to warn them about your friend."

"I'd sooner you didn't."

"I'll say you're with me," Corin said. "That we're bounty hunters tasked with finding these murderers."

Hagan laughed. "You are such an innocent. King Nogel is well aware of who I am. He's cousin to the Duke of Morwella, the same nobleman who wants me swinging from a noose."

"You don't have to tell the king your name."

"I'd sooner not risk being recognized—like yourself, I've a certain look." Hagan glanced up, hearing the sound of barking dogs and shouts. "Time we weren't here."

Full of misgivings, Corin followed Hagan out of the house, and the pair slipped back into the woods. "We'd best vacate the area," Corin said. "They'll be mad as hornets when they find Staveport's corpse."

"My horse is close by," Hagan said. "We should cross the border, me thinks, and make for Reln."

"What about your friends?"

"*Friends?*" Hagan crinkled his nose in disgust. "I don't know where they are," he said. "And I'd sooner not find out."

"That's fine, but I have to warn the king."

"Don't be stupid Corin," Hagan said. "Nogel will slice you up like bacon before you can squeak your innocence. By tomorrow these woods will be crawling with soldiers. Keel blew his chance by butchering that old man."

"Then why did he do it?"

"Because he's a wicked twisted bastard—you coming or what?"

***

Keel had no regrets. Killing the old fool had raised the game, making it more interesting. A diversion. His clumsy companions would be tracked and hunted down by the vengeful nobles, while he, Keel, could work on Nogel alone. A trick to lure the king away from his people. All part of Keel's masterplan.

He sprinted through the forest, the trees dripping and wolves howling in the distance. Far away, he could still make out the dull red glow of the room where Lord Staveport sat alone with his throat cut open. Keel smiled, he so loved the hunt. And stalking a king made a man such as him feel so alive. He reached the broken rocks where he'd arranged to meet the other three, the late arrivals from Reln. Caswallon's new recruits to his team, fresh from Kella City.

Keel sprang up the rocks, deftly jumping and climbing until he cleared the forest roof and had a sweeping view of dark foliage and deepening night sky above. The moon rode silver to his left, and three shadows emerged, blending into men who strode up to join him.

Quick-eyed Curlecot and his silent brother Blane both were skilled archers. Behind them loomed the hulking brute called Dastan. Keel had only received news of their joining him yesterday. The other men knew nothing of these newcomers, and Keel was determined to keep it that way. He liked the idea of running two separate squads in case one of them failed, or got out of hand.

"Where is the king?" Dastan asked, his flat gray eyes pinning Keel. The man was almost as tall as Postin, but broader yet, and his round face a maze of scars. Rumored half insane, Caswallon had spared him the rope and sent Dastan south with the brothers.

Keel matched Dastan's glare until the big man blinked and shuffled in discomfort. The tallest archer stood forward and introduced himself. "Curlie Cull," he said, "and this is my brother Blane, he doesn't say much on account of his tongue being missing. The High King ripped it out," he explained, though Keel wasn't interested.

"We've work to do," Keel said.

"Are there not others?" Curlie Cull glanced around. "Caswallon said—"

"—They are occupied elsewhere," Keel said, waving a hand. "I need you three to flush out the king."

***

"He's a beauty!" Young Tamersane whooped in delight as the white hart blocked their path ahead. "I've never seen such a noble beast."

"He'll make a fine trophy," Yail Tolranna said, fingering his bowstring. "May I, Your Highness?"

"You may not." King Nogel sat his destrier, the boar spear lashed to the saddle and his bow held ready. "This animal is worthy of a king. You boys should return to the lodge before this night greets dawn."

"Staveport ordered we stay with you, Highness," Tolranna said. "There are rumors of outlaws frequenting these woods."

"Lord Staveport is not my nursemaid," the king said. "And Dal Terini assured me only last week that he'd flushed such scum from this countryside. Besides, I'm well-armed." He flashed the pair an assuring grin. "Go back lads, you're cold and wet. Feast on pig and ale." The youngest one, Tamersane, looked relieved at that order, but Yail Tolranna appeared worried.

"Highness, I beg you . . ."

But the king wasn't listening; his eyes were on the white hart that was still watching them in the moonlight. The beast raised its antlers and then vanished behind a clutch of briar. Nogel cursed.

"Your prattle has driven him away, gentlemen. Leave us to our hunt, lads. Go!"

The youngsters exchange glances. "As you wish, my lord," Tolranna said. "Come on, brother, let's make sure those slugs have the pork well tendered in that kitchen. They guided their beasts off into the darkness. King Nogel barely noticed their departure.

He dug in his heels, urging his horse up the path, a broad track that cut deeper into the forest. The king was tired too, and soaked to the bone. But he rarely got the chance to hunt alone these days, and an opportunity like this was not to be missed. The hart appeared again, ghostly pale, its silvery hide lit by the moon as it emerged into a glade ahead.

Uncanny how calm the beast appeared, as though it was waiting for him. Nogel guided his horse forward with his knees as he nocked arrow to bowstring and pulled back. He released, and the shaft flew true, striking the beast in the shoulder. But when Nogel reached the place where it should have lain, there was no sign of the hart. Instead, a white owl watched him from a branch above his head.

"What trickery is this?" King Nogel heard wolves baying far away. He dismounted quickly, shrugging away any misgivings he was feeling. The hart must have staggered off to die, a trick of the light. He had only to search the undergrowth and he'd find the beast.

But twenty minutes later, the king emerged scraped and bloody from brambles, his search in vain. He cursed when he noticed that his horse was missing. Instead, a man stood watching him where the stag had vanished. A smallish figure, swords resting lightly in either hand.

"Who the fuck are you, and where's my horse?" Nogel strode towards the stranger, but the man faded off into the night before he could reach him. "Come back here," Nogel called, then dived low as an arrow thudded into a stump a foot from his position.

He rolled out of sight and scanned the clearing ahead. *Nothing.* No sound or sign of movement. Nogel cursed himself for a fool. Those boys had been right, he shouldn't have risked being out here alone. But rage gripped him at the thought of robbers lurking in *his* forest.

Bow in hand, King Nogel clambered and crawled through the undergrowth until he reached a broken cluster of rocks. These he climbed quickly and lay on his belly at the top of the biggest. He scanned the trees, a dark green canopy. Already the light was shifting from black to gray, the pre-dawn looming.

What was that? A flicker of movement below. Someone running beneath the trees. He turned his head, saw his horse had returned to the glade and was grazing head down at the grass. He waited. Somewhere an owl called out and the wolves answered. They were nearer now.

Nogel waited half an hour as a pink light filtered through the trees, changing their hue. The horse cropped down there in the glade. The outlaws were waiting for him to return. But their time was running out and come sun up his men would scour every tree for their lord, and these villains would be hanging from one. But how many were there?

Nogel determined to find out. He was a warrior king, not one to let his men deal with such vermin as this. He waited longer and at last he saw movement. A figure creeping back through the trees. An archer. Slowly, Nogel raised his aching body by his arms and then crouched in a position where he could shoot. The man was still visible, flitting beneath those trees, making for the glade where Nogel's horse stood silent.

The king set arrow to string and loosed in one swift movement. A scream cut short announced him on target. He glimpsed movement in the bushes, heard a thud. There would be others, including the swordsman he'd first seen. But after waiting another half hour, and the sun's first golden glow promising the first dry day in a week, Nogel stood up, swept the forest with his keen eyes, and then walked down to that glade.

Cowards usually skulked in shadows. *The sun has driven them away.* It was time for a new kind of hunt. Nogel smiled. He was going to enjoy this morning. He reached the horse, patted his neck and put one foot in a stirrup. He froze when a huge figure crashed out from the trees, a double-headed battle-axe held high.

Nogel freed his foot from the stirrup, dropping the bow and reaching out to slide the long heavy boar spear from the saddle. The axe man swung for him. The king blocked that cut with his spear, fending off with the oak shaft while distancing himself from his attacker. A giant clad in freshly oiled ring mail, not what he'd expected from outlaws lurking in the forest.

The big man swung out again with his axe. Nogel stepped out of reach and leveled the spear, lunging forward and forcing the enemy back. Someone laughed, and Nogel heard movement behind. He circled, the spear gripped in both sweaty palms. The swordsman stood watching him—beside him was an archer, arrow nocked and ready, his face red with rage.

"Put one in his gut," the swordsman said, and Nogel saw the shadow of the axe man rising behind him. He spun about as the string twanged and an arrow thudded into the dirt by his foot. The axe swung across. Nogel trapped its beard with the iron halter cross-piece of his boar spear and yanked, pulling the man forward. Nogel twisted around, and the axe man groaned as a second arrow thudded into his back. He sank to his knees, and Nogel kicked him hard in the face.

"That was careless," a casual voice said. The king turned, saw the swordsman smiling at him, the archer once more pulling back on his bow. Nogel cursed, nowhere to go this time. But just as the bowman made to release the killing shaft, his companion twisted his sword up into the man's belly, goring him open.

"I hate working with amateurs," the small man said, tugging his sword free of the archer's corpse. Nogel leaned on the boar spear, fighting for breath. To his right, the axe man struggled to his knees. Nogel rammed the butt of the spear into his skull and the man slunk prostrate again.

"Your turn," King Nogel said to the swordsman, who watched him with an amused expression from the edge of the glade. The man swung his sword in circles through the air with an arrogance that amazed Nogel.

"Our game has barely begun," the swordsman said, then looked up as the sudden sounds of horns and hounds baying announced that Nogel's men were arriving.

"Looks like we're going to have to postpone this visit." The stranger grinned at him again and vanished in the undergrowth. "I'll see you soon, my lord!"

"Who are you, villain?" Nogel roared at the trees, receiving no answer. A few minutes later his nobles arrived, their faces grim and alarmed at the corpses.

"I was attacked," King Nogel said. "That one still lives." He pointed to the prone axe man.

"That's not the worst of it, Highness." Yail Tolranna vaulted off his horse and approached his king. "Lord Staveport is dead."

Chapter 6 | Concerning Kings

Corin watched the road as a rider trotted his horse between steep banks, his green cloak resplendent and polished mail glinting in the sunshine. It was three days since he'd discovered the dead lord and made good his escape. Despite his gleaming attire, the rider looked worried, glancing anxiously along the high ridges leaning over the road, a perfect place for ambush as could be found between the border cities of Reln and Port Wind, and just three miles from where the road bridged the River Kelvannis, entering Kelthaine in a maze of woodland and high hills ahead.

"You doing this—or shall I?" Hagan was watching the rider too, both of them lying low, concealed by bushes, their horses tied, and the steep bank shouldering their shadows.

"I've got it," Corin said. "Just you keep both eyes out for his companions."

"Messenger, lone rider," Hagan said.

"For whom, I wonder?" Corin slipped from his hide as the horseman approached. He walked out into the open, standing with hands down his sides, Clouter slung across his back. The rider jerked his reins, halting his steed abruptly. The beast was skittish and danced this way and that until its rider steadied the pacing.

The horseman unslung a bow from his saddle sheaf and stringed an arrow. "You won't need that," Corin told him, but the rider pulled back on his bowstring.

"Bad idea," Hagan said, emerging from the afternoon shadows of the bank. The rider glanced about with wild eyes.

"Yes, lots of us lurking around here." Corin motioned the high ridges flanking the road. "A robber has to make an honest living. Now kindly dismount friend, and hand over your purse."

The rider hesitated, guiding his horse around.

"Do like he says and your throat stays uncut," Hagan said. "And, do it fast else we order our friends to fill you with arrows." The rider's eyes lashed the ridges again. He nodded, dropped the bow, and slid from the horse.

"Well done," Corin said. "Now I'll be taking your coin." The man reached for the purse hanging from his belt, untied the loop and passed the pouch across. Corin caught his arm, twisted it behind the man's back, and brought him to his knees. He unsheathed Biter and held it to the rider's throat.

"Grab the coin," Corin said to Hagan, and the Morwellan joined him.

"It's all I've got," the man coughed, as Corin nicked his skin with Biter's edge.

"We'll take it," Corin said. "But that's not what we want from you, old son." He removed Biter, allowing the man to clear his throat.

"I have nothing," the rider said.

"A fine-looking steed and nobleman's garb," Corin said. "A tad risky riding this road alone—must be a reason."

"I'm a messenger," the man said. "An envoy, and you need to let me go. King's business."

"What king would that be?"

The man looked at him as though he was mad. "King Nogel, of course."

Corin nodded slowly. "Well then, who's this message for?" The man looked uneasy, and Corin grabbed his cloak by the fur-lined trim. "Thing is, you're riding north. *Alone*. And rumor is King Nogel has returned to Wynais after some unfortunate business in the Wood between Waters, so it strikes me as odd you heading in the opposite direction."

"Told you I'm a messenger," the rider said. "King Nogel wants to inform the High King of Dal Terini's murder."

"Why would the High King give a toss about some low-life tax collector?" Hagan loomed above Corin and gazed down at the messenger. "I think you're lying."

The man shook his head but Corin prodded his cheek with Biter. "Your message is for Caswallon—yes?"

The man shook his head vigorously, but Corin dug deeper with the steel until he threw up an arm in panic. "Please, spare me. I will tell you everything I know."

"Good idea," Hagan said.

"I do serve Caswallon," the messenger said. "He sent me to Wynais a year ago to join King Nogel's rangers. There have been rumors of Nogel's disloyalty to his overlord, and Caswallon needed to ensure this wasn't so. I've concluded my audit and am now returning to inform the High King's councilor that his misgivings were unfounded."

"You're riding back to tell him the plot on Nogel's life failed," Corin said. "I want answers, matey. And quickly. You see, we lads have been blamed for some atrocity in those woods, and the only way we can prove ourselves innocent is by catching the real culprits. And I know you are aware of who these people are. Enlighten us, *traitor*, and I'll spare your life."

The man nodded slowly. "I accompanied the king to Cragowan Castle. My orders were to rendezvous with Keel, the man tasked with organizing Nogel's *accident*. Something went wrong, I didn't see Keel, but the king was ambushed and two men were killed, a third captured. Good men from Kelthaine, I don't know what happened."

"But Keel escaped?"

"Yes, and now Nogel is scouring Kelwyn for any sign of him and his surviving men. I have to report this failure back to Caswallon. His scouts were the ones I found murdered in the forest, and the man captured is an ex-Tiger called Dastan."

"How many men remain with Keel?" Corin asked, but it was Hagan who answered him.

"Five," he said. "Those others must have been late arrivals in case our crew didn't work out. I doubt they'll last the week unless they've slipped across the border."

"We have to find them," Corin said. "Especially Keel, and Nogel needs to know this was Caswallon's work and not some robber party."

"No doubt the captured one will squeak it out," Hagan said. "We need to get going, Corin—so slit that bastard's throat and let's move." The messenger paled hearing that.

"Dastan won't talk," the man said. "But I can help you." He screamed then as Hagan's sword cut into his throat, spraying Corin's face with blood.

"What the fuck did you do that for?" Corin leaped to his feet and squared on Hagan, who stood his ground, face a grim smear.

"This was taking too long. Achieving nothing. We need to cross that bridge and vanish into Kelthaine. Stay in this country another day and we'll be hung, or worse."

"Yeah, well—you go," Corin said. "I've a job to do and men to kill."

"If you mean Keel then you are deluded." Hagan's face was grim. "Even you're no match for that one, Corin an Fol. Come with me, we'll make for Fardoris and take ship south. Only safe thing to do. Then we'll get drunk in some godsforsaken tavern and I'll kill you in your sleep." He laughed briefly.

Corin ignored the barb and turned his back on Hagan, walking across to the bushes that concealed Thunder and the other horse. Corin stowed Biter and launched himself on Thunder's back. "Be seeing you Hagan," Corin called out to his companion, who was standing in the middle of the road, the corpse still at his feet. "Have a care, the king will be after you."

"He won't know unless you tell him," Hagan said. Corin urged Thunder to trot back down the road. "Corin!"

He turned and glanced over his shoulder, seeing Hagan still standing there. "Stay alive so I can kill you next time we meet," Corin called back, and Hagan saluted him, then vanished from the road.

***

King Nogel paced the throne room at the Silver Palace in Royal Wynais as his daughter watched him from the doorway, a week after his return from the hunt and the death of Lord Staveport. Young Ariane looked radiant in her green dress and coifed dark hair. Short of build, slender, and keen of eye—his princess, his precious jewel. The only one left alive that he loved.

"Father, what ails you?"

Nogel stopped pacing and turned to stare at his daughter. Ariane stood with feet braced and a determined look on her face. So like her mother. Yet Princess Ariane was tougher, shrewder. Those attributes came from him. Queen Cailine had been a dignified, peaceful soul, whereas her daughter was sharp and probing, not one to rest idle.

Today Ariane looked flustered and uncomfortable in the dress, and Nogel knew she'd prefer to be in riding leathers or practicing in the sword hall. After losing his queen, Nogel had doted on his daughter, even allowing her to train with his warriors, a thing unheard of in Wynais.

He smiled reassuringly. "I'm just restless child. Do not fret."

"Did the man talk?"

"What man?" Nogel felt a flash of irritation. He'd meant to keep last week's events from his daughter, but no doubt Ariane had charmed the details from his nobles. He'd have a word with Yail Tolranna and Tamersane later.

"The one you almost killed," she said. The axe warrior."

"He's told us nothing," Nogel said. "The man's half crazy. A rogue wolf and renegade, part of a bandit crew living in those woods."

"So he wasn't sent to kill you by that warlock in Kella City?"

"Ariane you really must stop this nonsense," Nogel snapped at her, but his daughter stood her ground, her lips tight and dark eyes determined. He noted her small fists clenched at her side.

"It's the truth—isn't it?"

"The truth is I'm no friend of Caswallon."

"Is that a joke—he sent men to kill you, Father."

"We have no proof of that," Nogel said, walking over to the high table to pour a brandy, his daughter's probing gaze following him. "There were other robbers in the woods, but we will hunt them down and justice will be done. Past time I cleaned up that border country."

"But the governor was murdered, and our dear Lord Rowan."

Nogel's face softened and he walked over and clasped his daughter close. "He will be avenged, my love. We will catch these villains." He stroked her dark coils and kissed her lightly on the forehead. "But I need you to stop worrying, girl. Leave this to our fighting men. Meanwhile I'll keep both eyes on the north—see what Caswallon's up to."

"He's wicked, Father."

"That he is," Nogel said. "And were we living near Kella City, I would be worried. But this is my country, Daughter, and you will rule here one day. You need to study statecraft, lore and court ethics, stop these idle musings."

"It is only that I worry about you."

"I know, and I appreciate that, child. If it's any consolation, I have people watching events up in Kella. Good people. Should anything happen to the High King, we will be ready. Now then . . . will you allow me to peruse—I've a kingdom to rule?"

"Of course, Father." Princess Ariane curtsied and left him.

The king watched her leave, a flood of emotions washing over him. Dearest Ariane had only seen twenty-one summers, and many of those had been without a mother. The girl was rebellious and headstrong, and he'd had complaints from court about her frequent ugly language, something that made him smile. Ariane would make a fine queen one day, but not for many years. The girl had a lot to learn, and Nogel would look for a suitable husband, maybe from Raleen or Morwella. He knew Tolranna had his eyes on Ariane, but no way would Nogel allow those raffish brothers to set hands on her. The boys were wild and irresponsible, especially the youngest, and like his daughter he indulged them too much. Lord Staveport had often told him so. "You'll rue that one day, Highness." *Poor Rowan.*

But what *had* happened in those woods? A botched attempt on his life by would-be assassins, or merely thugs as he'd told Ariane? Nogel knew she was right. This dark business stank of Caswallon. Only logical that he would go after Nogel, Staveport had been right about that. And Dal Terini murdered in his own chamber? That made no sense. Terini was a petty baron. Half thief, half tyrant—but useful. Killing him had served no purpose.

But having seen that swordsman in the woods, King Nogel suspected him the perpetrator. There'd been an uncanny look to the man. Not your common brigand or cutthroat. Almost, the man had a noble appearance, like some disinherited prince wanting revenge. A riddle, and one he intended to solve.

The name *Keel* meant nothing, which in itself was odd. Surely an accomplished villain like that would be known? Nogel's contacts knew every assassin and mercenary captain in the Four Kingdoms, yet this man was a mystery. A psychotic killer who enjoyed his work and had promised the king they'd meet again. Hopefully that would be soon and Keel would be swinging from a rope.

Nogel rubbed his tired eyes. He'd sent parties of rangers into those woods near Kelthaine, yet no word of the brigands had he yet received. Frustrating how they'd gone to ground. He watched from his window for a time, out at the wide vista, the city below and lake shimmering deepest blue beyond, framed by sunshine and mountains—his beloved Kelwyn.

After long moments perusal, Nogel sat at the desk with glass in one hand and quill the other. He wrote the note, then bid the guard outside the door arrange it be sent via pigeon right away.

***

Silon read the contents of the note written in King Nogel of Kelwyn's distinct and bold hand:

S

You were right to warn us,

Caswallon has showed his hand.

We need to act against him before all is lost.

I propose a clandestine council here in Wynais.

N. Kelwyn

So, what had happened? Silon leaned back in his study at Atarios and sighed. He'd been planning to leave for Vioyamis in the morning, but now it looked like he'd have to return to Kelwyn—and right away. King Nogel needed help finding these people, and then some kind of plan to counter Caswallon's actions. But how could they achieve that? The man was an accomplished schemer. To plot his downfall was potential suicide, but Silon suspected Nogel would want to act. And rashly, judging by his nature.

He sipped the iced tea and watched his daughter below. Nalissa was seated in a divan reading some tablet in the hot sun, her dark tresses covering her face. She seldom spoke much these days but seemed content. Silon would never forget how close he'd come to losing his only child. Corin had saved her. And yet, Corin was his other worry.

The man was a reckless storm of conflictions and not to be relied on. And he'd heard nothing from Corin in almost two weeks. Time to employ someone else to go see what had really occurred in that vicinity around Port Wind. Fortunately, Silon knew just the person for the task. And knowing her hatred for Corin an Fol, she'd most likely prove more than willing.

He strolled out to the gardens, the sun half blinding him. Nalissa looked up from her tablet. "Father?"

"How are you this morning, my girl?"

"Well enough—though I want to return to Vioyamis. I no longer enjoy city life."

"That's understandable, but I feel you are safer here."

She laughed. "You mean winged demon women are less likely to return to Atarios than elsewhere? That was months ago, Papa—yet still you fuss."

"You know what I mean, Nalissa. And you should be wed by now—gods know you've had enough suitors. Rubaan and the staff are here, and the city guard. Vioyamis is so remote, hard for me to relax with you alone down there. Indulge me please."

"Very well," she said. "How fares Corin an Fol these days?" Silon rolled his eyes and left her staring after him.

A brisk walk took him to the barbican and high crenulations of the city walls. Wedged tight against that stone was a maze of houses, hovels mostly—the poor quarter of the city. Silon made for the furthest of these and knocked firmly on the battered door.

The woman that opened it was hard of face and deeply tanned. She folded her tattooed arms and stared at him in disapproval.

"What the fuck do you want?"

Silon saw the curved blades resting against the lone table, and the small crossbow cranked and ready on the window sill. She wore her customary crimson, long tunic and leggings, her feet bare, and mass of dark hair disheveled. Her jet eyes were heavily kohled and she looked slightly drunk.

"I have a proposition for the Crimson Lady." Silon forced a smile. "One to our mutual advantage."

The hard-faced woman stared at him a moment and then nodded. "You had best come in then, merchant. It's been a while but I can't say I've missed you. What is it you want from me?"

"I need you to find someone."

"Who?"

"Corin an Fol."

Chapter 7 | A Score to Settle

She loved the sea, the movement beneath her feet and wind in her hair. It helped her to forget the past, the woman she had been before that terrible day. The day she almost died. Since then she'd contracted out and made a steady income that supported her various habits. She'd killed frequently, receiving coin from anyone with a grudge.

They didn't know her name, she'd almost forgotten it herself. These days she was *The Crimson Lady*, a pirate princess and killer in the dark. The old rage and betrayal she felt had almost faded away over the years until she saw the merchant from Raleen, a man she knew vaguely from having worked for him a few times. But her anger wasn't focused on Silon, but rather the man whose name he'd mentioned. The same individual who had abandoned her, left her to die in the desert.

I'm going to kill you, Corin an Fol. Cut out your heart for leaving me to die.

The merchantman had left Kador yesterday, bound for Reln docks. Once there, she'd slip ashore and ask questions, wait around until he showed up. Or else call in at Port Wind. He'd be holed up in those badlands somewhere. Silon hadn't explained why he wanted Corin removed from the game, neither had she asked. She'd never looked forward to a contract like this one before. Time had passed and she'd never sought him out. First it was the pain that kept her away, then the haze of fading memory brought on by those drugs and the bargain she'd made with the spirit woman that fateful day. It didn't matter. Her mind was sharp this morning. Clear as the sunlight dancing on the waves below. Find the Gray Wolf and kill him.

The ketch's sails trapped the wind, and she braced her strong legs as the waves mustered and swelled. Two swords swung from her broad belt, a dagger hidden up each flared sleeve, and the crossbow hung from a loop at her waist. She looked good, her customary crimson garb having received much needed attention from Silon's tailors in Atarios. Appearance was everything in this shallow existence. The sailors avoided her, knew her reputation.

The Crimson Lady grinned at the sunshine. The week ahead looked promising.

***

Corin downed his third ale as he gazed out the window, the rain beading on the broken glass of the tavern he'd found in the docks at Reln.

What to do?

He'd floundered since parting from Hagan, caught in a haze of indecision. Wanting to warn King Nogel, but preferring to hang on to his head while doing so. Hagan was right—they would be prime suspects, as would any mercenary type lurking in these parts. The king's men were scouring the country south of the border—the primary reason why he'd crossed over and was lying low in Reln. Corin hadn't been ready to follow Hagan, but after seeing how things stood, he saw this as his only choice.

He needed to contact Silon, though he didn't want to. The truth was he'd accomplished nothing, and the merchant probably knew more about what had happened in those woods than Corin did. So best to lie low and keep his ears peeled back. What better place for that than a fisher's tavern on the edge of the harbor? It was also an excuse to get drunk, which he hadn't done in a long while. *You have to make the most of any leisure time you get.* Besides, he needed time to think. Drinking helped the thinking.

Thunderhoof was being attended to in a warm, dry stable, the boy's eyes had shined when Corin gave him the silver.

The rain increased to a steady pour, and Corin leaned back in his chair, chugging at the thick dark brew, famous in this region. He could see the ocean, the white spray lashing the quay as the storm blew itself out.

Strange life. After leaving the Wolves, he'd worked for Silon these last six months. In and out of Permio, gleaning information on the bandit Krugan. Silon had left him be mostly, and their relationship—if cool—had been reasonable, dispassionate. Aside from that business with Nalissa.

Corin still had a soft spot for that girl. He'd only seen her twice since then, most his time being spent on the Krugan Gang stake-out. But even Permio hadn't been all bad. He'd spent many a week holed up in Silon's various taverns and coffee houses, listening while drinking. Each desert probe had to be well researched.

He'd fared north once to distant Car Carranis on the borderlands with Leeth, tasked with an important delivery Silon wouldn't trust to birds. The grim-faced commander of that vast stronghold had taken the parcel from him without comment. Corin had returned the next day.

It's been a busy few months. He sipped his ale and smiled as the warm brew helped wash the harsher memories away.

An hour passed. Another. The weather worsened to storm. Wind called shrill outside, and rain streamed and beaded against the shabby glass. Corin watched the ocean as a ketch pitched and rolled into the harbor. Hard to define, perhaps a local fisher daring the inclement weather, or else some durable skipper up from Port Wind to trade.

He saw men jumping ashore, striped clad sailors mostly. Was about to turn away when another figure emerged from the boat clad in crimson leather. This one walked with a confidence suggesting a fighting man, though smallish in build. Another mercenary sent by Caswallon, perhaps?

Corin would keep one eye on the door, but he doubted anyone would choose to stop here when there were better hostelries up in the town. He returned to his ale and drank deeply, wasting another hour and yawning as sleepiness stole upon him.

I need to contact Silon—there's nothing I can do here. Perhaps his best bet would be to book passage on the next ship sailing south. Return to 'Sarfe. Be expensive with Thunder accompanying him. But Corin still had enough coin left from that messenger's purse and could wait until Silon contacted him at the Crooked Knife. Seemed like a plan. He dared not ride back to Kelwyn, neither was there much reason to stay here. Keel and his cohorts would be long gone by now.

Corin had almost made up his mind when the door creaked open and a corpse walked in. He recognized her instantly. A sturdy looking woman clad in dark red leather, two swords at her side and a crossbow hanging from her belt. She saw him seated there and walked right up to him, her eyes hidden by a veil. Corin felt his jaw drop.

"You're dead," he said, his lips trembling.

A knife appeared in her left fist. She used it to knock his tankard from his hand and then shoved it point first in the table, a hair's breadth from his small finger.

"No, but you will be shortly." Yazrana pulled the veil from her face and stared down at him with icy loathing. Then she produced another knife and stabbed out at his eyes.

Corin caught her arm just in time and pulled her towards him over the table. She landed on top of him and bit a chunk out of his ear, the knife stabbing for his body this time, as he rolled sideways and tried to get away.

She stabbed his arm, a narrow slice. Corin kicked her in the belly and she rolled over, then climbed back on top of him and brought her head down hard on his nose.

Crack! Corin felt giddy and sick. He saw the knife moving and grabbed her arm again. She brought a knee up into his groin and he gulped at the pain. His fingers shot up for her face, one slid inside a nostril and tweaked the nose ring. He yanked, she let go and rolled off.

People surrounded them. He heard shouts—men were placing wagers despite the angry complaints of the patron bemoaning yet another fight in his tavern. Yazrana glared at him, a knife in each hand. Her nose was bleeding, but his was broken and his balls felt like balloons.

"You're a bastard," she spat in his face, readying for another attack.

"I thought you were dead." Corin wiped tears of pain from his eyes. "You broke my fucking heart that day."

"Liar!" Yazrana lashed out with one of the knives, narrowly missing his face. Corin refused to move this time. She clenched her teeth and hissed at him. "You left me to die. Abandoned me to hyenas and vultures."

"You *were* dead!" Corin spat blood out with the words. "I checked your heartbeat, felt for your breath. I lay there with you in the blood and shit, watched you fade in my arms. For fuck's sake, Rana—you were dead."

She wiped the blood from her nose and lips, rose to her feet. Corin looked up at her as the woman he had loved gazed down on him with icy contempt. She stowed her daggers up her flared sleeves and yelled at the patron. "Get me ale." Corin saw the man look at her askance and hurry off to comply. "You're full of shit," she told Corin. "You always were, and I was stupid enough to love you."

"I loved you too," Corin said.

"You left me to die," she said in a quiet voice. "And when I crawled back into Cappel Cormac on my knees and enquired after my love, they told me you were shacked up with some tavern wench. I would have killed you then, but by the time I found the place you were gone. I was starving and penniless, forced to beg for food. All because of you."

"It was Taskala that betrayed us that day," Corin said. "Not me, and I killed that bastard on Gardale Moor. I avenged you, Yazrana." Corin felt the tears streaming down his face. He had loved this woman and he had watched her die. Seen the wounds, the flies settling inside them. Now she stood before him—impossibly alive—her cruel Permian eyes full of hatred and her brown fists thrust into her waist belt. The innkeep appeared and slammed the large tankards on the table, spilling ale.

"I think it's time you two made up," the man said. Corin glared at him. *Small chance of that.* But then Yazrana laughed that throaty chuckle he remembered so well.

"You haven't lost that gormless expression I remember so well," she said, pulling up a chair and easing herself onto it. She leaned forward and slurped at her ale.

Corin rose shakily and took the seat opposite. "The girl was nothing," he said. "A lost moment. I was desperate and lonely and you were gone. The only thing that kept me going was my need to avenge you."

She stared at him in silence, sipping her ale. "You were always full of shit, Corin an Fol." Her dark eyes flicked across to the patron. "Have you a spare room, sir?" The man nodded, vainly trying to hide his smirk. "We'll take it."

"We . . . ?" Corin blinked in surprise.

"Have some catching up to do," the dark-eyed woman said.

***

"You've failed, and yet you seem smug—why is that?" Caswallon gazed at Keel coolly with those probing dark eyes. A lesser man would flinch or avert his gaze beneath that mendacious stare. But Keel was unfazed. He had nothing to fear from this man.

"I laid the plans down satisfactorily," Keel said. "Your men let me down. I appreciate it's hard getting reliable people these days."

"Is that so?" Caswallon leaned back in his chair. They were seated in the remote cold room he used for interviews, far above the High King's palace, a lone tower some called the "Astrologer's Roost." It was the second time Keel had been here. "I think you are over optimistic. That you made such a mess that the whole of Kelwyn is suspicious. Any attempt of surprise blown away by your incompetence."

Keel felt a flush of anger but held back from comment. He might not fear Caswallon, but there was no reason to provoke the man any more than was necessary. He'd heard the rumors—Caswallon had mysterious and powerful allies, and staying in with him could help Keel achieve his own specific goals.

"And why did you murder Dal Terini?"

Keel shrugged. "He'd told me what I needed to know, I saw no reason to let him live. And it diverted the militia's attentions, leaving me to look to the king."

"Who is still alive." Caswallon steepled his long hands and stared hard into Keel's eyes. "And unlikely to hunt any time soon. You've let me down Keel, and yet you offer no excuses. I'm disappointed to say the least."

"It was reconnaissance I deemed necessary," Keel said. "Time to lay the traps but not yet time to spring them."

"The *time* seemed perfect to me."

"If I'd killed Nogel in that wood, the suspicion would fall primarily on you. Close to the border, an act of war—enough reason for Belmarius's Bears and the remnant of Halfdan's scurvy wargs to rise up against you. Far better we strike when they are looking elsewhere."

Caswallon arrowed his gaze at Keel. "Where?"

"Wynais City, or there about. The least place they'd expect."

Caswallon laughed. "You amaze me, Assassin. Your arrogance holds no bounds. Your men are being hunted throughout the Four Kingdoms, and yet you expect to enter that city—alone, I assume—and kill its king, when you failed to kill him in a wood?"

"I wasn't trying to kill him," Keel said. "If I had been he'd be dead. This game has barely started, Councilor. As for those men"—he smiled—"decoys."

"*Lord High* Councilor," Caswallon corrected, his thick brows knotted together in studious thought. "You forget yourself, Assassin. I weary of your excuses. But I'm intrigued enough to allow you another attempt. Can I trust you not to fail me again?"

"I didn't fail you this time," Keel snapped back. "You'll realize that soon enough. But, yes, I will see this task through. You have my word on that, and in return I expect the gold you promised."

Caswallon nodded. "I will keep my part of the bargain, though I've heard you're already rich and wonder why you put yourself at risk in such a venture. Why not task out to others, reuse the men who escaped Nogel's vengeance? I believe they are still at large."

"It's not just about the gold," Keel said. "I've a reputation to keep." He gazed at the fire crackling by the door. "How fares your master, the High King?"

"Ailing, but not near quickly enough." Caswallon's shrewd eyes bored into Keel's and the killer smiled.

"You have only to ask."

Caswallon nodded. "We'll see how the game plays out. I need you back in Kelwyn, and on task."

"No problem."

"And none of your men have been captured yet? Seriously?" Caswallon laughed again. "King Nogel's people fail him. Kelwynians have always been soft, protected by their overlord. It's past time they paid for such indolence."

Keel shrugged, bored with the subject. "The three you sent were killed, but then you know that."

"Actually, I didn't." The smile drained from Caswallon's face. "That messenger should have reported back to you. The inside man—he was part of Nogel's hunting party."

"I've received no reports aside your own."

"I will look into this," Keel said. "And I don't like that Morwellan you sent last month."

"Hagan Delmorier," Caswallon smiled. "A rival?"

Keel barked a laugh. "Hardly, but the man's got a temper and he's clever, unlike the others we used who are all so predictably stupid. I don't trust the fucker—Hagan could risk warning the king, dicing his own head against the gold he'd receive. Man's a gambler, that much I know."

"Hagan's not important," Caswallon said, "and King Nogel will have heard of the man's crimes up in Morwella. The scar on his face makes him easy to recognize. I interviewed Delmorier. He's proud and vain. The man bares a grudge that will give him away even if his face doesn't. Hagan's got a death wish. Do not concern yourself with him."

"I wasn't," Keel said. "I just said I didn't *like* him."

"You can kill him next time you meet."

***

Yazrana snuffed the candle and let the darkness creep into the room. Outside, Corin heard the crash of breaker against the harbor wall. He sipped the remnants of his ale and lay back, tired and dreamy, head throbbing with too much ale and nose still hurting badly. The woman's musky scent filled the room, and her sweating body pressed against his own.

"At least you still know how to please a lady," she breathed in his ear.

"Lady . . .?" Corin smiled as she cuffed him.

"The Crimson Lady." Yazrana smiled back, her face just visible in the night. "Terror of the ocean."

"I've heard the stories," Corin said. He hadn't, but didn't want to spoil the moment. They'd made love passionately three times and he was beyond exhausted and strangely happy. Corin wondered if he were dreaming already. She had been dead in that desert pass. Cold and gone. But paradox or not, Yaz was back from the grave and warm in his arms.

I'll worry about that in the morning.

"I need to sleep," Corin said. "If I can with this buggered nose. Then tomorrow you can tell me all about your adventures, and how you returned from the black shore."

"Sleep?" Yazrana chuckled, the throaty deep sound he remembered so well. "We're only getting warmed up." Corin groaned as her hand slid down his belly and stiffened him below. Amazing how weariness can vanish in a second.

Next morning, Corin stood at the quayside watching the waves lash and boom against the stone. Yazrana stood beside him, a crimson headscarf masking her features, and heavy cloak keeping her warm. She was from Permio and not used to this climate.

"Need I assume you've a plan in place?" the woman asked him. Corin had told her about the botched attempt on King Nogel's life.

"Report back to Silon," he said. "Little else I can do—lest he send another wench to murder me." She punched his arm and he smiled, feeling very happy this morning.

"If he sends another woman, I will kill her first," Yazrana said, and Corin raised a brow. "Not that I've forgiven you, Gray Wolf. Last night's activity soothed my loathing of you temporarily, but I still could stab you at any time."

"I'll bear that in mind," Corin said. He reached down and kissed her full lips, pressing her body against his until she wrapped her arms around him and pulled him close.

"But maybe not today," Yazrana said.

"Silon sent you to kill me." Corin looked pained. "I find that a bit excessive—I saved his daughter from slavery. Funny way to show his gratitude."

"I expect you shagged her too," Yazrana said. "That merchant has a warped sense of humor, and I liked seeing the horror in your eyes. Owed you that much."

"I didn't think Silon had a sense of humor," Corin said. "Nor do I understand why you are so fucking angry with me."

"Because you fucking left me to die. The only man I loved! Gone. I woke cold and alone, my body wracked with pain, a pile of corpses everywhere and no fucking lover. And you wonder why I'm *hurt?*"

"You were dead, Yaz," Corin insisted. "I held you against me, felt your last breath fail and fade. I wept for hours over your corpse, woman. I just cannot believe you're alive." He felt the salty sting of tears cornering his eyes. "Gods—I loved you woman. *Still do.*"

Her tough face softened. She looked younger than her forty years, a handsome strong woman, never beautiful—but the warmest soul he'd ever known.

"For a while I thought I was dead," she said, allowing him to hold her again as the sea lashed with increased vigor against the stone. "My body was broken, my heart torn apart. This world and everything in it my enemy. Yet here I am, and still wondering whether I should kill you." She smiled a sad smile and he kissed her again. "I'm not the woman you knew, Corin an Fol. A made a pact with fate. And I'm getting old, and tired."

"You weren't last night, Yaz," Corin smiled. "At least tell me what happened, how you survived, and the years following, and how you met up with that shithead merchant in Port Sarfe."

"Perhaps I'll tell you that story one day," Yazrana said, her eyes dreamy and gazing over the high, crashing waves. "I'm cold in this drab country. Miss the sun." As he studied her face, Corin thought he saw the ghost of another woman gazing at him. A woman with eyes of green and gold. The moment passed and he shook his head.

"Something amiss?" she asked. He didn't respond so she turned away. "Let's return to the tavern and plan our next move."

Corin got his grin back. "You're staying with me?"

"At least until I've got a better offer." She smiled.

Two days later, Corin and Yazrana were seated in a crowded roadside inn a dozen miles north of Calprissa, the dour merchant facing them across the table.

"I'm glad you two made up," Silon said. *Was that a smirk on his face?* Corin repressed the urge to jump over the table and stick something sharp in the merchant's face, widen that half grin.

"You sent her to kill me."

Silon shrugged. "You needed a jolt, and I needed to know what happened in that forest. You are unreliable as a scout."

"I saved your daughter's life."

"That's your profession—it's what you do," Silon said. "And you're well paid."

"Not lately," Corin said. "I think—"

"Shut, up," Yazrana said, silencing the room as all faces turned her way. The dark woman wrapped in crimson cloth. Corin grinned at her, and Silon wiped his face with a napkin.

"Is there a problem here?" The portly landlord inched over and addressed Silon. He looked worried; Yazrana's curved swords and Corin's massive longsword had caught everyone's attention.

"Just friendly banter, good fellow." Silon waved the patron off to fetch more ale. "Time we discussed our next move," he said to the pair facing him across the table. Silon lowered his voice. "This mad dog Keel will strike again."

"You know the villain?" Corin asked.

"By reputation only," Silon said. "He's a clever, unpredictable killer, and Keel's not his real name. I'm not entirely certain, but suspect I know the rogue's true identity."

The innkeep brought the ale. Corin and the woman both took hearty sips, but Silon stared at his cup forlornly. Corin remembered how the merchant disliked ale, preferring his own grape in the distant south.

"Well then indulge us—who is he?" Corin asked, but Silon shrugged the question away.

"Nogel must be protected at all costs."

"He has an army." Yazrana wiped froth from her mouth and glared at some of the men still watching her from corners of the inn. They turned their faces away and whispered. This crimson-clad woman was causing quite a stir.

"Obtuse Kelwynians." Silon shook his head. "Soft and useless. Nogel's a warrior, but the king surrounds himself with nobles who don't know one end of a sword from the other. His daughter's a better fighter than most."

"He has a daughter?" Corin blinked at Silon, and noticed Yazrana's dark eyes flicker his way. "A princess?"

"Congratulations on working that one out," Silon said, the sarcasm lost on Corin. "We need to warn Nogel firsthand that Keel will strike again, and that the king needs to watch Caswallon closer than ever."

"By *we* you mean Yazrana and me," Corin said.

"Correct," Silon said. "But first you need to mop up his rag tag confederates and track down Hagan Delmorier. Kill them all and then close in on Keel. That one needs to be caught alive."

"Hagan's a former ally," Corin said. "I'm not killing him unless I have to. Besides he's quit the job. Gone back up north." Corin had explained to the pair how he'd met up with Hagan, and what they'd found in the forest, including Lord Staveport's suspected murder by Keel.

"You'll have to kill Hagan one day," Silon said. "Best you do it sooner, else he gets you first."

"Apart from the Morwellan, who else is there?" Yazrana swept the room with her cool gaze, one or two faces turned away again. The rest appeared preoccupied, and an awkward silence had filled the taproom. Corin eased Biter at his side. He'd greased the scabbard and could slide the short sword out in a nonce. Preparation is key. *This could turn dangerous.*

"Hagan mentioned five others apart from Keel," Corin said. "As far as I know, they stuck around. Hard to be sure, but Nogel was quick to set watches on all the ports and roads leaving this part of his country. And we watched the Kelthaine road. That's how we caught that messenger. The man could have been useful, but Hagan gutted him."

"Start with Postin," Silon said, his eyes sweeping the room carefully. "He's from around here."

"I heard his name mentioned," Corin said, but couldn't recall where. Beside him Yazrana nodded slowly.

"Makes sense."

"Postin's a local thug," Silon said. "He's a huge brute well known as a troublemaker. 'Postin the Hammer,' they call him. He recently escaped the hang man's noose and had a price on his head long before this sorry business. He'll be lurking in the woods, is my guess. You can start by scouring those and flushing him out. Once you've dealt with Postin, move on to the others. But hold off with Keel—we'll want to link that one back to his master in Kelthaine."

"The High King is our enemy?" Yazrana looked puzzled. "The Tekara—his crown. I thought it protected all Four Kingdoms."

"Not the High King, his councilor. And, yes—the crown has done so until recently." Silon looked bitter. "But Caswallon's no common schemer. He's deft at sorcery and I fear for Kelsalion III. The High King suffers poor health and his mind is feeble. If Caswallon takes out King Nogel—the only real opponent left since Belmarius and Halfdan have gone to ground—the High King will be on borrowed time. We need to act fast."

Corin downed his ale. It was stuffy in the room and the familiar sound of rain drummed on the dirty glass of the lone tavern window. "Ready when you are," he said. They looked at him.

Silon nodded. "Let's go." He stood, nodded to the innkeep and tossed some coins on the table. Yazrana and Corin followed the merchant outside, both had hands on swords. Faces turned away, except one character hidden in a corner who Corin glimpsed before exiting the room.

Outside in the rain, they mounted their horses and Silon bid them good day. "Find Postin," he said. "And when you do, watch out for that hammer he carries." Corin and Yazrana watched horse and rider vanish in the misty rain. *Time to go.* They spurred their mounts northwards, back towards the forest surrounding Port Wind and the wilderness beyond.

***

The inn's occupants resumed their business, the three strangers soon forgotten. As was the lone figure who stole from the busy taproom and saddled his horse. Keel smiled. This game was getting interesting.

Chapter 8 | Hunters and Quarry

The arrow passed an inch from his face and stuck in a tree trunk. The shaft quivered and stilled as Corin dived headfirst into the bracken. He'd left Yazrana and the horses a mile up the lane before he'd diverted towards the thin trail of smoke.

A crawl through bushes had revealed their quarry, a huge man sitting hunched by the fire. Postin the Hammer looked half troll. Shaven head with right ear missing, and massive bulk hunched in misery in the drizzle, the tell-tale hammer resting like an iron sapling against a nearby tree.

Corin made his move when sudden lightning struck close by, blinding him and making him jump in alarm. And also saving his life. For the briefest moment he'd glimpsed the archer in the distance, allowing him to dive before the shaft struck home.

Corin rolled to his knees and scanned ahead. Another lightning strike, this time further away. Postin still sat there like a stone carving. A trap to lure them in? But who had warned the giant, and where was the archer now?

Corin feared for Yazrana, still out on that road. The horses would give her position away and the bowman would turn on her. *I'm not losing you again.* Rage gave him strength as he surged free from the brush, pushed down on his legs and ran zig-zagging toward a thicker clump of trees. He heard another arrow zing close, a third a moment later.

At least the bastard was still focused on Corin. But what if there were more? He dare not worry about that. Lightning struck again behind him and the growl of thunder filled the forest.

Corin heard the horses neighing and cursed the bad luck. Poor Thunder—they'd be an easy target unless Yazrana found cover for them fast.

Clouter gripped in his palms like a paddle, Corin lay low and shuffled through the soaked bed of pine needles and mulch as he worked his elbows and knees toward the wispy smoke trail. He reached a clearing and looked down.

Postin had gone. Corin heard a bearlike growl behind him. Instinct saved him again as he rolled sideways, the massive hammer smashing into the dirt where his head had been. The giant tugged the weapon free and, legs braced wide, swung again.

Corin lashed out with a sidekick, catching Postin's knee and overbalancing the big man. The hammer missed again. Corin hoisted himself up with Clouter, blocked another swing that almost knocked him off his feet, turned and ran back into the thicket.

Postin swore and gave chase—a shaggy mass of bone and muscle, but slow moving—and Corin soon left him panting for breath at the edge of a rise. Let the giant rage—he needed to find that archer.

Corin watched as Postin glowered down below, making ready to climb the hill. Corin left him there and ranged sideways, keeping out of sight. That bowman had to be close, and he'd fired from this direction. Corin searched for several minutes to scant avail. Postin's curses informed him the wretch still looked for him nearer the campfire. But Corin had circled back to the road, and a quick run had him arriving at the place where he'd left the woman.

Yazrana had vanished, as had the horses, and Corin heard no sound. He cursed their ill fortune again, crouching low on his knees as he gulped down breaths. Then he smiled in relief, hearing hoofs on stone and seeing her emerge, riding the mare with Thunderhoof clomping behind, her gloved hands leading him by the reins, and her face veiled by scarf and mist.

Corin waved her back but Yazrana rode close then vaulted from the saddle. "He's not alone," Corin said, and the woman nodded. Then her gaze swept past Corin and her face whitened.

"Who is that?"

Corin saw a man standing in the lane some twenty yards away. He was smiling like a fool and held a war bow in his right hand. He took a step toward them and bowed slowly, his hands swept wide. Corin cursed, took brisk strides forward, but the archer vanished in the shadow of the trees. Out of sight, he had the advantage again.

They led their horses back down the lane before mounting up and cantering south toward Port Wind, Postin's shouts fading in the distance.

"What now?" Yazrana asked as they reined up and watched the lane. Nothing moved out there, and the only sound was the constant drip of water on leaf.

"That bastard nearly got me," Corin said. He explained how he'd seen Postin but had then been shot at. "He used that troll for bait."

"But who was he—another outlaw? Perhaps Postin has joined a gang?"

Corin shook his head. "That was Keel."

"How can you be sure?"

"Something Hagan said, the bastard's playing games with us."

"Well then, he'll regret that—won't he," Yazrana's eyes were large with anger but she looked worried too. They both knew how lethal an archer was in these woods. "Let's head back into town," she said. "At least we can take shelter and feed our horses. If this Keel's all he's rumored to be he'll follow us, catch up with us in a tavern. I hate this fucking country, so I'd rather cut his eyes out by a nice warm fireside while you replenish my ale."

"Agreed," Corin said. "Though Keel might prove hard to net. Whatever the bastard is planning, there's no point us waiting here for him to fill us with arrows." The two riders urged their soaked beasts to continue through the wooded lane until the trees parted and the valley revealed the stone walls and roofs of Port Wind in the distance, the thin gray line of ocean beyond.

Corin cursed. Keel had stolen a march on them. But this game had only just started and that wouldn't happen again. Let the killer come with his night-gangers in the deep of darkness. Yaz and Corin would be ready for them.

***

Postin looked up as the archer emerged from his hide. "Do I have to do everything for you?" Keel said.

"You told me to wait here." Postin leaned against his hammer, his round face red with rage. "I could have killed that bastard if you'd have warned me he was creeping about."

"I wanted to see how he worked, learn who this is stalking us."

"You let them get away?"

"I needed to give you boys some work," Keel said, waving a hand as the others appeared through the trees. "Keep you busy and the attention away from me."

"They're making for Port Wind," Rasheffan said, interrupting as he loomed before Keel. The other three stood alongside, shuffling their feet as Keel watched them.

"That's predictable." Keel felt slightly disappointed. "You'll need to draw them out."

"Why didn't you kill them when you had the chance?" Crall asked.

"Because I need to know who they're working for, and that means questioning them with a hot knife and some enjoyable leisure time. Your task, Crall. Postin can break the bones and you can work the knife. I hate missing out but I've more important matters to attend. So off you run—go do the grunt work and get details."

"Two men?" Torke asked. "Shouldn't be a problem. But why bother? This entire region's still crawling with soldiers and bounty hunters, all baying for our blood."

"Most of whom are inexperienced and clumsy," Keel said. "These two are different. *Professionals*. I need to know who sent them, so I can return the favor at a later time."

"We'll find them tonight," Postin said, fingering the metal shaft of his hammer. "I'll dent the longswordsman with this—just enough to make him squeak."

"What of the other man?" Rasheffan asked Keel.

He grinned. "A woman. She favors the curved sword. Had two scimitars strapped to her waist when I saw her. Cut a rare dash in her dark red attire, though a tad conspicuous for an assassin."

"A fucking woman?" Postin looked outraged, while Rasheffan glanced at Torke, who grinned. Crall shook his head slowly.

"A female mercenary," Crall said. "She'd have to be good."

"More recently a pirate," Keel said. "I'm sure you've heard of The Crimson Lady, latest terror of the ocean." Keel smiled at the irony. A woman posing as a pirate had set herself against the biggest pirate of them all. Of course, the men here didn't know that. Keel had no intention of revealing his true identity to nobodies such as these.

"I've heard rumors, no more," Torke said. "A Raleenian beauty who was once Prince Rael of Crenna's lover. They say she betrayed him, stole some gold from that pirate prince and set up on her own."

The kick sent him sprawling on his face. The second one had him groaning and clutching his groin.

"You shouldn't listen to fucking rumors," Keel said, kicking Torke a third time. The other men backed off, seeing the fury in his face. Torke groaned and coughed up blood. Keel saw the fear in the man's face and withdrew his boot. He forced a grin.

"The woman is a lone operator and a charlatan," Keel said. "A renegade from the Permian wars. But I want to question her at some point, gentlemen. Therefore, I need you to keep The Crimson Lady fresh and eager for my return."

"Where are you going?" Postin was the first to risk speaking.

"That's not your concern, Hammer," Keel said in a quieter voice. "Do this for me. Capture them both and find out who they work for—and keep them alive and talkative, especially the woman. I'll be back in a week."

"You're going after the king again," Crall spat tobacco. "You never explained what went wrong in the woods. It wasn't our call."

"Didn't say it was. But I need you to keep the attention focused on this country. So make some noise when you capture that pair."

***

Corin ran the cloth down the length of steel as he gazed out the window. Out there, a full moon spilled silver over the ocean. The wind had died back, and the sea was calmer, a few stars shone accompanying the moon. It was very late, and no sound could be heard save the distant thud of wave on stone.

Yazrana slept behind him, her naked body sprawled across the cot. He glanced her way, taking in the deep brown skin, the scars on her back, as well as the enticing curves and corners. She was a fine woman and he still didn't understand how she was alive. They'd made love late into the night after slipping back into the tavern, a nod and wink from the innkeep as he unlocked their room.

Corin was weary, finding hard to keep his eyes open, the monotony of his vigil only eased by his work on the sword. He gazed down the length of the blade, turning it this way and that, trapping the moonlight, the steely-blue glint shifting to silver.

Movement caught his eye—something white gliding past the moon. *An owl.* Corin tensed, felt a shiver. Pale and beautiful; the bird settled on a stone pillar down below, its huge eyes gazing straight up at him. *Eyes of green and gold.* Never blinking. Corin lowered Clouter to the bed where Yazrana still slept silently. He rose to his feet. The owl lifted, gave a long low call and then vanished into the night.

Corin nudged Yazrana and she stirred.

"What is it?" The woman blinked back sleep.

"We need to leave," Corin said. Yazrana looked at him and then nodded.

"You've seen them?"

"No—but I know they're coming. Call it intuition." She dressed quickly and strapped on her swords as Corin watched for shapes in the night.

"It's almost dawn," Yaz said. "Perhaps we should wait for the light . . . wait." She nudged his arm. "Over there." She pointed to the right where the street vanished behind a building, a lone lantern casting flickering shadows. A huge figure stood beneath it, the long-hafted hammer giving his identity away.

"I doubt he's alone," Corin said. "Best we slip out the rear." They waited a moment until two other men joined Postin, the three gazing up at the inn. Corin rubbed his chin. *Where are the other two?* He'd wager they were close, maybe Keel too—though that was unlikely. Were that so, he'd probably be in the room with them, the creepy bastard.

"Find a window out back," Corin whispered. "Get the horses ready and I'll see what they're planning."

"We leave together or not at all," Yazrana said. But Corin shook his head. He reached over, grabbed her shoulder and stroked her long thick hair, kissing her lips gently.

"I cannot slip outside quietly with a six-foot sword," Corin said. "You're lighter on your feet than me. Far better I create a diversion by making some noise while you slip out the back with the horses. Wait for me in the woods outside town." Yazrana looked worried but nodded her head reluctantly.

"Be careful," Yazrana said, and he blew her a kiss and turned back to the window. Postin and his friends hadn't moved. A slight creak behind announced she'd slipped out through the door. Corin let out a long slow breath. The three men were leaning close, as though locked in deep discussion. Postin shook his hammer at them and the other two faded from view. Corin smiled. These boys didn't have a clue. He could understand why both Hagan and Keel had distanced themselves from such amateurs. He needed to draw their attention away from the inn. Allow Yaz to free the horses and get away.

I'm going to enjoy this.

The other two returned. Corin heard a gruff shout and saw Postin shove the tallest one. All three looked up when the sound of hoofs clopping announced Yazrana was leading the horses from the stables. Time he intervened. Corin unfastened the latches and opened the inn door.

"Sorry I kept you waiting," Corin said, sliding Clouter free of its pommel.

"Get the woman," Postin said to the other two, who ran off immediately towards the back of the inn. Corin's tossed knife took the slowest in the back of the thigh. That one cursed and dropped to his leg, one less for her to worry about.

Postin grinned at Corin. "I'm ready for you this time, Longsword. No creeping up on me in the woods."

"Where's your master, Troll-face?" Corin walked closer, Clouter slung casually over a shoulder. He crossed over to where the wounded man was trying to staunch the blood. Corin kicked him in the face and the man sprawled. He brought his heel down on the back of his neck, crunching the bone.

Postin waited with hammer held ready. "Thought you'd need my full attention," Corin said. "Didn't want him stabbing me in the back." Corin flicked Clouter across his shoulder and swung out at Postin—a clever swing meant to disembowel. But Postin was quicker than he looked.

The big man jumped back, stepped sideways and swung his hammer, the huge mallet narrowly missing Corin's head.

Corin stepped forward to strike again, but the pointed end of the weapon stabbed at his eyes. Corin jumped back while Postin reversed the hammer and brought it crashing down. Corin dived to his left as the hammer smashed into the cobbles and sent sparks flying.

Corin twisted his body and sliced sideways, both hands gripping the blade on either side of the cross-guard.

Postin blocked that swipe with the iron shaft of his weapon and then forced the hammer down hard, the heavy weapon almost wrenching Clouter from Corin's grasp. He let go with one hand and allowed his blade to slide free.

Postin grinned and stepped forward again, thrusting the pointed end of the weapon at Corin's face. Stabbing and poking, stepping forward, the hammer held ready to swing. Axe for hewing, hammer to crush, the spike for mauling and maiming. Corin had never faced a poll-axe before, and this giant was a master of the weapon.

Another poke at his face. This time grazing his cheek, and the giant forcing him back to a wall. He needed to act fast before Postin's friends came back. Yazrana should be free of the town by now. Corin wasn't going to win this fight easily. *Cut your losses and stay alive.*

Corin blocked a thrust and jabbed Clouter low at Postin's groin, sending him off balance. Before the man could ready his pole-axe, Corin rammed Clouter's pommel hard into Postin's ear, knocking him back and allowing Corin to leap clear of the hammer sweeping at his head.

A dance to the side. Postin swung again but Corin was already sprinting up the lane. The third man appeared with a bow in his hand. He reached for an arrow but Corin shoulder charged him and kept running. He didn't look back, but the cusses coming from behind meant they were giving chase.

Corin reached the low wall separating the town from the fields and woods beyond. He vaulted the wall, crashing into bushes, and clambered free using Clouter to hoist his aching body forwards. Then he heard someone come crashing after him and saw the arrow strike a nearby tree.

Corin zig-zagged back and forth across the field until he reached the cover of the woods, the road barely visible through the darkness of the trees.

"Yazrana!"

***

She'd wasted no time. Had both horses saddled and was leading them up the lane when the first man appeared, blocking her way. Yazrana's tossed knife found his right eye and she led the horses past as quickly as she was able.

A second man appeared, saw his dead comrade and yelled. Yazrana let go of the reins and reached for her swords. The man facing her was gaunt and hard-faced. "You just killed my friend," he said, leveling his broadsword at her. He stepped forward, confidently sweeping hard and fast across.

Yazrana's blades met the sword mid swing. She pulled one free while chopping down with the other. Her opponent backed off, his eyes wild. Yazrana grinned at him. Stepped forward again and he turned and ran.

She led the horse through the gates and out onto the road. The shadows were lengthening as morning beckoned. Yazrana mounted up. She'd find a suitable place to hide the beasts and then return to help her lover. She made for a distant line of oaks, glimpsed the sun peeking out through their gnarly trunks. Was about to slip from her saddle when a stone struck her head and knocked her from the horse.

Blood streamed down her face as Yazrana tried to focus. She'd landed badly, tried to stand but a boot kicked her in the face and she was thrown back to lie sprawling. A face loomed above her. Cold green eyes smiling.

"I couldn't stay away after all," Keel said, reaching down with the knife.

Chapter 9 | Outlaws

A rare glint of sun cast glow on the road ahead. Corin sprinted towards the dark line of pines, the place where he expected to find her. The horses were there, the reins neatly tied to a tree. But of Yazrana there was no sign. Corin glanced around wide eyed. What had happened here?

He looked down at the muddy lane, sweeping his gaze back and forth until he saw boot marks leading off into the woods. He made to follow, then stopped, hearing shouts coming from the town gates behind. The sun blinding him, Corin slung Clouter in its scabbard, untied both horses and vaulted onto Thunderhoof's back. Yazrana must be around here somewhere. He'd lead the horses away and return to this spot. Yaz would catch up with him later, and Postin and his mates would think they'd cantered away.

But where was she? Corin didn't like the way this morning had turned out. He should have killed Postin, but had nearly been skewered himself. He'd badly underestimated the brute. That wouldn't happen a second time.

He reached a turn in the road and dismounted by a riverbank where the wide stream was dammed by a fallen tree, enabling Thunderhoof to ford across downstream of the logjam, Corin leading Yazrana's beast by its reins. Once hidden from the road, he dismounted and led the horses down to a clearing flanked by large pines. He lashed their reins to the nearest tree, making sure they were well hidden from the road.

"I won't be long," Corin told Thunder, and turned back for the river. He unslung Clouter and held the longsword high as he waded across, soaked from the waist down. The water was chilled, and he was sneezing and cursing by the time he got back on the road.

Corin waited, crouched and listening. Satisfied they weren't coming this way, he started running back down the road until he reached the spot where she'd tied them. There were new boot scuffs scattered around, the large ones must have been Postin's.

Corin wiped sweat from his face and gazed around. They must have gone back to town to plan their next move. No doubt they'd regroup later and try again. He sheathed Clouter again and slid the saex free. Time to find out where she'd gone.

Corin studied the road and verges, walking slowly back and forth. Crouching down he traced what looked to be marks caused by light shoes, hardly noticeable compared to the heavy boot scuffs back where the horses had been.

Closer inspection proved he was right. Someone else had been here. Then he saw the track left by her boots and knew what had happened. *They had Yazrana.* Keel must have waited for their return, using his thugs to lure them out. The arrow thrust in the dirt to his right cast away any remaining doubt. Corin cursed his judgement. He'd been outplayed again and now the bastards had his woman.

Corin followed the signs away from the road. Down below, the stream curled around rocks and then parted as a large stone resembling a granite egg sat in the center of the stream, looking like some reckless god had cast it there. The tracks led that way. Light footsteps and the marks of boot scuffs. She'd been unconscious, Keel dragging her.

He reached the river again and saw a rudimentary camp. Faggots still glowed and hoofs had left marks. Then he saw the crimson scarf stained with blood. Her blood he suspected. The thought of that killer holding Yazrana filled him with rage. But she had to be alive or why make the effort? Corin followed the hoofprints until they rejoined the road a mile south of where it split towards Port Wind.

Keel was heading south. Corin was left with a bleak choice. If he followed blindly, Keel would set traps, and the others would know where he was heading. He'd sooner not have Postin stalking him while he was tracking Keel.

Heart heavy, Corin walked back to the town gates. He'd get some information and then decide what was best. The road in was busy with carts and cattle as drovers and farmers led their stock into town. The gates were open and Corin strolled through as though he hadn't a care in the world. The lone gate guard was sleeping in a rocking chair. Things had returned to normal after King Nogel's visit and the murders. If anyone was aware of the fighting down by the harbor, they showed no sign. Corin got the odd skeptical look as he walked back down to the quay. He ignored those quizzical faces and entered the tavern where they'd spent the night.

The innkeep was dusting down tables. His face when he saw Corin was far from friendly. "You left in a hurry and without paying." Corin slapped two silver coins on the table. The innkeep stared at them, his face slightly less hostile. "There's a dead man outside my yard."

"It's the three still alive you need to worry about," Corin said. "They were going to attack your inn so I went out to meet them." Corin followed the innkeep out the back where the corpse still lay at the corner of the yard, well hidden from casual eyes.

"I moved the body," the innkeep said. "I'd sooner the soldiers stay away, and this man is known to me."

"Another archer," Corin said as he gazed down at the corpse. He hadn't noticed the bow during the attack and now realized how worse things could have gone. "One of Keel's men."

The man's face paled hearing that name. "Kulvin," the innkeep said. "He was a loner, an outlaw with a large price on his head. A renegade from Kelthaine who'd plagued this area over the last few months. I'd heard he'd got together with Postin the Hammer."

"Who is still at large, as are his friends," Corin said. "Far worse, Keel has my woman."

The man stared at him for a moment in shock. Corin didn't know why he'd told the innkeep, but he seemed no friend of these villains. "How do you know that?"

"He left a calling card, so to speak." Corin felt flushed with anger, thinking of Yazrana hurt by that bastard.

"You're certain she's alive?"

"Yes—I have to believe that. He wants to lure me close."

The innkeep shook his head slowly. "There is more to it than that. Keel doesn't care about you—why would he?"

Corin shrugged. "He's a warped wicked bastard. This is a game to him, or so it appears."

The innkeep awarded him a long careful look, as though weighing some heavy matter. Finally, he nodded. "Come inside and get some food in your belly. You look exhausted lad, and you'll not save her by getting yourself killed."

"What of Postin and company?"

"They won't be seen here during daylight," the innkeep said. "Big Postin's well known and there are still soldiers around. I expect they're out in the countryside looking for you."

Corin nodded and then cursed, thinking of Thunderhoof and the other horse still tethered by that stream. Another mistake he'd made this morning. *I'm losing my edge.* Corin pushed negative thoughts aside contemptuously. He needed to up his game if he retained any chance of saving Yazrana. The thought of losing her after finding her again was too much to bear.

Keel wouldn't kill her yet. Corin wished he could believe that.

"What do you know about Keel?" Corin asked the innkeep as he returned from the kitchens with a large haunch of ham and a tankard of ale. Corin launched himself at both.

"Very little—just rumors. They say he was the one who killed the governor. A shadowy figure who's united some of the worst villains in this region. He hasn't been around long and I don't know where he came from. One thing is certain, the man's no common villain."

"I need to get back to my horse," Corin said. "I left him with Yazrana's out in the woods."

"The Crimson Lady," the innkeep smiled. "Stupid of me not to guess her identity when I first saw her."

"What are you talking about?"

"Your paramour is a well-known pirate princess. Those curved swords and her red attire gave her away, though I didn't grasp it at the time. She's been raiding the coastal towns for several months."

"That doesn't make much sense." Corin pinned the man with his gaze. "I fought alongside her in the Second Permian War. We were in the Wolves. I thought she'd died back there."

"I've heard stories, nothing solid. There was a rumor going around that The Crimson Lady was in league with the Assassin of Crenna. True or not, this rogue Keel must know her value. She'd fetch a high price in Calprissa, I'll warrant."

"You think that's where he'll take her?"

"Only choice that makes sense, unless he'd away up to Kelthaine."

"No—he was heading south."

"Well then, it's either Calprissa or right on down to Permio—where I hear the new Sultan will pay considerably more for her."

"What?" Corin blinked, he was missing so much here. "*Why?*"

"Because she almost killed his father."

Corin didn't know how to respond to that. It was though a large chunk of his past was missing. Rather than question the innkeep more, he changed the subject. "I need to mop up around here before I can leave Port Wind," Corin said, his voice raw with emotion. "I don't want Keel's men on my back while I search for that rascal."

"I can help you with that."

"Thanks, but you're an innkeeper. I—"

"—was a soldier once based in Permio."

"You fought against Barakani?"

"No, this was earlier, twenty-five years ago."

Corin blinked. "You must have been very young." The innkeep didn't look a day over forty.

"I'd seen thirty winters, was a veteran even back then," the innkeep said with a wry smile. "I weather well. Fought in Leeth too, the barbarian fringes—when King Hal first seized the throne and sent his raiders into the Gap."

Corin shrugged. "Thanks, but I don't think you need concern yourself with this business. Even if you were a redoubtable warrior, you're long in the tooth and have a tavern to run. No offense, and I appreciate your support." The innkeep burst out laughing, much to Corin's surprise. "What is funny?"

"You fucking youngsters are all the same. *Know it all.* I could still knock you on your back longfellow, though I'd sooner not mess with that sword you carry. But let me tell you my reasons."

"Go ahead."

"Postin murdered some customers a while back. Trade used to be good here but over the last few years it's died away. A lot of that is due to Dal Terini's taxes, the king's turning a blind eye, and local outlaws terrorizing the neighborhood. I'm ready for payback."

The innkeep's name was Stane. He'd been a sergeant in the Tiger Regiment, but Corin had decided not to hold that against him. Stane produced a well-oiled broadsword from some hidden cupboard, three throwing knives, a wood axe and a longbow with a sack full of shafts.

"Going to war?" Corin raised a brow, impressed by Stane's armory.

"I like to be prepared." Stane grinned. The man looked a lot happier than Corin felt. "It's slow season in Port Wind. Dead, or dying. I'll close the shutters and tell my niece to mind things while we're gone. I'll come back with a sizeable reward and buy another tavern."

"Sounds like you've been planning this a while." Corin stared at Stane, not knowing what to think. But the old soldier looked durable, and his cheerful manner would prove welcome.

"He'll go after the king again."

"Who will?" Corin was still thinking about Calprissa and where Yazrana would be.

"Keel, of course."

"I thought you said you didn't know anything about him? Why risk another attack on the king? There must be easier targets now that Nogel's had his fingers scorched."

"True, but I don't think that will sway Keel. On the contrary, it will encourage him. That's if he's who I think he is." Corin gave Stane a strange look but the innkeep shrugged. "Just an old man's notion—let's concentrate on finding your pirate lady and dealing with Postin and the others."

"Sounds good," Corin said. "And thanks for your help."

"As I said, I can use the reward money." Stane smiled, and Corin knew he was hiding something. Why would a man in his mid-fifties risk all on a venture like this?

An hour later, Corin—after returning to the horses—led them close to the road. There he waited until Stane joined him just before dusk. The innkeep had had some tidying-up to do but had put the word out about Postin and the others. He hadn't had to wait long before the answers came.

"They're holed up in a cave," Stane said. "I know where it is—Postin's lurked there before. I suspect they're awaiting word from Keel, or else planning another visit into town tonight."

"How far?"

"A few miles inland, there's a lone hill that rises above the River Kelphalos. You can see for miles from its crown. The cave is near the top and well hidden."

"You're thinking we attack before nightfall? Won't that be risky?"

"Suicidal—they'd spot us a mile away. We need to climb the hill after dark and wait until they're back. That's if they don't decide to spend a night at home." He grinned.

***

Postin yawned as Torke worked the fire into a blaze. He could see Crall's silhouette outside as he leaned against the rock, gazing down on the road and river far below.

"You think he's right?" Torke asked, turning from the fire and staring at Postin.

"What's that? Who?" Postin had been trying to nap and wasn't in the mood for conversation.

"Crall. He reckons Keel's going after the king again."

"Who cares?" Postin said. "Doesn't concern us no more. Job was a fuck up."

"Keel seemed pleased with himself, even if we didn't kill Nogel."

"I said I don't care." Postin glared at his companion and then looked across as Crall leaped down to join them, his albino features and long white hair rendering him ghostly in the gloom.

"Be fully dark soon," Crall said. "What are our plans?"

"Sleeping," Postin said. They'd caught some rabbits earlier and he'd eaten his full.

"Those bastards killed Rasheffan and Kulvin," Torke said, his eyes glinting by the fire.

"Your friends, not mine," Postin said.

"We need to go back to that tavern and question its patron," Crall said. "He might know where they were heading, and I for one want to pay them a second visit. What say you, Torke?"

"Ready when you are." They were about to leave when Postin stood up and rubbed his eyes.

"I'm coming," he said. "I could use an ale." They extinguished the fire and slipped down through the bushes, gripping branches as they made the steep descent. Once back on the road, the three started the long walk into town.

The sky had cleared and the moon rode over the ocean as the three stood outside the tavern, staring up at its closed shutters and unlit rooms.

"Strange," Torke said. "Maybe the soldiers got word of our visit this morning and closed his establishment down. Best we keep moving."

They wandered through the empty streets of Port Wind as fresh rainclouds spilled droplets over the stone. "Back to the cave," Torke said. "We can start afresh tomorrow." Crall nodded, but Postin stood where he was.

"You go, I'm having a drink."

"The taverns are mostly shut. Any remaining open are likely to contain soldiers," Torke said.

"*The Last Drover's* most likely still open. I'll take my chances," Postin told him and left them staring at him as he walked up the hill toward the center of Port Wind. The rain had increased to a steady downpour. Postin leaned under a building and waited. He saw three soldiers leave the shabby tavern at the far end of the street, and after watching them depart, he strode across and pushed open the doors.

The inn was empty bar a sleepy-eyed patron, an angry looking girl, and a lolling wet hound that drooled over a bone by the fireplace. The man and woman glanced his way, their faces worried. The hound growled then returned its attention to his bone.

"We're closed," the girl said, folding her grubby arms. The man reached for something behind the counter and then froze as Postin lifted his hammer into view for the first time.

"You?" The man looked terrified, the girl confused.

"Who's this?" she asked, looking up at Postin, the hammer, and back to the man.

"I need a drink," Postin said. "Not after trouble, but if one of you squeaks to them soldiers outside, I'll split the pair of you in half."

***

Corin scanned the cave entrance for any sign of life. Clouds racked the sky above and the bushes sighed as the wind rushed through. Cold and dark as a tomb on this hill. "I'll go take a look," Corin said to his companion. Stane was still panting after the long steep climb. He could barely answer but shook his head. Corin wondered how useful the former Tiger would be in a fight. Time would tell.

He crept over to the entrance, keeping low and whenever he could, pressing himself against the large rocks to avoid leaving shadows. A narrow entrance that was hard to find in the dark opened into an expansive cavern. Corin let his eyes adjust. He noticed a faint glow over to the right. Remains of a fire stamped out. Just the odd faggot glinting red. Aside from that, there were blankets and cooking utensils. Corin saw a spear and some arrows stacked against a ledge.

He ventured further inside until he reached a brook, and leaned down and washed his face. Nothing here but a few fresh rabbit bones. Corin walked back to the entrance and whistled softly.

Moments later a face loomed out the dark and Stane stumbled in. "Now we wait," Corin said. Stane just nodded and stretched out against a damp rock.

"Sure you are up to this, old fella?"

"Enjoying myself so far." Stane's teeth glinted in the gloom. "Truth is I miss the life of a soldier, never really settled in the tavern trade. Too many tossers as customers, you have to swallow your tongue."

"I'll bet." Corin couldn't see himself as an innkeeper. Maybe a doorman, but not a proprietor. He thought of Rado down in Port Sarfe and all the nonsense he put up with. Not for Corin, that life. "So why did you leave the regiment? I've heard the Tigers cosset their older veterans. You could have enjoyed a cushy posting in Kella or Car Caranis. Lots of wine and lasses."

"Perani."

"I don't know the man, only his reputation." The Tiger's general was known as a martinet and hard taskmaster. His troops feared him more than the Bears feared their leader, Belmarius, and the Wolves feared Lord Halfdan. Halfdan had been a good commander, willing to do anything his men did. Belmarius was rumored to be the same. This Perani sounded like Taskala, who had given Corin such a hard time as a recruit—a score that had been well settled.

"Perani was always a bastard, but he's changed over the years. I used to respect him," Stane said. "Cool in a crisis and dependable. But some worm got inside him and he became cruel. And corrupt. I blame that conniving bastard Caswallon. Perani's a puppet to the sorcerer."

"So Caswallon really is a sorcerer?" Corin changed the subject.

"The worst kind."

"I didn't know there was a good kind." Corin hadn't believed such folk existed but he'd had to reassess his opinion of late.

"There are lots of different types," Stane said. "Wizards, warlocks, mages, magicians and enchanters—all have different skill sets. Caswallon deals in necromancy."

"That doesn't sound good." Corin had no idea what necromancy was but just hearing the word made the cave appear darker.

"We saw *things*. I've . . . witnessed . . ." Stane shook his head. "The regiment changed, Corin. The officers, some of the men. They became cruel like Perani, all eager to climb the greasy pole. I started to see bad things happening in the barracks. Not the usual coarse banter, but bullying and baiting, even the odd grisly murder. Some of my old comrades disappeared after a dust-up in Leeth."

"Men die in battle."

"True, but I found out they were ambushed after Caswallon tipped the barbarians off."

"Why would he do that?"

"Because he's in league with the enemy, both Permio's sultan and the King of Leeth. And I wouldn't be surprised if he's allied himself with those Crenise bastards. I learned a great deal in Kella, Corin—whispers in taverns and barracks. Caswallon's plotting something big. I'd like to do my part to stop him—however small—rather than grow old and useless in a tavern. It's another reason why I'm here."

Corin spat on the dirt. Crenise pirates had murdered his kin. He'd paid some back but still hoped to pay more . . .

"That's not the worst of it," Stane said. Corin stared at his outline as the wind whistled outside the cave accompanied by a new sound. Falling rain on leaves. "He's going to kill the High King."

"Seems a bit extreme," Corin said. Stane was bitter and obviously had fallen out with his officers. Maybe they'd blocked his pension, poor bastard. That said, Corin didn't swallow this conspiracy stuff. Too much time listening in taverns. Still he might as well humor the old boy, as there wasn't much else to do in this cave until the brigands returned.

"Caswallon's been working toward this for years," Stane said. "Ever since the High King's heir was drowned alongside his queen in that shipwreck. Kelsalion is weak and ailing and his only heir's a complete waste of space."

"Prince Tarin?"

"Wanker."

Corin looked up hearing the sound of movement outside. "Looks like we've got company." He reached for Clouter as he rose slowly to his feet.

***

Crall gazed at the rocks hiding their secret camp. Rain soaked his shoulders and face as he looked up there. "What's up?" Torke asked, inching alongside.

"Something's wrong," Crall said. "I can feel it." Torke knew all about Crall's instinct and didn't respond. The albino's sixth sense had saved the gang on several occasions. Crall knelt down and examined the soaking ground. At last he'd saw what he'd been looking for, the faint marks left by boots, to the left of the hidden track they always followed.

"Visitors?" Torke said, the grim smile just showing on his face. Crall nodded and slid his sword free from its scabbard. He took a step forward and then cursed as a blow knocked him from his feet.

"Wanted to meet you lads outside," a voice said. "Figured you would know your way around the cave better than us." Crall rose to his knees and groaned as a boot impacted his face, cracking his nose and spurting blood on the wet grass. Somewhere close he heard the brief clash of steel and then Torke begging for mercy.

"We only need one of them alive," said a second voice, sounded older.

"Kill him," Crall croaked as the blood streamed from his face. "He can't help you like I can."

"You fucking bastard, Crall!" Torke must have risen to his feet, as a brief thud announced he was sprawling again. A face loomed over Crall. Long and shaggy and something sharp pricked his ear.

"Don't think your mate appreciates your loyalty, strawhead." Crall froze as the blade point cut into his ear. "I can sympathize with that. You should be able to trust your friends in this life. So methinks I'll kill you instead."

Crall closed his eyes but nothing happened, until seconds later he heard Torke cry out as a blade silenced his vocal chords. "But then again"—the long face showed a nasty smile—"we might change our mind."

Crall nodded.

"Time to get up, loyal Crall. You can tell us everything you know inside the cave. Dry and cozy in there." That evil smile again. Crall staggered to his feet, trying to staunch the flow of blood seeping from his nostrils.

"We best light the fire again so we can heat the knife. Cauterize his hooter."

"I'm on it," the older man said. Crall heard him crash through the bushes. Back in the cave, he was forced to his knees and pressed back against the rock. A tall figure stood over him as the older man worked fresh life into the fire.

"I'll tell you what you want to know—what is it?" Crall asked, noticing the light growing outside. Dawn was approaching.

"You tell me?" Crall could see the face more clearly. A tough, unpleasant-looking individual with a faded scar splitting his right brow and vanishing into his shaggy mane, the hair smoky brown and disheveled. Bearded, a long nose, recently broken. That hard face was dominated by angry eyes. Tall and wiry, he was leaning on a sword almost as long as himself.

"You're Corin an Fol," Crall said, and he heard the older one mutter something behind him. "The Longsword. I was in Permio a while back. Heard stories about you."

"All true." The cruel smile again. "This is Clouter." He rammed the longsword point down into the dirt an inch from Crall's groin. "And this one I named Biter." The man pulled back his cloak, revealing a nasty-looking curved blade a little under two feet long. "Good for close-up work. Just sharpened it this morning. Tell me which body parts you're willing to lose first."

Crall felt panic seize him. "*Please*—I can help you get your woman back. I know where Keel would have taken her."

"You . . . know?"

"Yes, I am certain."

"Enlighten us, Sir Crall."

"Wynais, the Silver City."

"And why the fuck would he go there?"

"He means to finish what he started in the forest."

The man called Corin laughed. "In Wynais? King Nogel's city, surrounded by soldiers, guards, royal bodyguards, the king's rangers, and royal Kelwynian Cavalry? Sounds like a winning plan. Or maybe you're talking shit like I think you are."

"If I was trying to hoodwink you, I'd say Calprissa—it's the obvious choice being close, and Keel would expect you to seek him there."

"You think Keel knows who we are."

Crall managed a laugh despite his fear. "He probably knows how many shits you've had this week. Bastard's in a league of his own, Longsword. You, me, your mystery friend over there. We're not in his class."

The other man showed his face. And Crall vaguely recognized him. The innkeeper at one of the taverns by the quayside. "You haven't used a sword in a while," Crall said.

The man smiled briefly. He produced a well-oiled broadsword and pointed it at Crall's head. "It's coming back to me," he said.

"Shall I poke him a bit, Corin an Fol?" The man looked at his tall companion. "If I'd known who you were, I wouldn't have let you in my inn, Gray Wolf. A sodding deserter and renegade from Halfdan's crew."

"You shouldn't believe everything you hear, Stane." The Longsword's hard eyes flicked his way, and Crall felt a glimmer of hope. Perhaps he could drive a wedge here. But Corin looked down on him again and smiled. "He doesn't mean it. Stane's an ex-Tiger. They're all tossers. Besides, if he's going to kill me, he'll make sure you're dead first."

Stane snorted. "Bugger this conversation, I'm heating the knife—so this scarecrow bastard needs to start talking sense." He rounded on Crall. "Where's Keel now?"

"I'm not a fucking crystal gazer." Crall had recovered some of his habitual courage after the initial shock and pain. "But I'd hazard a guess he's riding the high road to Wynais, the woman in tow."

"Why take her?" Corin kicked him hard in the groin and Crall swallowed the pain, looking up unblinking at the tall figure standing over him.

"Insurance."

"What do you know about her?"

"Save as most people. She was a Permian assassin who's been playing at piracy until she had to lie low after upsetting Lord Rael of Crenna. Tough lass—but that's a man I'd sooner not cross. Last I heard she was doing contract work for that weasel merchant down in Raleen. Heard you'd worked for him too?"

"You are well informed for a lowlife scum bag," Corin said. "But you're still talking bollocks. Why wouldn't Keel sell The Crimson Lady at Calprissa, where they love hanging pirates? Dragging her all the way to Wynais seems like a lot of hard work, and too risky even for a wild card like Keel."

"He needs a scapegoat," Crall said. "For when he kills the king."

Stane loomed close. "He might be onto something there, though I hate to agree with the turd."

"Alright," Corin said. "I'll chew that unlikely cud in my mind while Stane gets his knife ready. Hot enough yet?"

"Almost." Stane wandered off again to check on the fire.

"Next I need to know where the big lad is so I can shove that hammer up his arse," Corin an Fol said.

"Postin stayed in Port Wind," Crall said. "I expect he's still there if he hasn't killed some bugger and had to leg it. He'll be drunk as a drowned rat in a cider vat, but that's when he's most dangerous."

"Good," said Corin. "You can go find him and I'll do the wet work. First though, I need to know everything about your leader. Stane here's a bit of a thinker. Too much time pulling pints, and perhaps his organ too. He thinks he knows your boss's true identity."

Crall paled. "You're better off not knowing."

"Try me."

Chapter 10 | Hostage

Yazrana crouched low and spat blood from her mouth. High above, she saw buzzards circling, hunting for carcasses. *You're not having me yet, you bastards.* Yazrana hated those birds and had good cause; they'd feasted on her flesh a year ago.

Her slender captor saw where her gaze led and smiled. A charming smile from a handsome face with almost perfect teeth. The loathing she felt for those birds paled in comparison to her feelings for this man.

"Think it's you they're waiting for?"

"I don't care."

"Tosh—that's a touch melodramatic. No one wants to be eaten by birds. Messy, noisy things." Keel dusted down his immaculate coat and tunic. He'd abandoned his outlaw gear and was dressed like a Kelwynian nobleman in russet and green, all smiles and pleasantry. "I'm inclined to think you care a great deal. You were tortured once, is that true?"

"Left for dead actually. Abandoned."

"Ah, yes. The same long-legged loon that you've recently forgiven. I'll never understand the fairer sex."

"And I've heard you've no use for women." She spat the words out, forcing a smile.

He looked pained and turned away. "I could hurt you in a special way for that. A lingering pain that would drain all your spirit, were you not part of my plan. But do have a care—I might change my mind if provoked further."

"I'm not part of any plan. Forget it, Assassin. I know who you are, remember—and I don't fear you." The latter statement was a lie and they both knew it. Everyone feared this man. Especially those who knew his proper identity. Yazrana had seen his handiwork before. But the man now calling himself Keel wasn't going to use her for his twisted games without a struggle.

He gazed down at her. "You're damaged goods, Yazrana. I'll bet you were a beauty in your twenties. Quite a stunner amongst the stinking hovels and fleshpots of Cappel Cormac. How many times did you raise your skirts for copper, or to service anyone at hand for a bite to eat?"

She spat at him and he laughed. "You're say . . . forty, maybe even older, and that beauty has faded like rose buds in frost. *Gone.* Nothing left but the long cold gray of winter—the silence of the grave." His expression hardened. "You shouldn't have taken to the waters, else I'd never have heard of you."

"What are you going to do—sell me?"

But he'd bored of the conversation, as he so frequently did. The man was quicksilver, his moods shifting effortlessly from almost amiable to sudden terrifying violence. She knew whatever he said, Keel could turn on her at any moment and slice open her throat. Perhaps that would be for the best—he was right after all. Her glory days were over.

But what about Corin? She'd always loved him in her way. At first when he was that gangly recruit she'd nestled after him, wanted to protect her protege from that sadistic bastard Taskala. But she'd been lonely too. Beneath her battle-hardened masks, Yazrana had been lonely, not only then but throughout her entire life.

Corin an Fol had been a brief glimmer of warmth in a cold empty world. She had no kin, no friends—save perhaps old Lord Halfdan, but that had turned sour when she'd become his lover for that brief time. Hard to be a fighting woman in a world of men.

She had been hurt when Corin abandoned her in the desert. She didn't blame him entirely, but the rage she'd felt inside had wanted to tear him apart. He'd told her she'd been dead and clearly believed it was so. *He should have made damn sure.* Not that that mattered now, as she would soon be hanging from some gibbet in Calprissa, or gutted open by the monster who held her captive. Nothing else was certain in this life. Only death. You take what you can while breath allows and hope the gods are kind. They weren't being kind today.

Keel was seated by the fire, ignoring her. The ropes chafed into her hands as she leaned back against the tree stump. She was thirsty and tired, and her sturdy but stiff body no longer recovered as it used to. Yazrana still had her pride, though. She could best any man she'd met with a sword, save perhaps Corin. He'd taken to the longsword like no other. A rare skill, and the passion to match. His wild anger and long limbs suited to the blade. Then there was this man—Keel. Yazrana doubted she could kill him even if she had her swords—now neatly lashed to his saddle, and doubtless to be sold along with her crimson garb.

At least he hadn't stripped her, or worse. The man seemed disinterested in that, which was strange, but then maybe the rumors were true after all. She dared not mutter his true name, allowed lest the demon awaken inside him. Best not to test him again.

She gazed down at her battered body. Her worn leather trousers and the vest badly torn, her tanned arms bare despite the damp chill, the intricate tri-colored tattoos spiraling up from wrist to shoulder, accompanied by the scars of ceaseless campaigns.

She'd gotten strangely lucky in Permio, but that had cost her. A bargain with a creature she tried to forget. Always there, waiting on the edge of consciousness. Smiling at her with winking eyes of gold and green.

And what rash actions. Stalking the sultan in his own palace—a madness had taken her and the memory was hazy, as was the brief time spent with her current captor, out there on the ocean. The place where he was prince.

The price placed on her head in Permio had forced her into that new, albeit abrupt career. Raiding the coast with a ship full of freed slaves. So romantic, it was as though a different person had resided inside her. Emboldening her, prompting her to reach out to aspirations worthy of far better folk than she. She'd owned three ships. They'd done well for several months and she'd looked the part with her crimson dashing attire. What a farce.

The Crimson Lady. Yazrana smiled at the irony. *I have never been a lady.*

He turned and caught her smile. "What's funny?" He seemed intrigued and ceased his constant prodding at the fire he'd just lit. Night had fallen and she hoped he'd toss a blanket her way.

"Life," she said.

He stared at her for a long moment until she feared he'd turn on her. Instead he almost smiled, not the cruel mercurial grin he usually showed, but rather a whimsical sorrow, as though they were alone in a world of emptiness and void. "Is strange, agreed," Keel said eventually. "But compared to what? I mean—what else is there?"

"The gods," she said, puzzled by this new mood. "The other dimensions, outside and beyond the gates of death."

"Hearsay. Maybe such places and beings don't even exist," Keel said. "Perhaps we are alone in this world. There are no gods and no other realms but this febrile filthy existence. We are lemmings rushing into endless dark, Yazrana. Why did you try to kill the sultan?"

She was shocked by the question, and couldn't answer at first.

"I was curious," he said. "Impressed even—why I accompanied you. Few professional assassins would dare the courts of Sedinadola, let alone a charlatan like you."

"I had nothing to lose, and a lot of hatred against the man who'd taken everything from me."

"The sultan? You were naïve, but I applaud your action. Enjoyed our venture, and for a while I was happy to let you roam the oceans in your stolen dhow. But when people started talking about you in taverns, and your renown spread, I decided to intervene—sent my men to sink your vessel. No offense."

"I assumed that was you," she said. "They killed everyone—I alone escaped."

"And joined my wonderful crew." He chuckled.

"I don't recall being given a choice."

"You could have done well in my service." His jade eyes narrowed. "I might have made you a captain, for you were sharp. But you lack ruthlessness and then acted squeamishly on that beach."

"Where you butchered everyone."

"We are all killers, Yazrana."

"But you enjoy it more than most."

"Which is partly why I've taken you captive. I never leave a job unfinished. It's bad for business."

"Are you going to trade me for coin in Calprissa? Those noble folks will love watching me swing, and doubtless reimburse you generously for providing them with the leisure."

"We're not making for Calprissa," he said, poking the fire again.

"Why not? Where are you taking me? Permio?" Again, she was puzzled, as Calprissa was both close and the main coastal city in Kelwyn—a land she'd raided for almost three months.

"Because that would be both boring and predictable," Keel said. "And I despise those two things more than anything else in this life. Besides, I'm rich already."

"What then?" She felt a cold quiver of dread in her belly.

"You are going to help me, my dear." He saw the strain on her face and laughed. "We're going to kill King Nogel, you and I—and I'll make sure you're the one they blame for such an abomination. They won't just hang you in Wynais, Yazrana.

They'll cut open your belly with red-hot steel and tug out your guts. It's nothing personal," he added after a moment. "Strictly business."

Yazrana closed her eyes and tried pushing back the fear. *I will escape, take my own life. Ruin your fucking plans.* But she knew he'd be watching her with those cunning jade eyes. This was a game to Keel. A sport and she was the bait. She felt tears of anger well in her eyes but refused to blink. "You're still working for Caswallon like a common lackey."

He didn't like that and rose with that casual grace he always possessed. He stood over her and kicked her hard between the legs. "Don't test me, cunt. Whatever they do in Wynais I can do better—make it last much longer. Now gets some sleep, if you can." He laughed as though at some private joke. "Sweet dreams, Crimson Lady." Then he removed a blanket from the horses' saddle gear and reached down almost gently, arranging it around her shoulders. Yazrana ignored the pain and stared at him in silence. Somewhere close by an owl spoke in a long deep voice.

Despite everything, she slept for a time. Waking when he kicked her ankles. "You look younger when you're sleeping." His smile now resembled a kindly father gazing down on his favorite child. "It's a clear blue morning. Rarer than hen's teeth in this shitty corner of the world. I'll bring you some gruel, it's almost warm—so I'm spoiling you this morning."

Throughout that day and the next they rode east along deer tracks and random paths flanking the southern banks of the Kelphalos and making for the low hills of central Kelwyn. Keel let her straddle the packhorse, her hands lashed behind her back and legs strapped tightly to the saddle with two leather belts. He rode ahead on his stolen stallion. Pilfered from a farm outside Port Wind, his deft gloved hands guiding the reins to the accompanying beast.

On the third day after leaving Port Wind, Keel's stolen food ran out and he dared a tavern. They rode in at evening, the sun's departing rays splattering the west like a discarded blood orange. He untied her arms and released the belts strapping her thighs. She almost swooned as the blood rushed back into her legs, setting off the pins and needles from ankle to crutch. She slid from the horse and staggered.

"Relax, I'll be watching you," Keel said. "Try anything stupid and I'll not only gut you but everything living thing in the tavern and the village surrounding." She felt her head nod, knowing that was no idle threat.

She followed him inside. A few faces turned their way and voices fell silent. Keel waved a hand when he saw a portly man wading through customers, a large plate of meat in his grubby hands. "We'll have some of that, Master Innkeep," Keel said, ignoring the stares.

"You'll have to wait," the fat man said, wiping sweat from his brow. He froze when the tossed knife struck a beam an inch from his right ear. It quivered and stilled as all eyes watched.

Keel smiled, and Yazrana saw the second dagger appear in his hand. "I'm not really one for waiting," he said. He pushed Yazrana forward and bid her sit at the nearest table over by the fire. It was hot and stuffy in here but she welcomed the break from the weather outside.

The patron hurried off to comply, his round face nervous and lips trembling. Yazrana doubted they'd ever witnessed excitement like this before. The food, when it arrived, was nothing special but tasted delicious after days of clammy gruel. Yazrana wolfed it down using her fingers to scoop up the last crumbs and liquid. He smiled at her.

"How elegant you are—and us with company too." As usual Keel looked immaculate, whereas her vest and leggings were stained and spoiled, his cloak and fur-trimmed garb was pristine as ever. The landlord hovered close.

"We need lodging too," Keel said.

"We're full, sir."

"Then you'll have to throw someone out—won't you. And I'd do that quickly, as we're weary and I get vexed when weary. I might be tempted to slice some of that bacon off your belly." The man's face paled as he hurried off to do as bidden.

The inn was almost empty, as most of the customers had mumbled excuses and left. Yazrana heard angry exchanges above her head and guessed the tenants had just found out they were sleeping in the street. Their curses grew louder and she wished she could run upstairs and slap them. What did they have to whine about? These people knew nothing about fear.

The innkeep led Keel up the stairs after the fuss had died down. Yazrana followed, her eyes glancing for anything sharp in reach. She'd probably not get a better chance of escape than in this tavern before they reached Wynais.

The room was shoddy but quiet, especially since the inn had emptied itself rapidly after their departure upstairs. She suspected it would be full tomorrow, as the entire village and surrounding farms would be huddled together discussing the sinister knifeman and his dark-eyed silent woman.

A single scruffy bed in the corner and a rickety window with two broken panes of glass; they awarded lantern views of some kind of garden below. Aside that, there was a drab chair and a candle burnt down to the stubs. She heard a horse shuffling about below, somewhere close by, and made of note of where the stables must be.

Keel stretched out on the bed and pulled off his boots, tossing them into a corner. Yazrana seated herself on the only chair, as far from him as she could get in that small room. He smiled, hinted the bed. "We can share if you wish." She glared at him and Keel shrugged, lounging on his back and staring up at the badly peeling plaster on the ceiling.

"These people need a decorator," Keel said, closing his eyes. "Enjoy your rest on that hard floor and watch out for the cockroaches—I saw a huge one under the bed when we entered." He shuffled into a more comfortable position and folded his arms behind his head, half closing his eyes.

Yazrana knew he was teasing her. Testing to see if she'd make a move. She shuffled, the chair creaked and he blinked, stared at her for a moment and then half closed it again.

Yazrana watched him from the chair. He'd have to sleep at some point in the night. But Keel was like a cat. The bastard would wake before she got near him, or close to the swords—both her scimitars and his rapier, he'd laid close beside the bed.

She felt giddy and sick with exhaustion and frustration, the fear of what awaited still griping her belly. She tried closing her eyes but it only made things worse. She'd felt better sleeping in the fields, the wind and sky—even the cold drizzle had lulled her senses into a false calm. Here in the gloomy silence of this room, Yazrana felt more alone than any time she could recall. She wondered how Corin fared. If he was seeking her, or had stayed to deal with the other scum. She hoped the brute Postin hadn't killed him. The man was half troll and the thought of that hammer crushing Corin's skull almost brought the tears back.

He's alive. She turned her gaze to the window as a white crescent moon chased shadows from bushes. Somewhere close an owl hooted again, moments later a second one answered. Yazrana shivered as a chill crept up her spine.

Something's out there . . .

A shimmer of light and she saw the shape of a woman, more than just a silhouette. A tall willowy figure cloaked in shadow, wrapped in a long deep dress of shifting hue. Her eyes glinted with tiny lights like distant lanterns flickering, sharp sparks of green and gold. Behind the woman, a white owl glided into view and settled silent on a fencepost.

The woman curled a hand in the air, drawing a sign. She spoke, and Yazrana heard those words echoing in her head, but no sound reached her from the garden outside.

Remember our bargain . . .

The woman's gown shimmered and faded, and her face fell into shadow. Yazrana watched spellbound and terrified as she vanished in the night, a final flicker from those gold-green eyes and she was gone. The owl blinked once then lifted and flew out beyond the silver moon.

A memory came back to torment her.

Flies crawling on my flesh. Hot sun burning down, her tongue black and heavy, mouth parched. And the terrible pain of a body slashed apart. The woman had come to her. The lady of the night. Queen of Owls. The two of them had made that terrible bargain, and when the deal was sealed, Yazrana had been allowed to forget. But now the memory came flooding back. What that woman had made her do. And poor Corin hadn't deserted her. That was the lie she'd invented to stay sane.

A life for a life. Save the beloved and be spared the sorrow of dying again. *He is in peril.* As she gazed from the window, Yazrana felt the tears spill from her eyes. It was all she could do to stop from sobbing out loud. Mercifully, the memory started drifting away as it had before. The Owl Queen's second gift—*lest memory steal your sanity too.*

She breathed out long and slow. Focused on the window itself, rather than the empty yard and bushes down there. As she stared, Yazrana noticed the split wood, half rotten in place and barely containing the glass. She turned, looked at the man. He was sleeping, she was sure of that.

She ran a blistered finger along the sill and up the side of the trim, the edges came off in her hand like crumby powder.

Termites. A few of the tiny grubs fell to the floor. Yazrana turned. He hadn't moved. His dark prone shape rested silent on that bed. She pressed both palms against the window's reveals and then, with a sudden angry violence, Yazrana pushed hard and fast until the window buckled, the glass exploded, and she fell out into the dark beyond.

She landed badly, the glass spraying her face and bare arms. Her left ankle twisted badly, and both knees knocking painfully. She heard a shout of rage above, turned and saw his face framing the hole in the wall.

Yazrana hobbled to her feet and made for the cover of the bushes. She half expected him to jump down after her, but instead he must have grabbed his weapons and was heading for the door. All the time she needed to disappear.

However near they'd sounded from the room, the horses were out of reach—neatly stabled at the other end of the inn. But even with a twisted ankle she managed to force her body forward to the low wall encircling the village. Dogs bayed and lights appeared behind her. Shouts faded off as Yazrana hauled her battered body over the wall, collapsing in gasps and then mingling with the darkness beyond.

She stumbled through a maze of low trees, using their branches to hoist herself along. *Keep moving—the pain doesn't matter.* The dogs had grown silent and she heard no sound of pursuit. Even a hunter as skillful as Keel would be hard pressed to find her before morning, especially as the moon had been swallowed by storm clouds and fresh rain spilled down from above.

She reached the road and crossed to the other side where taller trees loomed dark like silent sentinels of the night. These she entered, vanishing within, biting her lip and shutting the pain out again as she walked, tripping and slipping through that deep damp wood.

The owl flashed by her head again and settled white and silent on a branch as she passed beneath it. The bird called out, but Yazrana ignored it.

The race was on and she determined to win. Keel would kill the king, with or without her. Yazrana had to get to him first, and that meant she had to either stay ahead of Keel, or kill the bastard should chance allow.

When her legs could carry her no further, Yazrana hauled her battered soaking body up the trunk of a pine, climbing up using her knees and elbows until she was safely hidden way up amidst the shelter of needle and cones. She wedged herself into a knot of branches and locked her legs around the trunk, anchoring her position.

Far below, the owl glided past in silent vigil. She watched it vanish and felt her mind drift as the adrenaline faded, replaced by utter exhaustion. Somehow she clung on. Finally, Yazrana slept, despite her discomfort and soaked chill.

Chapter 11 | A Rough Plan

"Seems daft—us strolling into town with this paleface prick in plain sight?" Corin poked Crall in the back, forcing him forward. "Might as well wave a flag."

He pulled the cloak around his shoulders as one hand grabbed Thunderhoof's reins, the big horse clomping behind his master.

Stane shrugged. "I'd sooner deal with Postin now rather than later. Crall can help us with that, and he isn't known around here, despite his recognizable features—I can say he's helping me with renovations and that's why I closed the inn. *Plumbing issues.*"

"Yeah—sounds like a plan." *Gods help us.* "What about me, and this?" Corin tapped Clouter's pommel, half hidden beneath the blanket draped around the pack horse they'd just purchased at a trading stable on the way into town.

Stane shrugged. "We'll think of something."

I doubt that. Corin had a bad feeling. They were wasting valuable time and every moment lost meant Yazrana was further away from him, and deeper in the clutches of that madman. He gripped Biter's hilt beneath his cloak, expected trouble to break out at any moment.

"Postin has a drinking problem," Crall said, as they approached the main street. "He gets violent and sleeps where he drops. If we visit the inn first we can trace his steps and when he left. Doubt he'll have got far."

"Sounds like a plan," Corin muttered under his breath. Faces glanced their way but no one seemed overly curious. Just more strangers leading their horses through town—doubtless seeking lodging work. Crall kept his pale features half hidden beneath a deep cloak. One or two passersby recognized Stane and nodded greetings; he waved back.

They reached the end of the street, the harbor's water glistening below with its swaying boats and tossing waves. The sun was out this morning and gulls cried out as they ducked and weaved among the fishing vessels.

Corin felt a stab of loneliness thinking of his lost youth in the village Finnehalle, so far away in distance and time. Yazrana drifted into his head again and he chewed his lip. They needed to deal with Postin quickly and move on, lest Keel tire of his game and kill her.

Crall stopped outside a shabby inn. "Where he was heading last night." *The Last Drover* looked a cheerless establishment with fading green paint on the door and badly shuttered windows. The sign above was rusty and creaking from the incessant damp.

Stane shook his head. "The worst tavern in town," he said, and Corin believed it. "Postin could be passed out on the floor inside and no one would care."

"That would be too easy," Corin muttered. He grabbed Stane's arm. "You wait with the horses whilst me and Crall go inside."

"Suits me," Stane said. "I haven't set foot in this shithole for years, so why break a good habit? Be careful, and watch Crall. He's a crafty one."

Corin tapped Biter's hilt. "Any tricks and I'll shove this up his arse." He made sure Crall heard that and made for the green door. A push and it creaked open. Corin blinked as the stale smoke stung his face. Gloomy and drab inside with half-drawn curtains and a dead fire, a large hound sleeping in front. The hound looked up, showed its teeth and then lolled again.

Corin approached the counter and waited until a scruffy-looking girl emerged.

"We ain't open yet," she said. Perhaps twenty, she had a pencil tucked behind an ear. Her mousy hair was greasy but she looked bright enough, though not overly friendly.

"No problem," Corin said. "Looking for someone. A mate of ours. Big fella. He was drinking here last night."

"We had a lot of people in here last night," she said, and Corin found that hard to believe. "All of them drinking."

"Huge—face like a slug, and towing a bloody great hammer with a long metal shaft."

"Postin," Crall said in a low voice as the girl scratched her ear.

"I know who you mean." She looked sour. "He left before dawn. He was trying to hump the dog and father persuaded him to go."

"He didn't hurt anyone?" Crall looked surprised.

"Nope, he was weeping in the corner and the dog came and licked him. We said we was closing and he staggered outside. Gentle as a lamb. He must have down ten pints inside an hour. Gave us no trouble."

"You know his reputation?" Corin asked and she shrugged.

"No, we only took over the *Drover* a month back. Moved down from Reln—too much competition up there. Father's going to do this place up and make it respectable."

"Good luck with that," Corin said, receiving a scowl for his trouble.

"Those visiting soldiers like it here, as we let them have the first one free."

"Ale?" Corin looked at her.

"That and other things." She shrugged.

"So where is Postin?"

"How should I know," she said. She turned her back on them. Outside, Corin heard voices and cursed. Again, they were wasting time here. He wished he could forget Postin and move on, but Stane had convinced him the big man would be after them once he heard from Keel, or any of the gang still living. Best to clear up fast and move on.

"Where now?" Corin said to Crall, who shrugged.

"If he was in that state he'll be in a gutter or drain somewhere. Or in the guard house if the king's men caught up with him. Let's try the harbor first. Plenty of hiding places there even for someone his size."

They left the inn and ventured outside. Corin froze, seeing Stane standing with arms gesticulating and four soldiers addressing him in angry fashion.

"What's happening?" Corin asked, grinning as he approached. The four turned to face him, looking far from friendly.

"This yours?" The sergeant slapped the packhorse's saddle where Clouter's cross guard and pommel showed.

"What if it is?" Corin asked. *None of your damn business.*

"You're a mercenary," the sergeant said, and his men turned from Stane, their arms folded or brushing the hilts of their swords. "Why are you here?"

"Passing through," Corin said. "And visiting my cousin Stane." He tapped the older man's shoulder, who nodded. Corin hinted Crall. "This here's his maintenance man, going to fix a leak in his inn."

The sergeant stared hard at Crall for a minute. "Don't I know you, albino?"

Crall shrugged, and Corin forced a smile.

"He's a useful man to know," Stane said, and the soldiers were staring at him as though he'd lost his mind. "I use his services all the time."

The sergeant ignored that and stared hard at Corin for a moment. "I don't like you, Longsword," he said. "You look like trouble, and we've had more than enough of that in this town lately. This country needs cleaning up. We're here to do that. I suggest you and your cronies leave before we fall out." He turned towards the inn. "Hey Dalia!" Corin followed his gaze and saw the girl peeping from the inn door.

"Hello Syd." She blessed the sergeant with a lopsided smile. "You boys coming in?"

"You open already?" Syd the sergeant smiled at the lass.

"Always open for you," the girl replied.

I'll bet, Corin muttered under his breath.

The sergeant turned to Corin and pointed. "Us lads are taking an early lunch. If you're still around when we come out, we'll introduce you to the clink. Give us trouble and you'll swing. That or spend the night explaining what you're really up to." He turned away. "Come on lads—time for some ale."

The four soldiers filtered into the inn. Corin shook his head in disgust, and then froze, hearing a hoarse shout coming from further along the street. He glanced that way and saw Postin limping up the hill toward them, the two-yard hammer slung over his left shoulder.

"Crall!" Postin croaked again, then he saw Corin standing next to Stane. "What's that bastard doing here?" Postin swung the hammer and gripped its iron shaft with fists held apart. Corin smiled at him.

"Round two," Corin said, glancing at Crall. "I thought you said he'd be sleeping?"

"Must have woken up," Crall muttered. The soldiers reappeared, having heard the shouts. They saw Postin and reached for their swords.

"Looks like your lunch has been canceled," Corin said, reaching forward and sliding Clouter out from beneath the blanket.

Postin roared as he ran at Corin. *No time to think.* Corin leaped backwards, swinging Clouter in a wide arc, just as Postin's mallet sliced through the air he'd departed. The sergeant yelled, grabbing his sword as his men rushed into the fray.

Corin ducked beneath another wild swipe from Postin's hammer. He stabbed down with Clouter, piercing the big man's boot. Postin yelled and pulled his foot free, the leather boot half ripping in the process. The point must have missed his toe by an inch. He glared at Corin, kicked the boot off and raised the pole-axe again. Behind Corin, the clash of steel meant Stane was fighting the soldiers.

"Time we weren't here," Corin said, leaping forward, ramming his cross guard into Postin's face and cracking his jaw. He stepped sideways, bracing his legs and readying Clouter to finish, when a soldier crashed into his back and Corin tripped over Postin.

He rolled and found his feet, sweeping wide with Clouter. Stane had the horses and Crall was still fighting the soldiers. Corin hadn't the time to wonder why.

He vaulted on Thunder's back and urged the big horse up the street. Accompanying hoofbeats announced Stane's mount was following, and a backwards glance announced Crall had come too.

The sergeant yelled but his men had no chance of catching them. Corin reined in at the top of the hill. He saw Postin regain his feet and shamble off into the harbor area, the soldiers having forgotten him, all their fury focused on Corin and Stane.

"Bastard's sloped off," Corin spat as Stane eased his horse alongside.

"Can't help that now," Stane said, his eyes on Crall, who cantered up on the pack horse behind them.

An hour later they reached the crossroads where the Calprissa road met the Wynais highway. An old gibbet marked the way. Corin stared up at the creaking chains with distaste. It was colder here and a stiff wind ruffled his cloak. The other two reined in alongside.

"Well that was a fuck up," Corin said.

"Could have gone worse." Stane grinned, his flushed features hinting he'd enjoyed the fight. "Those soldiers were in shock—why we got away so easily. And I think Postin's out of action for a while. Though I doubt we've seen the last of him."

"So why are you here?" Corin glared at Crall. Without the albino's help, they couldn't have escaped the solders, but Corin wasn't about to feel grateful. This dour scarecrow had his reasons.

"Nowhere else to go." Crall shrugged, then waved his hands in the air as they stared hard at him. "Seriously. I can't stay around here, either Postin will talk or someone will link me to the gang. My face is not an easy one to hide indefinitely. Those soldiers are going to be more determined than ever. Besides, I want to kill Keel."

Corin glanced at Stane, who shrugged. "Seems logical."

"Keel played us for fools and used us for bait in those woods," Crall said. "He had no intention of killing Nogel. I suspect he's planning something special in the Silver City. And your woman is a part of that."

"How did you get that sword?" Corin saw the weapon hanging through a loop at the pack horse's side.

"Providence," Crall said. "One of the soldiers was clumsy and got too close. Expect he'll be on latrine duty all month." He offered the sword to Corin.

"Keep it," Corin said. "But know that I sleep with one eye open."

***

Postin leaned on his hammer as he staggered toward the warehouses. Gulls soared and dived, and the pungent stench of rotting fish was all around. He eased open a door and fell inside, his face streaming with blood and his jaw a flame of agony. He collapsed onto a pile of ropes and passed out.

When Postin woke, it was dark and the pain in his jaw was worse than before. He reached up, placing one hand under his chin, the other at the side of his face. Then he cracked them together hard as he could and his jaw snapped back in place. Postin made a strange gurgling noise and passed out again.

When next he came to, Postin leaned forward and spewed. After that he felt better. Hungry, and very angry. He reached for the pole-axe and pulled himself up. Postin cranked the warehouse door open and stared around. *Dark.* No sound except the water lapping and sloshing against the harbor wall. A lone lantern creaking and a flickering amber glow hinting a second one away at the far end.

Postin tore off a section of his shirt and tied it around his face, soaking up blood and keeping his chin in place. The pain was agonizing, but nothing compared to the rage he felt. Only one thing mattered. Find that Longsword bastard and split him down the middle. First he needed some food, and that would prove tricky with his jaw all messed up.

Having no other plan, Postin walked back up through the town. No one around except the odd stray cat or hound growling at him. He stopped outside *The Last Drover,* rammed his bulk against the shabby door, forcing it in, and then wandered through the gloom toward the kitchens.

The hound was there; it wagged its tail. Nice to know someone loved him. A face appeared, and a lit candle revealed the girl. She held a dagger but almost dropped it when she saw the state of him.

"Need food," Postin's mouth squirted more blood as he struggled with the words. The girl's expression ranged from disgust to morbid fascination. Footsteps announced her father shifting alongside. He carried an axe and held it out in front, as though worried he'd hurt himself with it. And most likely he would, in Postin's opinion.

"Him from the other night," the girl Dalia said. The father nodded, too stunned to speak.

"Food," Postin worked his mouth again. "Beer!"

The girl nodded. "I'll make you some broth," she said, a twisted grin on her face. "Don't think you'd manage a sandwich, just don't break anything or upset father." Postin nodded and the girl left for the taproom.

"Fight," he said to the father, who nodded and then sat down on a rickety chair, the axe almost forgotten in his hands.

"The sergeant has men scouring the countryside for your friends," Dalia said, reemerging with a tankard of ale spilling over. Postin tried to grin. He reached across, seized the mug and down the contents—washing his face with froth. "Broth's warming up," she said.

"Why you help me?"

"Dog likes you."

After the ale, he had a second and the pain started to subside. She brought the broth and Postin took his time sipping at it, the girl even spooned some into his mouth. "Thag you," Postin told her.

"He's misunderstood," she said to her father, who nodded, his face anything but complying. "A gentle giant." She turned to Postin with a crooked smile. "You can rest upstairs, lovely. Spare room—no one need know you're there. We can poultice that wound and you'll be good to go in a day or so."

The jaw mended fast—it must have been badly mashed but not broken. He'd lost a few teeth but could still chew on one side of his mouth. Postin felt almost content as he said farewell and thanks to Dalia. The girl warmed his soul, she'd even performed a brief service for him after he'd spent several hours chopping logs for her father.

"Stay safe," she said, "and come back." Postin promised that he would, after he cleared up a spot of necessary business that couldn't wait.

He left three days later, before dawn when the town was sleeping, the only movement the trails of smoke rising above chimney and thatch.

Postin strode from town, a cloak holding off the damp, and a sack containing food and a large flagon full of ale—neatly tied by Dalia to the shaft of the pole-axe, sloping over one shoulder. He walked all that day and into the next, stopping at a tavern on the road to Calprissa.

Postin kept the hood over his face and listened to wayfarers. There was no news of Crall and The Longsword, nor of Keel. That seemed odd to Postin, as they would have stopped here on their way to the coastal city, Kelwyn's second largest town.

Next morning, he stole a pony from a farm nearby. Riding south, his feet trailing low and almost scraping the road, Postin kept both eyes out for travelers and especially soldiers. But the roads were quiet. He entered Calprissa at market time, blending best he could with the dozen or so traders hustling to get through the gates.

Postin—though a stranger to this city—remembered the place he'd first met Keel. The landlord to that establishment was in Caswallon's pay. That man might know something. Postin entered and took seat in a corner. A boarding house, the small man approaching looked familiar.

"You seeking lodging?" The thin moustache and wispy gray hair were the same as he remembered, as was the ponytail. *Carne Dooly.*

***

Dooly had been a wealthy merchant once. But he'd fallen into misfortune after trying to outbid another trader from distant Raleen. A man Dooly still hated beyond any other. He'd gotten in debt so bad he approached Lord Caswallon for a loan. He'd known the High King's councilor from earlier times when he'd traded in Kella City.

Caswallon had feigned sympathy and bolstered him with coin. The price for that support was high. Dooly became Caswallon's new man in Calprissa, and Kelthaine's master-spy liked results. The contract signed, Carne Dooly had to report back once a month with details of all who passed through the city. He made it his business to be thorough. So, he'd known when his enemy Silon had been here, meeting with the Longsword mercenary and the infamous *Crimson Lady*. Word he'd swiftly passed on to his master up north.

Carne Dooly recognized Postin the instant he walked in. Hard to forget a brute that size. He'd heard about the botched attempt on Nogel's' life and assumed Postin was on the run. He looked a mess, his jaw strapped up and clothes a shamble. And, of course, he had no money. But Carne Dooly smiled and bid him welcome, ordering his servants prepare a room out back.

"You know Caswallon's not happy with Keel," Carne Dooly probed gently as Postin wolfed down his meal. They were alone, the servants had seen to it that they wouldn't be disturbed. He couldn't be seen talking to a man like Postin. Wanted up north, and with a face like his, the noose usually follows.

This business needed discretion. Dooly knew Caswallon wasn't liked in Calprissa. Especially by people like Silon. Him and the Kelwynian king. Carne Dooly's task was to undermine Nogel's authority here, albeit with subtlety.

"What went wrong up there?" Dooly hadn't heard from his master in weeks, not since before the assassination attempt. He was getting nervous and had no fresh news to report. Hence Postin's arrival proved timely and convenient.

"Don't know," Postin said, between chews. Carne Dooly winced, the man was a pig in the swill. He hated dealing with bruts such as he. *Needs must these sorry days*. "I did my job without thanks or payment."

"I have money," Carne Dooly said. "But I need to know what happened and where Keel went."

"First tell me the name of that bastard with the longsword." Postin spat a fishbone on the table. Carne Dooly stared at it for moment.

"Is this someone I know?"

"Crall did, before he ran off with him."

"Crall betrayed us?"

Postin shrugged. "I didn't know there was an *us*."

"We all work for Lord Caswallon here," Carne Dooly said. "You included."

"I work for myself," Postin said, and Dooly decided to leave that alone. He changed tack. "I think you mean the mercenary Corin an Fol. A northerner—works for Silon. My enemy." Dooly smiled. "That merchant would be saddened were something bad to happen to his daughter's savior."

He told Postin about some strange happenings down in Permio. Events he'd had a part in, while dealing with Sulimo the Sultan's man until the fool had got his throat cut. Dooly had stayed away from Permian affairs since.

"I'll kill him," Postin said. "And Keel, Crall, and that fucking witch with the swords. All of them!"

Dooly smiled. "I knew I could count on you, Postin. I shall write Caswallon immediately, then get you sufficient supplies and money for the long ride east."

"East?"

"Wynais. Have you ever visited the silver city?"

"Nope."

"Well here's your chance—they say it's beautiful this time of year." Carne Dooly smiled again, though the sentiment was lost on Postin.

"Why Wynais?" Postin rubbed his nose with greasy fingers. His jaw clicked as he gulped down the last chunk of soup-soaked bread.

"Because that's where this game will play out," Dooly said. "Caswallon means to strike the adder in his nest. Nogel is a fool, and believes the threat is over. Keel has proved reckless, a maverick, and Caswallon needs insurance. Hence your new task. Kill the king and those others and Lord C will shower you with gold."

Postin stared at him as though he'd lost all reason. But Dooly held out a hand. "Wait—we can get you there. I've two men who will accompany you. Good fighters and loyal to the cause, they won't betray us like Crall. One is from Wynais and the other's a Kell. They will get you close to the king and help you get away."

"What about this Corin an Fol?"

"Kill him in the Silver City, and the others. Anyone you must. Just make sure you do for Nogel first. Once that's done, ride north for Kelthara and Caswallon's people will take care of you."

"Sounds risky," Postin said.

"No riskier than hiding in hedges until someone like Crall turns you in. You're a wanted man, Postin. Word will out for coin."

"I've scant cause to wonder who would spill them." Postin glared at him until Dooly turned his gaze away.

"I'm a businessman," he said, waving his hands. "*Besides,* this is perfect for you. Chance to avenge your hurt *and* get filthy rich. Sound like a plan?"

"Gold and retribution."

"As much as you like."

"Done." Postin thrust out a huge paw. Carne Dooly spat in it, and his own hand was swallowed by Postin's fist. Postin grinned.

Very early next morning, Carne Dooly watched Postin and his two companions ride out amid clatter of dust and hooves. He'd already bribed the gate guards so no questions would be asked. He'd given his men precise orders: *Use the giant to kill the king. See that he gets the blame and is caught. If he fails, do the job yourself. And bring me word of Keel.*

Chapter 12 | The King's Will

"You look well, Highness," Silon said as he sipped the excellent wine. They sat beneath a veranda at the end of a balcony awarding panoramic views beyond city and fields, the lake shimmering blue in the distance, framed by snowcapped mountains reflected in that water. A beautiful summer morning in a far corner of the palace where they wouldn't be disturbed.

"Good of you to come old friend." King Nogel snapped his fingers and the guard nodded, bidding the servants depart through the gilded double doors and then closing them behind him. The king waited until he heard the footsteps fading, then he smiled. "An interesting month."

"Dangerous, Highness. And tragic—I was saddened to hear about Lord Staveport. As honorable and decent a man as I've been fortunate to meet."

"And sadly missed," King Nogel said. "Ariane is upset, she loved Rowen. Almost like a grandfather—first her mother, then Staveport. I worry for her, Silon."

"She is tough like her father," Silon said. "And clever."

"Aye, she's sharper than me." The king laughed. "That's her mother's blessing. Cailine was a thinker, whereas I always preferred hitting things with swords."

"I've heard the same said of Ariane. Her tutor, *Squire* Galed, doesn't approve."

"Galed? Foolish little man. But, yes, I do indulge the princess more than I should. There are several at court who disapprove.

Despite the controversy it causes, I'll continue. Ariane's quick with a rapier, faster than most my guards."

"I think you are wise in that, Highness. Your daughter will need those skills one day."

"I hope not." The king sipped his glass. "But fear you may be right. The times grow dark around us."

"That's what happens when weakness allows."

"Evil creeps in through the cracks." Nogel nodded. "Kelsalion III is a disgrace, Silon. An insult to his forbears."

"A weak ruler, yes," Silon said. "But not a wicked man, and not the first feckless monarch to wear the Crystal Crown. Or to allow a manipulative advisor to steer his throne for him."

"Were Caswallon just that I wouldn't worry," Nogel said. "But you and I know the man is steeped in twisted lore. He's studied the darker arts for years—a well-known fact, though few dare mention it. Caswallon's a necromancer—the worst kind of sorcery—and he's undermining everything the Tekara stands for. I fear the crown's magic is fading under his stain. Tarnished by those shadows he's allowed in the palace. A thousand years of peace could be shattered in a day."

"You think he'll seize the throne?"

"Not directly—Caswallon knows the Tekara will only accept a direct descendant of Kell. He'll use that worthless boy, Tarin. The by-blow of one of Kelsalion's whores. Arrange for the High King to have an accident. All too easy, considering the state of Kelsalion. It's only a matter of time before that canard sorcerer shows his hand."

"What do you suggest?"

"We—or rather I—confront him. Face Caswallon down, while rallying the nobles to see sense. Kelthaine needs a damn hard shake. The Lords Belmarius and Halfdan can assist us."

"What about Perani, and the Tigers?"

"Staveport believed them Caswallon's puppets. I think he has a point. Seems Perani can't be trusted, but many others can."

"But—forgive me—you, Highness, are the king of Kelwyn, not Kelthaine," Silon said, choosing his words carefully. "You shouldn't be directly involved up there. Caswallon is looking for another excuse to destroy you. Don't enter his game."

Nogel smiled grimly. "He needs better agents. Those assassins he sent were amateurs, the one we captured half-mad."

"They were just throwaway pieces," Silon said. "I fear the key player is still at large."

"The sly swordsman—yes, I wondered about him. Tell me what you know." Nogel placed his glass on the table and stared hard at Silon.

"He calls himself Keel," Silon said. "An assassin in Caswallon's pay. The man who killed Dal Terini, and Lord Staveport. A psychopath and sadist who just wanted to show off his hand in those woods near Port Wind."

"In a badly staged attempt on my life."

"He was playing, Highness. I had my own people up there and they were witness."

"You had people in my forest?" Nogel's dark eyes narrowed dangerously.

"Caswallon tried to take me out," Silon said, waving a placating hand. "He attacked my family and nearly destroyed my beloved daughter. We were lucky but I realized he would strike again one day. This time aiming higher."

"Continue."

"I sent a man north to find out all he could. Hagan Delmorier—you may have heard of him."

"Indeed, I have! The man's a villain. A *murderer*." Nogel frowned, his face reddening in anger. "Duke Tomais banished the rogue from Morwella. Seems like Caswallon's gathering an army comprising of outlaws and villains."

"And thus, was able to infiltrate the infamous gang operating in those woods," Silon persisted, despite misgivings. "It was Hagan that told me about Keel and his plot on your life."

"Why didn't you report that back to me?"

"There wasn't time, Highness—when Terini was murdered I guessed the killer's true identity and sent my best man north to warn you with another. Keel struck before my pieces were in place. He vanished soon after, so I approached another contact in Calprissa and together we guessed the killer's name."

"Enlighten me."

"Rael Hakkenon of Crenna. The self-styled Lord Assassin."

Nogel laughed. "Rael the Cruel? The pirate prince? What nonsense is this? That rogue spends all his days terrorizing Permian galleys and hapless traders from Vangaris. That's when he's not torching his own people on that distant island."

"It now appears he works for Caswallon too."

"What evidence have you got for such an outrageous assumption?"

"It actually makes sense, Your Highness," Silon said. "If you know the man's history."

"I know enough to know I'd rather not hear more." Nogel rubbed his eyes and sipped his wine. "But why would Rael Hakkenon need the work, or more importantly the money? Man's rumored rich as a Permian sultan."

"It's not about money with him," Silon said. "Never was. It's vengeance he wants—against all humanity. You know what the former rulers did to him in Kranek Castle?"

"One of many macabre stories from that awful island."

"But one that's true to a point." Silon drew a deep breath, their conversation proving hard work. Nogel blocked out things he didn't like hearing. He had a warrior's impatience that bordered on downright foolishness. Silon sipped slowly and continued. "Rael was unsuccessful in his first rebellion against House Kranek. He was caught and tortured with exquisite precision. I won't go into the details, but suffice it to say, Rael repaid the debt with dividends when he stormed the castle some years later and burned every single occupant alive."

"That still doesn't explain why he'd ally himself with Caswallon."

"Rael despises the High King, holding him ultimately responsible for his own misfortunes. In his twisted mind, *House Kranek* was but a vassal of Kelsalion, therefore his task wasn't complete."

"You're implying that Rael Hakkenon—if this Keel character really is him—is going after the High King, and at Caswallon's bidding. Just because of some personal vendetta against authority. That's a trifle tenuous my good fellow."

"How else would you explain the murders, other than a madman loose in Port Wind?"

"Perhaps that's what happened," Nogel said. "I blame myself for neglecting that part of my country. Allowing some rough types to settle there."

"Keel must have heard about Postin the Hammer. A giant butcher with a pole-axe who'd been a former Bear, before getting kicked out the regiment for some atrocity. A local legend. The man was hung once but the rope snapped under his weight. Since then he'd taken to the woods between the waters and gathered some like-minded villains to his cause. They'd been haranguing locals for months."

"I know about these people. You forget whom you are addressing."

"Please indulge me, Highness."

"Go on."

"Hagan infiltrated the gang easily enough. He reported back that a man calling himself Keel had arrived one night and swiftly taken control of affairs. He said they were all afraid of this 'green-eyed newcomer' and that even Postin—well known for his lack of fear—was browbeaten by Keel."

"And that's not all," Silon said. "I met with a certain lady in Calprissa."

King Nogel steepled his hands. "Indulge me."

"Her name is Yazrana. She's Permian, but a former Wolf. Served in the wars under Halfdan. Good fighter. You might know her as *The Crimson Lady.*"

"I know a thorn in the foot." The king swore and rammed a fist into his palm. "You test our patience, merchant. Hagan the freebooter and The Crimson Lady—your contacts are as bad as our enemy's. Have a care lest you outstay your welcome in Wynais." Nogel stood and slammed his glass down on the table. He paced up and down, gazing out at his city below.

Silon waited until the king's pacing slowed and Nogel turned to him again.

"I know you mean well, Silon, and Lord Staveport always valued your council. But this is not tenable."

"I'm sorry, Highness—but needs must. Caswallon is playing a dirty game. We have to match his methods."

"By using scum and outlaws."

"In Hagan's case yes. But Yazrana's story is different. She—"

"—I don't want to hear it," the king said. "That woman's a murdering whore who's responsible for raids all along our coast. Poor fisher folk mainly, unable to defend themselves. That bitch will lose her head if she comes in range."

"Yazrana's the only person I know who's met Rael. When I showed her Hagan's note—the description of this small neat individual with piercing green eyes—she said that described perfectly the Prince of Crenna. He is like a cat, she said. Silent, swift and deadly—a hunter who sports with his victims."

"What is the point of this rambling?" Nogel said. "Caswallon wants the throne and is prepared to use anything and anyone to get it. We have to stop him, and that means confronting the knave head on and sorting this out, once and for all. The time for sly subtlety is past. I'm riding to Kella in the morning."

"Highness, I would advise strongly against that."

"Somebody has to make a stand, merchant. Agreed—I'm a foreign king, but still a descendant of Kell. Who else is there to face down this would-be impostor?"

"You will be riding into a trap."

"I disagree. Caswallon's spies and assassins are probing *my* country, the last thing he'll expect is our presence in the High King's courtroom. I will take enough men to protect my person on the roads but not so many as to cause alarm. We are done discussing this."

"I should come with you at least."

"No sir—this is not your affair. Return to Raleen and remove your players, else my soldiers learn of their whereabouts and string them up with the rest. I bid you good day."

Silon took the hint and rose with a bow. *The king's a bloody fool.* He swallowed and clicked his tongue nervously as he left the room, heart heavy as a stone. The door opened to let him through and the dour-faced guard nodded him go to a table. There Silon reclaimed his knives and satchel, his constant travel companions.

He left the study behind and walked briskly through the long corridor, the tall arched windows spilling silver light on statues and urns, and allowing stunning views of the city far below. Wynais was rumored the most beautiful palace in the Four Kingdoms.

Not that Silon took the leisure to indulge in that beauty. He was angry and disappointed. He'd expected more from King Nogel, and wished Staveport was still alive. The old warrior would have heard him out and seen the sense of his tactics. Nogel was impetuous and hasty, just the sort of character that would play into Caswallon's hands. And where was Roman Parrantios? The king's famous champion had been missing for months.

He, Silon, had to do something. Not just for Nogel's sake but for the whole realm. There was still one man he could speak to here in Wynais. The High Priest of Elanion was someone even Nogel had to respect. With that in mind, Silon decided to prolong his stay in the city. He would seek an appointment with Lord Dazaleon in the morning down in the temple, or wherever else the High Priest desired.

Silon was chewing over these thoughts when a voice called across to him. A young woman appeared from behind a chair, in one of the sumptuous lounges he past.

"You are Silon of Raleen?" She was dressed in jade and amber, small of build and pretty. Perhaps twenty, her hair dark and coifed neatly around her face. Her eyes were as black as her father's and keenly perceptive. She wore an impish smile. Silon bowed, this could only be Princess Ariane.

"Your Highness, I'm honored you would have heard of me, just a lowly trader from the south."

"Your reputation precedes you," Ariane said. "Lord Rowan always spoke well of you."

"I was so sorry to hear—"

"—we will avenge him." The princess's eyes were chipped flints of coal.

"I am certain of it," he said, thinking how like her father this girl was.

"Will you share some tea out on the veranda?" The princess's eyes brightened and she awarded him a winning smile. *You, Princess, are a charmer.* Silon thought of his own daughter Nalissa. Poor Nogel—fathers and their daughters, what chance did he or the king stand?

"I . . . *of course*, Highness. Again, you honor me."

"Tosh." Ariane waved a hand bidding him follow. A servant floated into view and nodded with a curtsy as she went off to arrange the tea. "It's a beautiful day and my solarium awards the finest views of the city. Did you not know these are my quarters?"

"I did not," Silon said, following the princess through wide spacious rooms until reaching double doors that opened out on a terrace and balcony that dwarfed the one where he'd left the king. This room faced east, where the shoulders of the mountain range known as the High Wall stood magnificent and crisp, the dark line of conifers marching up to greet the snowline, the sun pinkening and casting glare.

"Father prefers the lake view," she explained. "I like the mountains, to watch the sun's rise over their heights."

"It is magnificent, Highness. I am overwhelmed."

"That I doubt, and call me Ariane." She bade him take seat at a table and wait as more servants appeared, bringing a silver pot of steaming liquid and two silver-traced china cups engraved with some strange beast. Silon studied them with interest.

"I heard you are a collector." The princess awarded him that smile again, and Silon cleared his throat, embarrassed.

"I am," he said. "Apologies, these are beautiful. I—"

"—I wish to be frank with you, sir."

"Of course." Silon nodded and leaned forward to take a slow careful sip of tea. Strange drink, but not unpleasant. She poured a drop of milk in hers and one small lump of sugar. Silon was fascinated.

"My indulgence," Ariane said. "Father disapproves—says my teeth will rot." Silon chose not to respond, she waved a hand. "Time will tell . . . We need to do something about Caswallon," she added, her expression serious again.

That came as a surprise. Ariane looked stern, again reminding him of her father. "He is very powerful, Highness."

"Ariane," she corrected. "And are we not without strength? My father is a king after all."

"He is."

"But you don't approve of his manner?"

"It's not my place . . ."

"Neither do I," she said. "Father wants to tackle Caswallon as though he were an honorable enemy. The man's a snake in the sod and needs stamping on. One does not parley with a snake. One cuts its fucking head off."

Silon blinked hearing that. He'd heard how she liked to spend time with the captains in the barracks, learning bawdy jokes along with her sword lessons. Ariane laughed at his serious expression.

"I have little time for courtly nonsense," Ariane said. "I'm worried about the king."

"Your father is a redoubtable warrior," Silon said. "A strong ruler." *But stupid as an ox, and I'm worried too.*

"But not a subtle one, and Caswallon knows it. What really happened to Lord Rowan?"

"I . . . don't . . . know. So unnecessary."

"Your people were there." The smile again.

"Excuse me?" Silon rubbed his earring.

"I make it my business in this city to vet any visitors to the palace," she said. "Father has no time for such intrigue. Lord Staveport confided in me that he was worried Caswallon would go after the king. He said you'd placed spies up there and that comforted me. But now dear Rowan's dead, I'm at a loss. Who did this and why—surely Caswallon would have struck directly at my father, and not a loyal retainer?"

"I think there are several threads here, Highness . . . apologies, Ariane, I mean. Caswallon is using all manner of thugs to do his dirty work. Among them, I've reason to believe is the so-called Pirate Prince of Crenna. I had cause to mention this to your father."

"Who won't listen," Ariane said. "Father's impatient and random. Without my mother's calming influence, he's likely to do something rash."

You're telling me . . . "Like ride north for Kella City on the morrow?"

"*I knew it.* Silon, we have to stop him!"

"Ariane—Princess, I'm just a merchant from Raleen. *Of course* I'll help in anyway— but there's little I can do. Besides, your father the king is not pleased with me at the moment."

"He'll come around—blows hot and cold. I know that he holds you in high esteem." She crinkled her nose and winced slightly. "Hot." She hinted the tea and he nodded agreement.

"But very good," Silon said. "Princess Ariane, I'm sorry but I don't know what to suggest."

"Leave it to me," she said, waving a beringed hand for the servants to come and clear the table. "I've sword training this afternoon, and then historical studies with Squire Galed, my mentor. After that I will seek out my father the king and persuade him to think again. He usually listens to me."

"I wish you well with that, Highness." Silon smiled, though doubting it would make much difference. "I, too, worry for your father."

"I will deal with this," she said. "But that's not the only reason I wanted to talk with you." That winning smile again. "We need to set up a council that doesn't involve Father. He's too stubborn and blunt and certainly wouldn't approve of my involvement. But I'm old enough to govern my own thoughts. And to worry about what's coming. I've spoken about this to Lord Staveport, and our high priest, Dazaleon. The wisest men in Wynais. They were both in accord."

"It's a sound idea," Silon said. "Though to go behind the king's back . . ."

"—is the only way it can happen," she said with another imperious wave of the hand. "A clandestine passive council to watch events in Kelthaine and prepare for the worst should that villain Caswallon show his hand, as I believe he will. *Especially* if Father gets involved. I'm inviting you, Silon of Raleen, to be our leader."

"Ariane, I'm a merchant. A business man."

"Do not bandy words with me, sir. I know who you are—the craftiest, cleverest spymaster throughout the entire Four Kingdoms. I know how you tried to topple the sultan in Permio using that poor woman as bait."

Silon was impressed and smiled. "You know about Yazrana and the failed assassination attempt. You've done your homework, Ariane"

"Someone has to. It's why she took to the seas, they say. *Too many enemies.* That woman deserved to be treated better for all her troubles."

"We had an agreement," Silon said, concerned and baffled by how such information had leaked. He'd been very careful about the whole affair down there in the desert. Yazrana had contacted him soon after he'd returned home after that awful business with poor Nalissa. The woman wanted news on his man Corin an Fol. She was angry, and Silon knew her reputation. An accomplished fighter and survivor who'd been an asset to the Wolves, but was rumored dead. How could Princess Ariane know about all that? Though edgy, Silon was encouraged. This girl was one to watch.

"Yazrana blamed the sultan for all her woes," Silon said. "Him and one other individual. It was her that suggested that bold move in Sedinadola. I was to pay her a huge sum, but things went sideways and I lost contact with her. Bizarrely, she turned up as a pirate in league with Rael, until that fragile alliance fell apart. I found her in Calprissa, a fallen woman and renegade."

"And you think Rael Hakkenon murdered Lord Rowan?" Her dark eyes flashed at him angrily, and again Silon was impressed. Ariane proving far sharper than her father.

"I do. Yazrana gave a good description of Rael and it fits our prime suspect perfectly. A man calling himself Keel who recently appeared in the wooded country. No one knew from where, or anything about him—so my people tell me."

"Then we have to kill Rael Hakkenon as well as Caswallon."

"Princess, that's beyond our ability. Even if we could prove this was Hakkenon's work, we'd have to find him first. And we cannot act openly against Caswallon. Not unless he directly undermines the High King's power, or we can prove his connivance against your father."

"Who else is there?"

"We still have to *prove it,* Ariane. I'm in—but only if we do this my way. By using caution. Watching and waiting. This is not the time for hasty action."

"What do you suggest?"

"If this killer is Rael then I'm sure he'll be back. He was just shaking things up in Port Wind, sort of announcing his presence without revealing his identity. A game, in his warped mind. My feelings are Keel the Killer will show up closer to Wynais and then make his move. A bold strike that clears Caswallon of any involvement."

"And why would he do that?"

"Call it a hunch."

Ariane stared at him for a moment and then nodded slowly. "Then you are with us and will bring all your legendary spymaster skills?"

"I think any skills I might have are more than matched by yourself, Princess Ariane. It seems I have a new player to watch in this dangerous game."

"I stay awake and listen." Ariane smiled. "I might rule here one day."

"You are wise to do so," he said.

The princess nodded. "Are you hungry? I can call the servants back to provide you with lunch. You must excuse me—I'm late for sword drills, should have reported to the barracks ten minutes ago. But I'm so glad we had this discussion." She flashed him a smile.

"An honor, Your Highness, and thank you!"

Princess Ariane rose swiftly and with a swirl of cloth departed the balcony, leaving Silon alone, his busy mind racing. Outplayed by a girl the same age as his daughter. How had she known about Yazrana, and who else knew?

Where are you, Corin an Fol?

Silon had an unpleasant feeling that something dire was about to happen here in Wynais. He wanted to return to Vioyamis and study his papers, make plans and brief his staff. But his inner voice warned he'd be needed here.

The servants brought him an excellent lunch accompanied with more tea, a drink he decided he liked well enough in this chilly northern climate. He thanked them and let his mind wander as he ate, while watching eagles soar above those distant peaks.

Silon doubted Ariane would persuade her father to remain put, despite her assurances. Nogel was a reckless ruler. They had to have a buffer, a way of stopping him cross the border. Once King Nogel reached Kelthaine, the nets would trap him.

Where was Yazrana and The Longsword? They were needed here, and fast. *I'll seek out the High Priest this afternoon.* It was all he could think of for the moment.

Chapter 13 | Weavers of Deceit

Prince Tarin was fourteen years old, bored, and misunderstood. Life in the palace drifted aimlessly from one monotonous day to the next. His father doted on him, and that should have been all that mattered. But his father wasn't the man he'd been. High King Kelsalion III was assailed by nightmares and shadows, his reasoning and self-esteem almost lost and driving him to the brink of madness. Tarin blamed the Lord High Councilor for feeding that doubt. Not that he would dare air such an accusation.

Lord Caswallon was the only man he feared. A prince shouldn't be afraid, but Caswallon was half-man, half-shadow. A creature of the night. He delved where others dared not go. Alone in the high tower, recently sequestered as his own. Draped in a dark cloak with the low fire flickering, Tarin had been up there, seen the scrolls, maps, and charts, the smoky orbs, and the baroque talismans from some far country, and the array of pots all venting steam. A stale smell lingered in that room. None dared enquire why. Servants and guards stayed away as much as they could. That suited Caswallon, who was also a loner.

But the High Councilor seemed to enjoy Tarin's company. It was the reason why he'd gone up there on numerous occasions. Invitations, and conversations. Few ventured that arduous climb out of choice, winding up the spiraling stone-cold tower, a half hour's steady climb, the odd sconce or arrow-slot allowing brief hints of light. Barely enough to banish the shadows that always seemed to muster on those stairs. An arduous, thankless task, navigating the worn and dangerously slippery-steep stairwell to that forgotten room.

The "Astrologer's Roost," men called it. Kelsalion's father had used it to watch the stars and consult with the gods. Even the present ruler had done so in his early days. Back when his wife, Coranna the High Queen, still lived, happily together with their two sons, years before young Tarin had appeared.

Tarin wasn't sorry they were dead. Drowned off the coast of some barren realm. Were it not for that disaster, who would he be? Another bastard, forgotten and ignored. Instead Prince Tarin was the heir to the realm and the only living descendent of the hero/conqueror Kell, discounting Wynna's line that ran throughout Kelwyn's monarchs, therefore diluted by the weakness that emanated from that land.

Tarin knew he should feel grateful. Instead he felt bored. Outside the window, it was snowing. Early summer and yet the white powdery substance settled on those empty streets, the sky deep and heavy as his dreams. Tarin shuddered. *Is someone watching?* He turned and wasn't overly surprised to see Lord Caswallon standing there.

"Prince Tarin, you appear sickly." Caswallon's smile was barely visible beneath that dark close-cropped beard. He sported a long gown of russet, the sleeves flared, his hands buried inside deep gloves and a scholar's cap covering his thinning crown—fashioned in matching cloth and trimmed with silver fox fur. The High King's councilor was smallish in build but seemed bigger than most men. A constant creepy presence like a companion shadow awarded him height.

Tarin tensed. "I'm just bored," he said.

"Well . . . that's no way to be." Caswallon's coal-dark eyes swept the library. The servants had vanished the moment he'd appeared. The dust-filled room was empty save the two of them; a sparkle of motes shimmered briefly as the sun emerged and sky lightened above. The snow stopped.

"Don't you think it's odd?" Tarin turned to watch the window and sky outside, anything rather than face Caswallon. "Snow this late in the year."

"Tis but weather." His voice was low and sonorous. "Of small concern. *Look at me.*" Tarin turned, saw Caswallon standing beside him, though he'd not heard any movement. Caswallon smiled again, rested a cold hand on his shoulder. Tarin almost jumped at that touch.

"Your father is not a well man," Caswallon said. "You should prepare yourself for what is coming—not idle away your days in this constant state of sloth."

"Father is still strong in body if not in mind," Tarin said. It was true; the High King still rode a horse and occasionally hunted, though far less frequently than before.

"Kelsalion rots from within." Caswallon's tone was full of contempt. "He ignores his subjects who rebel against him."

"Rebel?" Tarin looked shocked. He masked his anger at Caswallon's words. Tarin hated Caswallon criticizing his father but knew he was right. The High King was tortured from within.

"Of course—*rebel.*" Caswallon removed his hand and strode off to gaze out the window. The sun had vanished again, replaced by wet, sliding sleet splattering the glass. "The Four Kingdoms are vulnerable, the people's safety at risk."

"Who is rebelling?" Tarin was puzzled, he knew nothing of such insurrection.

Caswallon shrugged. "Lords, generals. Petty nobles—*what does it matter?* A direct result of your father's ineptitude. Chaos approaches. Our only salvation is a change of direction. A breath of wind sweeping the dust from the shelves." Caswallon reached across and lifted a parchment blowing dust to prove his point. "When was this last read?" he said, and then tore the scroll in two. Tarin gasped.

"Idleness breeds insurrection, my young prince. Peril paves the way."

"Why are you telling me this?"

"Because you can help me do something about it, my boy. Shape up! We need to save our people, protect them from what's coming."

"I thought the Tekara did that?"

"The Crystal Crown?" Caswallon laughed. "Do you honestly believe that?"

"It has for a thousand years, since the Aralais granted it in gratitude to Kell after his saving them from the twisted folk."

"That's pure folklore, Tarin. *Myth*." Caswallon's dark eyes were intent, boring inside Tarin's skull. "The Tekara has no real power. It's a symbol, a statement, and superstitions have allowed it to become what it is. A *lie*, and a deception. Real power comes from he who wears the Tekara. Or . . . not, as in your father's case. The Tekara has failed him. Trust not in the crown, Prince Tarin. It is a false charm."

"If not the Tekara—then what?"

Caswallon smiled again. A sinister smear of his bloodless lips. "Your intuition. You're a bright boy, Tarin. Stay close to me and learn all you can. I'll be your mentor and guide. You should feel honored—prince or not, it's a valuable service I offer."

"I don't need a mentor," Tarin said, blinking. *Do I . . . ?*

"We all need direction in this life." Caswallon's hand brushed his shoulder again. Tarin shivered. One moment the man was standing by the window, the next instant he was leaning over him. *How does he do that?* Uncanny. "And you will be High King soon enough I fear."

"What do you know?"

The cruel smile again. "Time will out . . ." Caswallon turned away and, heedless of the cold damp, strolled out to the palace grounds without further word. Tarin wanted to question the High King's councilor further but was afraid to do so. Instead he stood hovering and hesitating until Caswallon had vanished in the shadows of bare branches, shrub, and gloomy snowfall beyond. Prince Tarin shivered as a blast of cold air reached him from outside. He felt a rush of excitement mingled with dread, fear. *I'm to be High King soon . . .*

***

A faint red glow on the horizon. Postin reined in alongside his fellow riders. High above, a skein of geese winged south through flinty skies, freckled with fast-moving clouds. Dusk was falling on the road ahead. It would be dark inside an hour.

"A campfire?" The man to his left sniffed the air. Strowd was lean as a whip, with a large hooked nose and the sense of smell to match. A good tracker, but irritating companion with his know-all ways and frequent bantering. The other man was broad as Postin, though short in build. An ex-mercenary out of Permio. He knew of Corin an Fol and claimed to have his own reason for seeing him dead. "No friend of mine, that long-legged twat" was almost the only thing he'd said in the three days they'd been out of Calprissa.

Tolc had no neck, just a large square head resting awkwardly on broad shoulders. He carried two short swords and a sawn off spear, the handle just three feet in length.

Postin didn't care for his companions but was content to put up with them for a few days. Once he'd been paid, he'd cut their throats and disappear. If Carne Dooly came after him, he'd do for that snake as well.

They rode closer to the glow until it revealed itself as an abandoned fire that the wind must have rekindled to flame. No sign of anyone near, but there were hoof tracks leading off back to the road close by.

Strowd crinkled his nose and sniffed. Postin glared at him. The man was half-dog, and stank like one.

"Any signs?" Postin asked him.

Strowd shrugged. "Three men, and three days ago. This breeze must have lit those faggots, no one's been around since."

"That will be them." Postin kicked the faggots, spraying hot dust at his companions' faces. They didn't complain, so Postin grinned at them, leaning on the pole-axe, his massive fists bulging and knotting. *I'm the boss here.*

"They'll most likes be in Wynais by now," Tolc said, voicing a rare opinion. "That's if they didn't stopover at a tavern or such."

"Yeah, that's helpful," Postin said. "I'm happy you're here." The pair looked at him and he shrugged. "Set up camp. We'll start again before dawn."

***

"How far to Wynais?" Corin led Thunderhoof along the grubby street. Little children stared at the huge horse as he clomped by. Corin grinned at a little girl and she ran off crying.

"Think she liked you," Stane said behind him.

"Shut your face," Corin replied. "Is there a tavern in this dump? I don't need another night camping outside with you two."

"I for one have enjoyed our sojourn," Stane said.

"That looks like one." Skinny Crall led his beast alongside Thunder and pointed to a large, square wooden building bulging out across the street.

"Doesn't look very inviting," Corin said.

"I can always ask them to hang some drapes," Stane said, and Corin turned to stare at the older man.

"Are you sure you're up for this, innkeep?"

"Loving every minute." Stane flashed him a grin. They stopped at the inn and bought fresh supplies. Corin learned they were only twenty miles from the city and, although the afternoon was wearing on, they decided to press on.

"There's a few towns on the way," the stable boy said as he groomed Thunder and checked his hoofs. "The biggest one has a bath house—it's just five miles from the city, before you get to the lake."

Corin didn't like the sound of a bathhouse but let that go. He thanked the boy and tossed three coins his way. One for each horse. Two hours later they were on the road again, pressing into night and cantering past towns and villages until they saw the sparkle of lanterns in the distance, revealing a sizeable cluster of dwellings, and beyond it the faint shimmer of silver hinted water. Far beyond that and hard to discern, Corin glimpsed distant lights. Like floating diamonds, they hung in the darkness, suspended in the void.

"Wynais?" Corin had never been to the city, but Stane had said he knew it well.

"That's the palace," Stane said, nodding. "The walls are traced with silver, it's why it glows. Also the reason it's called the Silver City."

"Never would have worked that out," Corin said.

They reached the town by the lake and stopped at a large establishment where music filtered out into the street. It was wide and cobbled—another sign they were close to civilization. The distant palace shimmered and hovered a few miles to the east, the walls etched by firelight and gleaming faint silver at the far side of the lake. Corin could just make out the shapes of mountain frowning down beyond, a horned moon riding high above.

It was colder here, and a fresh wind whipped from those heights. They stabled their horses and retired to the common room after Stane paid for their lodging and discussed news with the proprietor, a man he said he'd met long ago.

Corin huddled close to the fire, Clouter thrust up between his legs and many a pair of eyes glancing his way. Crall nodded at the sword, and Corin reluctantly placed it on the floor beside their table.

"You never know," he said. "I might need it."

"These fellows appear harmless enough," Crall said. Away to the right, beyond the shadow of smoke and fug, a large man was playing pipes and a skinny girl with gold hoops in her ears was cavorting around with a small drum. Men watched her dance but Corin shut his ears from the racket.

He tried to think. Yazrana would be in the city. But how would he find her before that bastard Keel did something? His mind had been clearer in the wilds. Now they were close to Wynais, he realized he hadn't a notion what to do next. Couldn't ride up to the guards asking if they'd seen a crimson pirate wench and an assassin.

Stane returned and took seat. He brought three large tankards, all spilling ale. Corin seized his and smiled. He felt better. Ale would help him think.

"Name's Corogan." Stane pointed at the proprietor. "Good fellow, sound as a pound. Knew him in my younger days when we were stationed down here. This hostelry's been in his family for years. Good to see him again."

"I'm happy for you," Corin said, taking his first slurp of ale. Better by far than the watery crap they'd put up with in Port Wind.

"Corogan says a stranger dropped by two nights ago."

Corin and Crall looked at him. "So?"

Stane shrugged. "Was the way he said it. Small fellow, hard green eyes. People started leaving after he arrived, made them uncomfortable. Took lodging upstairs and left before dawn. He paid with one gold coin."

"Keel." Corin glanced at Crall, who shrugged.

"Fits his description," the albino said. Corin felt a stab of worry. If Keel was alone then where was Yazrana? Dead in a hedge with her throat torn open, crows and foxes tearing at her flesh. He closed his eyes and gripped the table.

She lives and I have to find her.

He had to believe that else he'd lose momentum. They had a king to save, and his woman to find. Once that was done, Corin needed to clear her name. It had all been some big misunderstanding, though Corin wasn't sure how that had come about. He'd find her and they would return south. That was all that mattered. And the gold Silon owed him. That too.

***

Her feet were bleeding but the hot water felt good. She had kept to the woods, skirting the lakeshore and staying well clear of the road. Yazrana had seen no sign of her pursuer and dared to hope Keel might have given up on her. He had bigger tasks to attend than her.

But she hadn't dropped her guard. Her clothes were filthy and torn, and she hadn't had any problem convincing the City Watch she was just another beggar woman seeking alms inside the walls. Making for the temple of Elanion where all the poorer folk gathered, waiting for High Priest Dazaleon, or maybe young Princess Ariane. Both were said to bless the sorry folk and occasionally spray them with coin. Lord Dazaleon had even taken in strays and trained them as priests or retainers.

One of these had greeted her outside the temple. The vast spacious dome of studded silver and jade, its arched double doors open, and the priests within all clad in green attending the many devotees and acolytes.

"You are a fallen woman?" The priest addressing her leaned over her bath and washed her filthy feet. He looked half her age, pale as moonlight, his expression disapproving.

"My husband was a soldier," she said. "Killed in the desert war. No pension, left me penniless so I must seek work in the city."

The young priest nodded his head without much interest. "The Goddess knows your faults, yet she is merciful."

Pompous little shit. His hands started rubbing her knees and thighs and she closed her eyes. Later, dressed again in her shabby but cleaned clothes, Yazrana watched the priests line up to light the green lanterns, the tall impressive figure of Dazaleon leading the procession in the evening ritual.

Dazaleon was known as both a wise and honest man. He was perhaps the only individual who could help her in this city. He was walking closer, blessing onlookers and lighting candles as he passed. She took a step toward him, making sure no one noticed. Another, his leonine hair and mass of gray hair stood out like an island surrounded by the shaven pates of the priests of Elanion, clad in their shimmering green.

He was a few feet away from her so Yazrana forced herself through the crowd until she stood in plain view, capturing his attention.

"Daughter, come to me and receive our Goddess's blessing." The High Priest's voice was rich and deep, and he smiled kindly at her. A look far different from the priests and soldiers gathered close; their scowls were mocking and cruel. One or two of the younger priests stared at her brown legs where the trousers had torn. She ignored them and walked up to Dazaleon.

"My lord, may I whisper in your ear?" she asked.

"This is irregular," a priest said behind her, but Dazaleon waved back the protest.

"Something to confess, my dear?" He beckoned her close and she gazed up at those kind brown eyes. She tiptoed and spoke quietly in his ear.

Dazaleon's eyes widened and he gazed about. But before he could speak, a loud shout reverberated across the temple.

"Arrest that whore!" Yazrana glanced around and saw a squad of soldiers had entered the temple and were rushing her way. The High Priest was gazing at them in surprise and the gathering opening like a curtain to let them through. The captain's face was red with rage. "There's a rope waiting for that one," he yelled.

Yazrana held up her hands in denial, and then she stopped, seeing the small figure slipping out from the temple behind the soldiers. Keel flashed her a brief smile and vanished in the streets outside.

"What is this?" Dazaleon rounded on the Guard Captain as the soldiers surrounded the High Priest and Yazrana.

"This woman is wanted for piracy and murder," the captain said. "The Crimson Lady. Forgive this interruption, Your Eminence, but we received a tipoff that she was in the city, and we believe planning an attack on the king's person."

"You're a damn fool." Yazrana spat at his face as the Guard Captain pushed alongside and seized her.

"Is this true?" Dazaleon's huge eyes studied her. "You are the woman responsible for those terrible atrocities along our coast?"

"My lord—there is a killer in this city after your king. Time is running out."

"Is it true?" The High Priest's voice boomed in her ear as the soldiers grabbed her arms and pulled them behind her back. She saw a few of the priests smiling at her discomfort. *Bastards.* The sight most likely turned them on. "Answer me!"

"Yes." Yazrana dropped her eyes from his gaze. "I am she."

"Then our Goddess cannot help you." Dazaleon glanced briefly at her dark red attire and nodded to the soldiers. He turned away and continued with his duties.

"Dazaleon, stop! The king is in danger." A fist rammed into her ear and she fell sideways, another blow had her on her knees, and then a boot impacted her face and Yazrana pitched face first onto the hard-polished slate.

"Take her to the oubliette," the Guard Captain said. "We'll hang her at sun up."

***

The following morning Keel watched the city guard drag their prisoner through the streets toward the guard house shadowed beneath the east wall, the huge arm of mountains looming close. A bright sunny morning with eagles circling high above the city, and gonfalons of green and gold rippling in the summer breeze. *A good day to be alive.* And a fine morning for a hanging.

Crowds gathered close as they dragged the disheveled woman into the square where the gibbet stood surrounded by a dozen well-armed guards. Keel folded his arms and leaned against the wall, a tankard swaying in his hand. He'd started early today—a few drinks to watch the show and then on to the main business of the day.

A guard pulled her along the square by her thick black hair. Her clothes were badly ripped, exposing those tanned muscular thighs, and one breast. Her face—when he glimpsed it—was a mask of rage beneath that disheveled tousle of hair. Dark eyes huge and filled with contempt for all those gathered around her.

"You were a fine woman, Yazrana," Keel said, watching with a smile from his pillar. "But you shouldn't have crossed me." He wondered what they would do to her before the hanging. Could be interesting and the crowd was placing bets.

A tall, hard-looking soldier appeared with a whip in one hand. Keel grinned. *Good choice. Entertaining.* He sipped his ale and grinned again as the whip cracked and lashed her shoulders, ripping the shirt open amid yells of approval from the bystanders.

She fell to her knees, blood seeping from her back. The soldier with the whip stood over her grinning. He raised it high then stopped. He looked shocked, and then Keel noticed the knife sticking between his shoulder blades.

What's this?

The soldier dropped his whip and fell on top of the woman. Someone kicked her to the ground as shouts filled the square and soldiers seized their weapons. Keel faded back into the shadows. Time he wasn't here.

Chapter 14 | The King Rides Out

Corin swung Clouter in wide threatening arcs as the square erupted into angry life. Yazrana was half naked and bloody, with those laughing guards and crowd baying all around. Rage had filled him, but disbelief had slowed his reaction. Crall had acted quicker than anyone.

Corin had seen the whip rising a second time, the grinning crowd waving, their tongues hanging out, and then as he'd gripped Clouter's scabbard and tugged, he'd seen that flash of steel and realized the whip holder was dead.

That did it. Corin's wild sweeps with his two-yard sword kept the soldiers at bay, the city folk were already making for the safety of buildings and doorways for cover. From there they looked on as their hitherto game took a more serious turn.

Stane ran a city guard through with his sword. Albino Crall sprinted over and reclaimed his dagger, ripping it free form the corpse's back and stabbing out at another soldier close by. The man fell back, his throat ripped open.

Corin reached Yazrana. She blinked up at him. No tears there—just blood and rage. "Took your fucking time," she said, her voice barely audible, and her proud face contorted with pain.

"I'm sorry," Corin said. The solders surrounded them, but he reached down and hoisted her up with one arm, Clouter thrust point down in the dirt, and helping him pivot her up.

"Back off," he snarled at the guards. They all carried swords, a few shields, but Corin saw no bows or spears in sight. They seemed unsure what to do. Ill disciplined, lackluster and shabby in Corin's opinion. Used to a life of ease and comfort. Corin doubted they'd seen much action. These were too young to have fought down in Permio. Tossers, the lot of them.

They watched his blade in morbid fascination as Yazrana stumbled to her feet. She slipped Biter free from the scabbard at Corin's belt. "I'll borrow this," she said, and started limping toward the Guard Captain, who backed away, his face white with shock at what had happened, a routine hanging gone so awry, and he'd be the one held accountable.

Corin saw the panic on his face and grinned. "Let us leave quietly and no one else gets hurt. Sound the warning and I'll kill you first." He grabbed Clouter with both hands and swung the blade in another arc, the steel whooshing close to the captain's head.

The Guard Captain backed away again. His men looked at him for a decision, but none came. Ten soldiers stood facing Corin and Crall, with Stane somewhere behind. And the woman still limping toward the captain.

"We'll report this," the young officer said, and flicked a hand at his men. They nodded, relieved, and departed the square with as little fuss as was possible. Some of the citizens jeered as they left, but most had made themselves scarce.

"Come back and I'll stick the lot of you with this," Yazrana said, her voice croaky. She collapsed to her knees and Corin lifted her again.

"We need to get you out of harm's way," Corin said. "Give you time to recover."

"Nowhere to hide," she said. "And we have to stop Keel. I know who he is, Corin. I'd shut out that part of my life—but I fought alongside him once. I'm cursed, my love . . ."

Worried, Corin glanced at her face. "You're babbling, not making sense." She looked far away, barely conscious, her dark eyes blinking. What had those bastards done to her last night? She needed water, and then rest, and he needed somewhere close by to heal those wounds. Yazrana's eyes were closing and she fell again. He picked her up. It was no use; she'd lost a lot of blood. They needed help, and fast.

"This way!" a familiar voice called down from somewhere above. Corin glanced up and was amazed to see Silon standing alone on a balcony overlooking the square. *How?*

"Hurry now, I hear more soldiers coming," Silon said. "If the king or his advisors are alerted, we are all dead men."

Corin nodded and half carried, half dragged Yazrana across to the far side of the square. Stane covered his back and Crall held a dagger ready in each hand. But the square was empty, the last stragglers having taken the hint and left behind the departing guards.

A door opened on a well-lit room that appeared to be some large private dwelling. A hallway lead to wide stairs sweeping up and around with alabaster pillars carved flanking either side, a crystal chandelier winking silver light from above. Stane helped Corin carry the unconscious woman up until they reached another hallway with three doors at the far end. The one on the left was open and they brought Yazrana inside.

Crall followed behind. "I'll wait outside," he said. "In case we have visitors."

"Bring her in here." Silon emerged and hinted an anteroom.

"Nice gaff," Stane said, without introducing himself. Silon ignored him.

"I've sent for a physician," Silon said, motioning a table. "We need to talk."

"Why are you—"

"—Because I'm needed," Silon said before Corin could finish his question. "Your friend . . .?" His sharp dark eyes flashed toward Stane, currently gazing from the window to the empty square behind.

"A recently retired innkeep from Port Wind," Corin said.

"I was a former Bear," Stane said, turning to address Silon with a grin.

"King Nogel rides into peril," Silon said.

"What... again? Doesn't have much sense, that king." Corin looked through the side door where he could see Yazrana, prone and motionless on the cot.

"He wants to tackle Caswallon face on."

"I don't know much about Caswallon, but I'd say that was a bad idea," Corin said.

"Yep." Stane nodded behind him.

Silon, looking irritated, motioned the former innkeep. "Can you make yourself useful and pour us all a large brandy—there's a flask full of the stuff by that other window. And you'll find glasses there too."

"I'll go see," Stane obliged.

"We have to stop him," Silon addressed Corin again.

"We?" Corin shook his head in wonder.

"You," Silon corrected. "You, Corin an Fol, have to ambush the king and dissuade him from this rash and hasty course of action."

"Are you possessed? How can I—a lone mercenary, and a foreigner—stop a king's party and full troop and tell them the road's blocked?"

"You'll find a way."

"I haven't been paid for my last job yet. You owe me for Krugan—weeks, no—months of careful work."

"You'll get your money, so stop harping on. This has to be done and you're the man on the spot. There is no one else." Silon folded his arms and glared at Corin.

"It's a bad idea," Corin said, wondering if he'd ever see that gold.

"Very," Stane said, nodding and rejoining them and placing the flask and glasses on the table.

"Is there an echo in here?" Silon muttered. He poured himself a large glass, ignoring Corin and Stane. "Nogel rides out in the morning. I spoke with the king earlier today, advised against this but he's not to be swayed. Headstrong as a mule."

"And clearly just as stupid," Corin said.

"You're talking about a king," Silon snapped at Corin, who shrugged. "Show some respect, damn you."

"He's not my king," Corin said. "Nor is he my problem. I have to get Yaz out of this city once she's fit enough. Then I'm riding back south and waiting in your office until you pay me. Gold—and lots of the stuff. I spent months in that desert tracking those bandits. They almost hung me for my efforts."

"That was your job." Silon wasn't listening.

"After you've paid me I'm quitting," Corin said. "I'll resign."

Silon ignored him and gazed down at the square, which was starting to fill again as folk chattered excitedly about the events that had happened earlier.

"Nogel is my king," Stane said suddenly, and both Silon and Corin looked at him. The older man looked thoughtful. "He's a good man. A strong, decent ruler, though rash and hasty. Rare these days. *Noble Nogel* we used to call him. His queen was so beautiful, bloody shame what happened."

"What did happen?" Corin asked, but the other two ignored him.

"I'll help if I can," Stane said.

Just then Crall the albino appeared and loomed over them. "Soldiers are back, and some high-ranking officer. There's a huge important-looking priest with the officer and they're all heading this way."

"That will be Dazaleon," Silon said. He looked relieved. "I'll handle this." Crall nodded and took a seat beside them, taking Stane's glass and draining the contents. Stane hardly noticed, seemed lost in thought.

"You did well down there," Corin told Crall. "I was so shocked to see her in that state, I lost concentration. *Unprofessional.* Your action saved us."

Crall shrugged. "You were involved. To me it's just another job, and your team's better than the last lot I worked with. I expect Postin's heading this way," he added, after a moment's silence.

"You think?" Corin asked.

"Call it a hunch."

"They'd welcome him like they did her." Corin motioned Yazrana in the other room. He got up and went to see her. She opened her eyes and the ghost of a smile showed.

"I can hear you talking in there," she said. She looked awful, but at least she was alive.

"Silon sent for a healer," Corin told her, brushing hair from her face. "What happened, Yaz?"

"It was Keel—he's here somewhere. He sent the soldiers to get me when I was warning the High Priest . . ."

"Who should have listened to you," a booming voice echoed outside. Corin turned quickly, cursing as Clouter rested in the other room. He reached for his saex as two soldiers appeared outside, followed by a huge man in a green robe, trimmed with gold at the hem and hood, a shock of white hair framing his large handsome face.

You must be the High Priest.

Silon appeared. "She's in here, Dazaleon," he said. The huge figure entered a bald-headed priest and the two hard-faced guards followed close behind. The guards wore green and gold unlike the ones in the square had worn earlier. They also had breastplates and round steel helms, the visors open. The pair looked like veterans, their flat eyes flicked at Corin with distrust. He ignored them.

"Who is this fellow?" High Priest Dazaleon stopped and appraised Corin for a moment. His deep violet eyes were hypnotic and Corin felt a power there, almost as though the old man was reading his mind.

"Corin an Fol," Silon said. "Good man, though not a team player. He's volunteered to help us persuade the king from his present folly."

"Good of you," Dazaleon said before turning away. "Now let me see that poor woman." Silon motioned the bed where Yazrana lay, sleeping again. Dazaleon leaned over her. He stroked her head and parted her hair. "She has a fever and two broken ribs," he said.

"The physician's coming," Corin said, still wondering why he hadn't objected to the last words spoken to him.

"I am the physician," Dazaleon said. "You will not find a better one in this city, boy. She needs rest, and then I will talk to her before she's placed on trial."

"On trial?" Corin glared at the High Priest.

"This woman has committed serious offenses along our coastline," Dazaleon said. "She will have to atone."

"A misunderstanding," Silon intervened as Corin reached for his saex again. The merchant's dark eyes flashed him a warning, and Corin left the room, returning to the others sipping brandy at the table. The two guards glared at him so Corin showed them a finger. He reached for the bottle and took a hard slug.

"What the fuck is going on?" Corin said. His companions just stared at him. Silon emerged moments later.

"Dazaleon will heal her easily enough, and I've persuaded him to let matters be for the moment, though he is angry, and rightly so. I told him there was more to those dreadful events on the coast, that Yazrana was mostly innocent of blame but implicated by another."

"Keel," Corin said, nodding. "About time we found that bastard and turned him inside out. Yazrana says he's here."

"We cannot help that," Silon said. "Nogel rides out at first light. You and your new friends need to get to that border fast and stop the king from crossing into Kelthaine. Caswallon will have men watching—once Nogel's in his power they'll strike, we can be certain of it."

"What are you saying?"

"You need to leave tonight," Silon said.

"With half the City Guard looking for us?"

"Dazaleon has informed Yail Tolranna, the garrison lieutenant. No one will stop you at the gates."

"Tolranna? That hothead boy?" Stane's look was disapproving.

"Aye, the king promoted him after he lost Staveport," Silon said. "No one else suitable since his champion's gone missing. Go get some food in your bellies and grab what rest you can. I need you sharp and prompt at dusk." Silon addressed the words to Corin but his companions seemed more willing than he was.

"What about Yazrana?" Corin asked.

"I'll see she's safe until you return. I promise—just do what you can to save Nogel, Corin. If he's rides anywhere near Kella City, we're all sunk. *Understand?*"

"Understood."

***

Keel watched the light fade from the battlements as the sun sank beyond the lake, flooding that wide expanse of water with orange and gold. So beautiful. The sight touched him with its profundity. Dramatic and serene. *It reminds us how small we are.*

He felt a fleeting sense of sadness wash through him. It could have been so different. *He* could have been someone else. But the Fates had shaped him thus. They were to blame—and other mens' wicked deeds—for the monster he'd become.

Ironic. He had everything, had gained everything a man could wish for. And yet he lacked the fundamental forces which flowed throughout humanity. *Love and joy*—the reason for living. For him there was only cruelty and pain. A substitute for something lost . . . And *anger*, so much rage and lust for hurting others. When he saw happiness, Keel wanted to drive it away. Scrape the smile from those faces. No one should be happy. Living meant enduring pain like he'd done. The agony he'd suffered under that tower, their hot knives and pincers, the things they'd done. And him alone down there. Cold, body caked with shit. The fear of that hot cutting knife doing its awful work, their flushed, excited faces watching eagerly under torchlight. His screams, muffled, vanishing into the blood-soaked walls.

Keel shivered. The sun had gone. Extinguished beyond the water. That sheen shifted to purple then faded to dark silver as he watched, alone at the end of the east wall. Guards stood silent close by. They paid him no heed; a citizen seeking solace, swabbed in cloak and hood.

How Keel hated this life. This world—*Ansu*, had cheated him. Robbed him of his rightful destiny while others rode on his back. King Nogel was part of that hierarchy, thus partly to blame, but ultimately the fault lay with the High King in Kella. Caswallon alone knew Keel's vulnerability. But that cunning player needed to be careful. Keel smiled wryly. *You might be a sorcerer but I'm so much more.* Their new alliance made sense, but Keel was well aware Caswallon would betray him in a second.

Mood lifting, he walked briskly to the far gate. A guard blocked his way and Keel smiled at the man. "Beautiful evening— I'm out for a stroll, soldier."

The guard stared at him for a moment and nodded. "Peace be with you, citizen." He raised his halberd and Keel ducked beneath, passing through the tower doors and walking further along the wall until he could see the west gates far below.

Keel stood there in watchful silence as darkness fell and a chill breeze drifted down from the mountains, together with a fret that coated the crenulations with slippery damp. Keel hardly noticed the chill. He watched for another hour until he heard the gates creak open and saw three horsemen ride out. Even from this distance he recognized the albino Crall's lean shadow cast by torchlight. The gates cranked shut and the riders urged their mounts along the road toward Lake Wynais.

Caswallon's man had told him about the merchant's gambit to save Nogel. A fool's errand. The young priest had been witness to the discussion in the villa where the merchant held lodging. His master, Dazaleon, had seen to Yazrana.

A survivor, that one.

Keel considered returning there and stabbing her through the heart. But The Crimson Lady was small fry and he had better things to do. His actions would change the destiny of all Four Kingdoms. This game was about to play out, and soon everyone would know who was responsible for the change.

A new order. As Caswallon rose, so would he. The priest had sent a bird north informing Caswallon of Nogel's plans. The king was leaving at dawn. Keel could strike anywhere, but decided to let matters be. *Watch and wait.* Carne Dooly's man Tolc had sought him out earlier in a tavern outside town, informing Keel that Postin and another were lurking in the woods outside the city. Keel had told Tolc about the three riders.

"They'll be waiting at the border," he said. "Tell Postin to deal with them before the king arrives." Tolc had slipped out the gates that afternoon, allowing time for them to ride north before Silon's people got there. Keel grinned. Crall and his friends were in for a shock.

As for Keel, his quarry would be leaving in a few hours. Everything was in hand. Satisfied, Keel retired to his rented room and spent several hours resting—he rarely slept—in the shabby lodging near the gatehouse. He rose as soon as hoofbeats sounded on cobbles. Keel watched from his window as the king rode out with a score of men, all cased in silver armor that glinted beneath the stars. Keel waited a few minutes then slipped outside. He made sure no one was watching before trotting along the deserted streets until he found the young priest waiting outside the temple.

"Make sure the king crosses the border without trouble," the priest said, his tone aloof. Keel reached out and grabbed his throat. He tugged and threw the man to the floor and then kicked him hard in the face. The priest sobbed and held up his hands in feeble supplication.

"You don't give me orders, cunt." Keel kicked him again, harder this time, making the priest cry out. "Inform your real master I'll be in touch." Keel smiled at the weeping priest, kicked him a third time, and then left him lying bleeding in the street.

Keel departed Wynais later that morning. *No need to rush.* Once again, he would let others do his dirty work. *First King Nogel then* . . . Keel smiled as he rode, the birds chirping cheerfully in the bushes and the blue cloudless sky high above.

***

Yazrana woke and gasped at the sharp pain in her chest. She swore hoarsely and rolled free of the bed. She was naked and clean. Fresh clothes were folded neatly over a chair. She reached for them, wincing again as she slipped on undergarments, trousers and tunic, then woolen hose and long suede boots. A sword hung from a belt by a hook on the door. She strapped the belt around her waist, and then froze as a knock tapped the door.

"Who?"

Silon entered with a smile. "I heard movement, so thought you'd be awake. And dressed." He smiled. "Going somewhere?"

"Well I cannot stay here."

"You're safe for the time being."

"No one's fucking safe." She winced and sat back down on the bed, cursing again. "That bastard Keel is out there. *I saw him*, Silon. He'll be after the king—to finish what he started."

"The king has vacated the city," Silon said. "Nogel left silently this morning."

"Then Keel would have followed close behind."

"How would he know? The king told no one of his plans except the Captain of Guard, Lord Dazaleon, the princess and myself—and only because I was witness to his anger yesterday."

Yazrana bit her lip as pain stabbed at her chest again.

"You need to rest," Silon said. "Don't worry—the High Priest vouched for your safety, if not an immediate pardon. They don't like you here in Wynais, Yazrana."

"They have cause not to," Yazrana said.

"It wasn't your fault."

"You don't know everything, Silon. Things happened on that beach. Terrible things that I'm responsible for, however indirectly." She rubbed her eyes. "Where is Corin?"

"Gone."

"*What . . . ?* Where?"

"North." Silon reached down and checked her bandage beneath her tunic. "You'll mend," he said. "But you need more rest."

"Where has Corin gone?"

"I sent him out to wait for the king and stop him from crossing the border."

"How will Corin achieve that?"

"I have no idea," Silon said. "But the man has capable wit when he cares to use it. I couldn't think of any other way to stop Nogel. He'll have heard of Corin an Fol—Lord Halfdan was close to the king, and would have mentioned his favorite protégée. And you too, Yazrana. That's part of the reason why Nogel despises you. He believed you went rogue and lost your mind in the desert."

"That's partly true," she said. "If Corin is in danger, I need to be with him."

"You need to heal and stay put until I can persuade Dazaleon—and later the king—to allow you a safe return to Raleen."

"What about you?"

"Staying put, for the moment at least. Princess Ariane has a proposal for me. We've a meeting later today."

"She's a girl, a mere whisper."

"With a shrewd head on confident shoulders. Ariane believes her father is riding into a trap." "I'm sure she's right, and most likely the whole country would agree were they to know. Nogel is a damn fool."

"He is honorable and therefore believes others are the same. A king's pride. I agree it's a chink in his armor. Ariane worries that she will inherit a big mess soon and wants to set up a secret group to counter Caswallon's rise to power."

"What about Keel?"

"I expect he'll leave the city when he hears of the king's departure," Silon said. "A lone operator and rogue wolf."

"That assassin is no *Wolf*." She spat the words out and Silon apologized.

"I forget myself—a sensitive area. I should have chosen a different word."

She shrugged. "Doesn't matter. I'm no longer in the regiment. Unfit to use that word. I'm tarnished, Silon. *Lost.*"

"It wasn't your fault," Silon insisted.

You weren't there. "Keel will strike soon—I feel it," she said, after a moment. "Corin will need help. Whatever happens on that Kelthaine border, I'll wager Keel will play a part."

"We cannot help that."

"I can."

"Yaz—you need rest, woman."

"Nope." She smiled. "I need to atone for what I've done. I can think of no better opportunity. So be a good friend, master merchant, and find me a swift horse, a bow, and some knives, this sword will work though I'd prefer a curved blade. I'll need coin and food too."

Silon stared at her for long minutes and then sighed, knowing he was defeated. "You are incorrigible, Yazrana of Permio," the merchant said. "At least do me the honor of having lunch before you depart."

"I will." She smiled, feeling better now that she had a plan. The pain was nothing compared to the memory of those children screaming on that beach. *I can make a difference up there.* Perhaps then she could live with those memories again.

A few hours later, a fresh bandage wrapped tight around her ribs, Yazrana rode out between the city gates under the bright afternoon sun. She wore dun-colored trousers and a shabby cloak of faded gray, a horse bow slung across her shoulders, and two full sacks of arrows strapped to the saddle. The sun warmed her face as she let the mare canter toward the dazzling shimmer that was Lake Wynais in summertime.

Chapter 15 | Close Encounters

Corin gazed down through the trees at the wide river churning below. Further back, the road wound over hills and vanished into hazy distance. A bridge stood there, the great stone stanchions arched and engraved with symbols and gargoyles; all were lost on Corin.

The color wasn't. The bridge gleamed alabaster. A white hue so bright it both hurt his eyes and yet pulled his gaze in. Whitestone Bridge was a marvel; not like the huge expansion that crossed the Liaho leagues to the south, but impressive nonetheless with its arches, rails, and the chalk-like cobbles neatly paved together to make a level and polished roadway.

Lanterns shimmered silver, mingling with the white and distorting his vision. Hard to see movement down there. Corin counted twenty lights, all mounted on bastions thrusting up from the rails.

"Beautiful, is it not?" Stane appeared beside him and grinned. *At least you're happy*, Corin thought. Stane had the ability to shrug off concerns—or at least hide them from others. But Corin was worried enough for both of them.

"What are we doing here?" Corin said, shaking his head. "Trying to stop a stupid king from crossing into Kelthaine. Like emptying a well with a leaky bucket."

"He might listen," Stane offered, and Corin just looked at him. "It is *possible*."

"Yeah," Corin said. "And about as likely as myself getting gold from a certain merchant. Moreover, Heroic Nogel might decide to remove our heads—he doesn't like lurkers in woods as I recall."

"That's possible too."

"Likely, I'd say," Corin said. At least Crall would stay hidden. That might give them some small chance—if one of Nogel's loons recognized the albino from Port Wind then they'd all be trussed up quicker than flies in spider's webs. Cheerful thought.

A rustle behind. Corin turned, Clouter ready, but Crall waved his arms, his shaggy white hair matted and covered with bracken from where he'd been crawling hand over fist to remain hidden from any prying eyes.

"They're coming," Crall said, rising to a squat and hinting the road behind. "Twenty horsemen—no more."

"Best make our way down," Corin said to Stane.

"We'll meet you back at camp," Stane added, and Crall nodded before vanishing back into the undergrowth.

The way down to the road was steep and slippery. Corin had to stow Clouter lest he poke himself. Stane carried a heavy-looking axe in both hands—his favorite choice of weapon he'd explained, and a generous gift from one of Dazaleon's guards. The man had known Stane in his younger days.

They clambered down onto the road and walked warily toward the bridge, scarce more than a hundred yards distant. Nothing moved, not even a bird winged overhead as Corin cast his eyes at the clear blue sky.

They reached the bridge and took cover in the long grasses flanking the road. No point exposing themselves until necessary. It wasn't long before the sound of hooves reached them, coming from the south beyond the bend.

Riders emerged, their faces obscured by hoods and helms. They wore long green cloaks and armor glinted beneath. The man at the front was heavy set and tough looking. He reined up as Corin and Stane strode out in front of the bridge. Corin's hands were held wide and Stane grinned like a loon.

The riders reined in, bunching close. The horses snorted and steam showed from their noses. *Here we go.* Corin started walking toward them. He stopped twenty feet from the horsemen who watched him in silence. Finally, the burley one spoke, and Corin noticed for the first time the thin gold crown adorning his half-covered helm.

"You are bold for a highwayman." The king's voice was deep and calm. *A warrior.* Corin approved of his tone. "We are twenty—so state your business, fellow, and I'll decide whether you get to keep your head."

What to say...? Corin bowed slowly then took a step forward before blurting, "King Nogel, you need to go home." Not the best opening when addressing a king, but Corin knew little about herald etiquette. The king looked at him with raised brows. Some of his men scowled and Corin saw two reach for their swords.

Then Nogel laughed. "You are a strange fellow to be sure. On what authority do you state your purpose?"

"Common sense," Stane said, appearing alongside Corin, who flashed him an irritated glance.

"I've heard the mummer's fair is underway in Kelthara." King Nogel hinted across the bridge. "You two clowns should go hence at speed. Those northerners will pay well for such tomfoolery."

"Highness, let me deal with these rogues." A sharp-faced officer rode alongside the king, his dark eyes hostile and distrustful as he glared at Corin, and then at Clouter strapped across his back.

"Where did you steal that glaive?" The officer pointed to the longsword.

Corin glared back at him, trying to keep a lid on his temper. "Who might you be?" he asked eventually as tension rose among the riders. Corin saw the young officer stiffen under that question. He looked at his king, who nodded. Corin ignored the younger man deliberately and instead studied King Nogel, who also was staring at Corin's longsword with interest.

"General Yail Tolranna," the officer said after a second nod from his monarch.

"Well, General . . . *whoever* . . . Please shut up and let me speak with your king."

The general kicked his spurs in fury, but the king placed a gloved hand on Tolranna's horse, calming the animal. "You shouldn't let this man goad you, Tolranna. Maybe he can use that thing."

"I'm happy to let him prove it," Yail Tolranna said.

Try me, shithead. Corin folded his arms and counted to ten. Beside him, Stane stepped forward again, his arms wide, palms out. "Highness, we are—"

"—from Port Wind," the king cut in, still looking at Corin but addressing Stane. "I recognize that rustic accent. But your moody-eyed friend's from further north—yes?" He looked hard at Corin.

"I'm Corin an Fol. It's a little country—"

"—northwest of Kelthaine—yes, I've been there." The king smiled at what must have been some distant memory. Again, Corin was impressed. No one visited Fol, and he'd certainly never heard of any king dropping by. *Why would they?* There was nothing in Fol except seabirds and wind, and the occasional standing stone carved with hieroglyphics no one understood. A timeless ancient country he'd left over a decade ago.

"You were a Wolf." King Nogel smiled. "And a reputable one, I'd warrant. Lord Halfdan doesn't hand out many golden broaches to his lads. Nor are there many longswordsmen around these days. Weapons like that are too unwieldy for your average modern-day warrior."

"It's just practice," Corin said. "And you need strong forearms."

"I'll bet." The king smiled briefly and then drove that expression away with a scowl.

"What do you know of our *business*, Corin an Fol? And more importantly—who is paying you?"

"I work for Silon of Raleen."

"I see." The king looked at Tolranna, who shook his head.

"He—and others in your city—sent me and Stane up here to stop you crossing the border. Believed that you are riding into a trap."

"This man is a lying villain, Highness." Tolranna dug in his heels again, and again King Nogel calmed his horse.

"And why should a king heed the word of a merchant's lackey?"

"It's a fair point," Stane said, but was ignored.

"I told them you'd be too bull-headed to listen," Corin replied. The man Tolranna swore and even the king looked shocked.

"You have a reckless tongue, longswordsman. I'm surprised it's still in your mouth."

"There are people out to get you, Your Highness," Corin persisted, despite the hostile looks from everyone except his friend. The king's hard face was no longer friendly. "They work for that sly councilor in Kella City. They failed in Port Wind but they're going to strike again—probably in Kelthaine itself. You cross that border and you're vulnerable."

"I weary of this," King Nogel said. "Stand aside." He urged Tolranna and the score of riders to spur their mounts and canter towards the bridge. Corin and Stane leaped for cover as the horsemen bore down on them.

"I'll be speaking with Silon on my return—Corin an Fol," King Nogel said as he thundered past, the horse kicking dust in Corin's face.

"Arsehole," Corin said, wiping dirt from his eye.

"He's a king," Stane said. "What did you expect?"

"That went well," Corin said. "What do we do now?" He tensed and grabbed Stane's arm. "Up there through the trees—did you see it?"

"I did." Stane cursed. Corin stared hard for long moments until he saw it again. A glint of light. Someone was watching them from across the valley. Not Crall, as he would be out of sight at their camp way up behind them. *Keel?*

"We'd better get back to the camp quickly," Stane said. "Whoever that is—there'll be reporting back the king's actions. Maybe we can cut them off before they do any harm, send word to Caswallon?"

"Or maybe we shouldn't give a shit," Corin said. "If that king wants to ride to his death then let him, I say. Arrogant prick."

Stane gave him a hard look. "This is bigger than Nogel, Corin an Fol. We have to stop Caswallon's poison spreading. Any small action can pay dividends. Besides—most kings would have ordered our heads. Nogel is a good man, though hotheaded. You should show some respect."

"Bollocks," Corin muttered, but he knew Stane was right—there being more at risk here than a king's rash pride. Corin's prime irritation was down to his habitual dislike of authority—and that pompous arseling, the general had riled him. He shrugged after a moment. "Come on then, Sage." He smiled. "Whoever's spying over there doesn't know we've seen them. Let's get Crall and the horses and go pay them visit."

***

Keel placed the spyglass on his lap and crossed his legs. Amusing watching the fools down there. But puzzling too. The king had ridden up close to the two men as they'd jumped out in front of the bridge. A rash stupid action which should have cost them their heads. But Nogel had conferred with them briefly and then ridden past at speed. *Strange.* Who were these men? Keel was intrigued. He twisted the spyglass so it caught the light, allowing those fools below to see it.

He saw the taller one glance up and then look away quickly. The man looked vaguely familiar even from this distance, and Keel smiled. *Yes, I'm here. Do come pay visit.* Keel twisted the glass again and then stowed it in his belt. He rolled to his feet and stepped back into the bushes. Down below by the bridge, the two men faded back into the undergrowth. Doubtless making back for the camp.

Keel grinned again. They'd be in for a nice surprise when they got there.

***

Crall lit his pipe and waited, crouching low, expecting his friends to return at any moment. Instead the huge bulk of Postin the Hammer emerged through the trees and grinned at him.

Crall leaped to his feet but someone grabbed him from behind and held a knife to his throat. Crall twisted and wriggled, butted his head back and stamped down on someone's foot. He broke loose, but the knife tore into his throat and blood sprayed his garments.

Postin roared, and Crall saw the terrible hammer swinging toward him. He staggered, his hands staunching the crimson flow from his torn neck. A deep slice—he'd weaken soon with blood loss. Must warn the others. Crall forced his aching legs forward, twisting to the right as Postin's hammer flashed past. Ahead lay a gap in the trees. *Escape!* He hobbled that way, then a boot tripped him. Crall fell, his face impacting the dirt.

He rolled over just in time to see that hammer sailing down. Crall's face exploded. Agony flooded him, he caught the briefest glimpse of Postin's smiling face and then nothing. *Oblivion.*

***

"You shouldn't have double-crossed me, Crall." Postin kicked at the mangled mess of his former friend. "We had a good thing going once. But it seems you can't trust anyone these days." Tolc loomed close, saw the horror and backed off. "You squeamish?" Postin grinned at him. He thrust the hammer head in the dirt to wipe off the excess gore.

Postin felt happy for the first time in days. They'd reached the city and Tolc had entered, sought out the contact Carne Dooly used—a priest apparently. Tolc had returned with word that Keel was in the city, and the king was riding north to Kelthaine. They were to watch his departure and report back. *Boring fucking task.*

Postin couldn't understand why they didn't ambush Nogel and cut his throat open. *Job done.* But yet again it seemed Keel was playing games. Not with Postin the Hammer, though. *No more games.* That green-eyed bastard had to sleep sometime. Postin could wait. But then when they'd arrived at the border and seen the king's men riding up, Keel had been waiting for them. He found a camp and three horses and then they'd waited until Crall returned.

Keel ordered them lay low and do nothing as he slipped off to watch the road, and the king's approach from the south. But Postin had gotten bored. And as he'd watched Crall puffing contentedly at his pipe, he'd become angry. Crall had deserted him. Betrayed him and joined sides with that bastard Longsword.

When Keel emerged minutes later and saw the mess, he didn't look pleased. "I wanted him alive—all of them," Keel spat at Postin, who leveled his pole-axe and glared down at the smaller man.

Keel looked at him calmly for a moment and smiled. "Keep testing me, lardy lad," he said. "You're seconds away from a sliced gullet. Go on . . . *swing* . . ." Those green eyes probed Postin, unsettled him, like greasy worms slithering inside his skull. His rage faded, replaced by doubt. He stored the pole-axe against a tree.

"I meant no offense," Postin said eventually.

Keel smiled again. "I sleep light," he said. "Best you behave yourself." The other two men had kept their distance. Now Strowd loomed close.

"Two men coming this way."

Keel nodded. "Let's greet them properly," he said, then turned to Postin. "I want them kept alive—understand?" Postin nodded. They waited until the soft sound of boot brushing leaf announced the strangers' arrival.

***

Corin's first warning was Thunderhoof blowing steam in the distance. The big horse had sensed his approach and Corin knew something was wrong. Then he'd seen Crall's mashed skull—a mess of blood and brains, the pale lean body broken too, as though a rabid bear had torn upon him. Stane crashed into his back. Corin turned, saw the horror in his friends' eyes, then a voice spoke.

"You seem to be always crossing my path, longfellow." Corin turned slowly to his right. Three men stood over the campfire. Two he didn't know, but Postin hadn't changed a bit, and that hammer was badly smeared with blood and dirt. Corin ignored the brute and his silent companions. Instead his gaze focused on the small, neatly dressed individual seated cross-legged on a log, a rapier resting across his lap, and a comradely smile on his lips. His eyes were jade-green and cold as a serpent's stare.

"You'd be Master Keel," Corin said. "At least that's the name you're using at the moment."

"And yet I don't know you, Longsword" The smile widened. "You interest me. Such an ungainly weapon. Indulge me, will you—who do you work for? Despite your evident clumsiness one assumes you're a professional." He smiled and flicked his gaze to the other three still standing motionless by the campfire.

"Big Postin there wants to split your skull like he did poor Crall. The Hammer hates you, Longsword—isn't that strange? I can feel his rage throbbing through the trees."

"Why did you let the king live?" Corin didn't reach for Clouter. *Why bother.* He knew how quick this bastard was. If Keel wanted them dead then it would be over already. Best play his game for the moment.

"I'm sorry?" Keel feigned puzzlement. "I . . . *let the king live?*"

"In those other woods near Port Wind," Corin said. "You could have killed Nogel easily. Instead you sent those bungling fools and that fat bastard." He pointed at Postin who brindled with rage, seeming about to burst. "Why the charade—and why bother killing that old man in the lodge?"

"Oh . . . I enjoyed that," Keel said. "Like an opening theme to the main performance. A touch macabre, I'll grant you—but then we do live in a violent world. Take Postin the Hammer here. *So much anger.* No one loves him, you see." The sly smile again.

"Careful, Corin . . ." Stane's voice whispered close by.

"Your friend looks worried." Keel hinted behind Corin. "Think he might have shat his breeches."

"I know who you are," Corin said and saw a quick flash of irritation flicker across those green eyes.

"You know nothing of me—fool!" Keel rose to his feet in a smooth graceful movement. The smile ran from his face. "Tolc. Relight that campfire and start heating a knife. I'll work on the older man first, maybe take an eye."

"What about King Nogel?" Corin asked, and Keel turned toward him again.

"On his way to meet the High King, I'll warrant." He smiled again, evidently enjoying their discussion. "None of our business, Longsword." Tolc was already blowing on the faggots, crouched down and busy. The other man watched in silence, a curved sword clutched in his fist. Postin still stared at Corin as though willing him dead.

Sometimes when you don't have a plan you have to improvise. It's all about the timing.

Corin winked at Postin and grinned. "I'll bet your mother was a fat lazy sow with eight saggy tits." Corin winked again, slowly this time. *That did the trick.* Postin roared, leapt at him, the pole-axe swinging out.

"Postin!" Keel yelled as he leaped behind the giant. Corin dived sideways as the hammer thudded into a stump, Postin grunted as he yanked it free.

Corin glimpsed Stane making for cover to his right. Keel yelled at Tolc and the other man who gave chase. Corin forgot about Stane and those others. He had enough to contend with.

The pole-axe swung, and Postin crashed close. *Where was Keel?* Corin glimpsed movement to his right. He slid Biter free and jabbed down quick and hard as Postin swung the hammer a third time. That cut caught the giant's wrist, slicing along the forearm. Postin grunted and his blow swung wide. In rage he flicked blood at Corin's face—a shallow wound but useful. That arm was bleeding profusely and would hamper Postin's swing.

Corin heard laughter behind him. "Well played, Longsword." Keel clapped his hands. "I didn't notice the saex. A useful gut ripper when you don't have room to swing that monster, hey? Clever move."

Corin kept circling, glimpsing Keel's movement flitting from bush to bush. Postin sucked blood from his arm and lifted that hammer again.

He swung out lightning fast and hard. *Too damn quick for such a lardy lump.* Wind whooshed over Corin's head as he ducked, then cut in close again with Biter, but Postin's boot caught his knee and Corin skidded sideways. Postin braced his feet, grinned and swung again, this time in an overhead arc meant to split Corin like kindling from axe.

Corin saw the weapon descending and leaped backwards barely in time, only to trap his foot in a root and trip face-first in pine needles and dirt. He heard a laugh—*Keel.* And a roar—*Postin.* He tried to move but the giant's massive boot pinned him.

Postin kicked Corin with his other leg, sending shots of pain through his gut. The giant stood over him, pole-axe held ready. Corin saw Biter lying in the dirt. *No good.* He reached back for Clouter. No chance freeing the blade in time, but at least he could try. The hammer thudded down and then stuck in the earth an inch from Corin's head.

Postin was stumbling forward, Corin seized his chance and rolled free, picking up Biter and launching his body at the giant. But Postin had turned and was limping away. It was only then that Corin noticed the dagger sticking from Postin's thigh.

He heard a woman's yell and the clash of steel somewhere close. Corin turned, saw the man called Tolc sobbing, his back against a tree, a second dagger protruding from his groin. "Help me . . . *please!*" Corin ignored the dying man. He heard a hoarse shout, a scream, and the woman's voice again.

Then he saw her—*Yazrana.* She looked a mess, her dark hair disheveled and her face streaming blood.

"Yaz?" Corin ran toward her.

"I'm so tired of saving you," she breathed and leaned back against a tree. "That bastard Keel—he got me from behind." Corin saw the trail of blood running down her leg. "I'll live," she said. "Just kill that green-eyed fucker and make it painful."

Corin nodded. "Where is he?" He unslung Clouter from the scabbard on his back—better late than never. Corin looked around, seeing nothing until the brush moved and Stane appeared limping, the knife he gripped dripping blood.

"I got the other one," Stane said. "He's still alive so we can have a word with him." He blinked when he saw Yazrana.

"Keel?" Corin yelled at Stane.

"Haven't seen him lately."

All three of them turned when the sound of hooves thudded off into the distance. Minutes later, they saw a horseman cantering across Whitestone Bridge and vanishing into the hills beyond.

Corin searched for Postin, following the trail of blood, but he too had got away. It could have been worse—*much worse*—if Yazrana hadn't saved him, yet again. Corin staggered back to join the others. Stane had dragged the prone body of the wounded man close to the fire, now blazing.

Stane slapped his head. "Wake up, Boyo—we've sharp things to stick up your arse."

"That's Drowd," Yazrana said. She pointed to the silent figure slumped against the tree. No longer sobbing on account of his being dead. "Tolc." Yazrana smiled. "Carne Dooly's men."

"Who?" Corin asked.

"A sleazeball merchant from Calprissa. These two loons are his cutthroats. Dooly must work for Caswallon too." She stumbled slightly and caught herself against a tree.

"You feeling alright?" Corin asked her, and she nodded.

"Just a shallow cut to the back of my thigh—I'm full of bloody holes but fortunately none of them should prove lethal." She smiled. "It felt good, Corin. That scrap. Just like the old days."

"What do you two lovehearts suggest we do now?" Stane asked. He had a bad slash on his arm but wasn't complaining.

"You need to bind that," Corin insisted, as he stooped to examine Yazrana's leg wound.

"I'd just recovered from the whipping." She grinned at him and he kissed her.

"I don't know what to say," Corin said. "I'd be dead, or dying slowly, were it not for you."

"You're a weakness of mine, Corin an Fol." She bit back the pain as he wiped her thigh clean with a ripped-off part of his shirt.

"We need clean water," Corin said. "I don't want you pair dying of fever."

As evening's gloom crept low through the woods, Corin stood beside Thunderhoof, patting his mane as the other horses grazed, and his hurt companions took their ease by the fire. Drowd sat there too. Awake and very miserable, having just received a thorough interrogation conducted by Yazrana. She still gripped the hot knife in a fist, the blood dripping from its point. Two of Drowd's fingers were bleeding, the nails having been prised off. He was missing a molar too, his mouth oozing blood. Just one tooth—they wanted him to speak.

"Owe it all to you, boy," Corin told Thunder as he shoved a thatch of grass in the big horse's mouth. "You and the lass— what a team we are." Thunderhoof snorted indifference. Corin left him and joined the others.

"What did he say?" Corin walked in and stood over the weeping Strowd.

"I'm just getting started," Yazrana said, poking the hot knife up Strowd's nostril and forcing his head back. "You've no idea how many bits I can cut from you before sun up." She grinned at the wretch, and Corin almost felt sorry for him. Then he looked at Crall's battered corpse where the flies were crawling and felt the hot surge of rage returning.

It didn't take much. An hour later she put the wretch out of his misery. Strowd had told them all he knew. This traitor Carne Dooly had sent them to assist Postin in killing King Nogel. After that they were to do away with Postin and keep the gold Dooly had promised the giant. Yazrana was right. Carne Dooly worked for Caswallon, seemed that villain had an army of spies.

"So what's our plan then?" Stane asked as Corin sat down. They'd just finished digging a hole for Crall and burying his body with stones. A brave man who Corin would miss.

"Will you stop fucking asking me that," Corin grumbled. "I'm a mercenary, not an oracle." Over by the fire Yazrana was sleeping, her wound and busy knifework having drained her.

"Fine woman," Stane said, hinting her tanned sleeping body with a nod.

"You don't know the half of it," Corin said. They'd found two more horses in their search of the woods. Postin must have taken another, and Keel had stolen Crall's mare. As to where that villain's original horse was, Corin couldn't hazard a guess.

"Three choices," Corin said, after a moment chewing jerk-beef he'd retrieved from Thunderhoof's saddlebags. "Back to Wynais. Ride after Keel. Or . . . Calprissa."

"Calprissa?"

"Aye—we need to talk to this Dooly character."

"I know of him—a shifty bastard," Stane said. "I'll wager he'll get word of this event and do a runner."

Corin nodded. "I'm sure you're right, but we need a plan, and I for one do not want to ride back to Wynais with my tail dangling between my legs."

"We did our best," Stane said.

"Silon won't see it that way—I want payment sometime this month, and he wants results, first. Returning to the Silver City is not an option."

"Keel then." Stane looked unhappy about that choice.

"Fuck him," Corin said. "That one's a mad-crazy hound. Let that assassin go after Nogel, play his stupid little games until he unravels himself. My quarrel's with Postin."

"He could be anywhere, ranging the hills and woods. Take months to find him," Stane said. Yazrana stirred and raised her head.

"Will you two numbnuts shut the fuck up?"

"Sorry," Corin and Stane responded together.

"Postin's going to visit Carne Dooly who promised him gold. We go after him—shouldn't be hard. Big ugly man on a small nervous horse."

"We hunt Postin down?" Corin liked the idea.

"No," Yazrana said. "We track him to Dooly and kill them both. Now shut up and let me sleep."

"That was easy," Stane said, closing his eyes. "I like strong women. But I still think someone needs to contact Silon. *Just saying*..."

Corin ignored him and crawled over to the fire. He watched the flames flicker in silence then heard a shuffle beside him. The woman leaned close.

"I'm not sleepy now," she said, her lips parted slightly, and he reached for her and they crumpled by the fire. If Stane heard their moans that night he had the decency to stay silent. Next morning, they would ride south again.

Part Two
Kings and Sorcerers

Chapter 16 | Kella City

"Keep your mouths shut and fingers flexed," King Nogel said gruffly as he reined in, his men bunching their horses around him. "We need to be sharp today, lads."

Tolranna passed him the spyglass, and the king scanned left and right until he found what he sought. A black needle thrust like a vengeful spike into the deep blue of that Kelthaine afternoon. They were five days out of Wynais and they'd reached their destination. Kella City lay hidden behind stark hills, but the Astrologer's Roost was visible for miles—a single tower that rose above the city like a warning finger.

A sinister sight—especially when you knew who occupied the remote room at the top. The only room. Nogel had scaled those winding stairs as a child. A dare placed on him by the young Kelsalion. A long, arduous, and torturous climb led to a cold, drafty room, circular and dark, just the one window winking lamplight on the city, so very far below.

A grim place back then, but surely far worse now that Caswallon used it for his dreadful purpose. Of course, no one said that. And few would dare think it. Caswallon had a way of getting inside mens' heads and shaking them up. Especially the High King.

But not this king. Nogel's face took on a grim turn as he rammed the spyglass back in General Tolranna's palm.

"No one is to speak when we enter the city," he said. "You stable the horses, three to watch over them. The others will accompany me to the palace. From there I'm on my own."

"You plan to enter the palace alone, Highness?" Tolranna looked shocked, and not a little dismayed.

"I do," Nogel said. "Nor is there any other option, as soldiers are not permitted inside that building, just the High King's personal guard and Caswallon's people—which amounts to the same thing," the king added wryly.

"You're taking a risk." Tolranna forgot himself for a moment and the king glared at him.

"You are my general, boy, not my councilor, so hold your bloody tongue." This was said loud enough for everyone present to hear. In a softer voice Nogel added, "That leech won't show his hand inside the palace. He'll be wanting to study my resolve and weigh up his options. I mean to give him few. I'm going to confront that snake and then shake some sense into Kelsalion."

Tolranna nodded but looked unconvinced.

They rode up through the dark hills, the lane curving and cambering through wooded slopes, a glint of summer sun settling on the riders' armor and helms and sparkling off into the trees—a brave sight they must've looked on that sharp clear day.

Once through the hills, the city sprawled before them, dark and vast. Gloomy and despondent, it seemed to suck all light from that brave day. A granite city. Its dour inhabitants rumored hard and cold as the stone they dwelt in. Durable or not, they weren't impervious to fear, Nogel thought grimly.

The king reined in again and frowned. What had happened to this place? Nogel had never liked Kella City, but he couldn't recall it ever being so dark. That stone had had a certain sparkle, trapping the light—especially on a sunny summer's day like this one. As they rode closer he noticed all the windows visible had been shuttered, and the crenulations were painted black and resembled forbidding cliffs of coal, the gates tarred black as well.

Nogel cursed silently as he rode up to those huge wooden doors, his men close behind. A horn blared from somewhere above. Nogel, staring up, saw a face framed by steel, the helmet painted black and dull, such a contrast to his own.

"State your purpose!" The cold voice reached him and Nogel felt the fresh heat of anger rising inside him. He spurred his horse and pointed up at the guard, currently looking down at them from forty feet above.

"Is this how you address a king?" Nogel shouted up, challenging the guard until face and helmet disappeared. He heard shouts then nothing.

"This is intolerable," General Tolranna muttered behind him.

"Shut up," Nogel said without turning, as he tried to keep a lid on his temper. Eventually a grinding creaking sound announced the gates were moving. They waited as steel bars were slid back and the huge door parted just enough to allow them through, albeit in single file. The king glared at the dozen or so gate guards, who backed away, their long pikes raised in salutation.

A captain stepped forward, the broad crimson sash marking him clearly as the man in charge. "Your Highness, you do us great—"

"—Send word to the palace, I've business with the High King." Nogel glared at the man as he rode by. The captain looked shock.

"Highness, the Lord High Councilor doesn't permit visitations to the palace."

"I don't give a shit what Caswallon does or doesn't permit," Nogel said, bringing his horse to heel again. "You address a king, soldier!"

"Forgive me, Your Highness—but we have our orders." The captain looked anxious, as though he would be held to blame for any break of protocol. "The High King is unwell, Lord Caswallon seeks only to protect him. May I advise you and your men to make for the tavern quarter where you can be housed and treated with due courtesy and respect—as of course you deserve." He tried to smile; the expression didn't suit him.

"Fuck off," Nogel said and spurred his horse at the captain, making him jump back. "I know the way to the palace," Nogel said to the captain and his guards, all clustered around like agitated ants, their nest kicked by some clumsy stroller.

"You'd best tell your 'High Councilor' that King Nogel is in no mood for his prevarications." He rode from the gate, entering the huddled sprawl of the outer city, where narrow lanes weaved and twisted toward larger buildings ahead. The king and his men rode in silence as the dark city swallowed them whole.

Kella was a tangled thread of thatched leaning wooden homes, thrust together and squeezed narrow by the lack of space. Haphazard and random; this city was ancient and had outgrown its walls. The streets were grubby and dogs snarled as they cantered by. Nogel frowned again. Those lanes seemed dirtier than he recalled.

Eventually they cleared the maze of home and tavern, reaching a more open, wealthier district. Here were gardens and spacious parks, the grass cut low and verges neatly trimmed. A wide avenue led to a huge manse, its surrounding walls and gates hinting more gardens hidden beyond. The High King's palace and home of the fabled Tekara—his revered crystal crown. Nogel had played here as a boy.

Though he'd never seen the crown. Such honors were forbidden to children, even royal ones like himself. The Tekara was a legend. An ageless artifact that emanated a raw power throughout the Four Kingdoms. That beneficial force held evil at bay—so they'd told him as a child. King Nogel looked around and shook his head. The Tekara must have lost its magic.

They reined up by the gates and Nogel smiled for the first time that day as the warm glow reached him, and a sense of grateful relief. *It's still here. Even Caswallon can't harm the crown.*

The Tekara's crystal emanated rays of silver light, casting a glow that dispelled the customary dark stalking this troubled city. *Untarnished.* Nogel's real fear had been that Caswallon had polluted the incorruptible. But the Tekara was a thousand years old. The gift from the dying remnant of a legendary race. Folklore of course—but Nogel knew there was power in that crown. And that power remained, although contained here and blanketed by the gloom of the city surrounding it. Here, at least, was a bastion of hope.

An alien aura. Nogel recalled how that silver glow used to filter through the entire city instead of just the palace and its grounds. The sun shone bright here, the stone sparkled, and as more guards approached them Nogel held up his hand to shield his eyes from the glare. He felt encouraged and emboldened, he was right to come here despite earlier misgivings.

The guards crunched their steel boots on stone and halted in front of the gates. Nogel sat his horse until a stocky, tough-looking officer walked out from the ranks. They parted like wind-blown corn to let him through. A hard face, heavily lined and broad set was framed by close-cropped graying hair, a badly broken nose, and a narrow scar running for the corner of his right eye.

General Perani appeared in good health. The men gathered behind him wore the easily distinguishable spotted orange cloaks of the elite Tiger Regiment. Once, they had been the finest warriors in the world. But they'd fallen from grace, yet more victims of Caswallon's corruption.

Perani was rumored the finest swordsman in Kelthaine, though in his day, Lord Halfdan, the High King's younger brother, would have easily bested him. The general was clad in plain dun-colored leathers and fur, a short sword hanging from a belt at his waist. He wore a cool smile and bowed slightly as Nogel gazed upon him.

"Perani. You appear hale enough." Nogel's tone was cold. This man had betrayed his ruler, sold out, and was directly responsible for the coup that had seen both rival generals and their regiments driven from this city.

"My health is good, Your Highness—I thank you for noticing." A second bow; this one slightly ironic. *The bastard's mocking me.* "But you come unannounced, My Liege, thus I fear you will be disappointed. The High King often sleeps at this hour."

"I can wait," Nogel said.

"Then come this way, my lord," Perani said, flicking his fingers to order his men open the gates to the palace. "The Lord High Councilor will see you, I'm sure. But those men will have to stay put. We don't allow soldiers in the palace."

"The High Kings never did," Nogel said, reminding the general that he'd been here many times.

"Quite so, Highness." Perani smiled slightly, again the mocking sardonic glint showed briefly in those gray eyes, cold and flat as a serpent's gaze.

"My men will need stables and an inn for rest and leisure," Nogel said. "I assume you have this in hand?"

"At once, Highness." The bow again, and again he clicked his fingers. "You there—captain." Perani pointed to an officer. "Escort King Nogel's soldiers to a reputable tavern. And ensure their mounts are groomed and rested by the regimental stablemaster." The officer thudded a fist into his chest and strode off, shouting for half a dozen men to follow behind.

"Your horse too, Highness, if you please."

Nogel gazed down at the general coldly for a moment and then slid from his mount. He handed the reins to one of the men. "Keep your eyes open and stay fucking sober," he whispered in the man's ear. The soldier nodded and led the king's mount off to join the others with Tolranna, already making for their temporary quarters. Nogel saw Tolranna turn and glance his way, those dark eyes worried as before. He waved him on and turned to face the gates, the general stood aside and allowed him through.

"We are most honored by your visit, Highness," General Perani said, almost as an afterthought.

Nogel ignored Perani and his men and strode into the palace grounds, the warm sun flooding his features and the brightening silver glow of the Tekara bolstering his confidence further and casting back the gloom that had filled him during their ride through the city. He and his men were safe here. The crown would protect them even if its wearer could not. Even Caswallon dare not commit atrocity in the Crystal Palace.

Nogel walked briskly through the gardens, Perani uninvited by his side, a dozen soldiers too. Evidently the ban of armed warriors in the palace didn't apply to the Tigers. Another machination by the councilor. The High King's guard had been made up of volunteers from all three regiments. The highest honor a soldier could attain. Soldiers had to apply to join, undergo a tough selection process, and most were rejected. Evidently that was no longer the case.

Servants bowed and vanished into folds of brush and green as King Nogel strode toward the palace entrance. To his right were cloisters. In a corner shrouded by alabaster arches, Nogel saw a young man, pale of face and slender of build. Prince Tarin placed down his scroll and gawped as the King of Kelwyn walked by.

"Greetings, Prince," Nogel called across to him, but the boy just stared. *Little shit.* Nogel returned his gaze to the ornate doors ahead. A retainer appeared, bowed deeply and let him through into the cool sweeping expanse that was the Palace Hall. Nogel froze as he entered. A man stood there clad in a shimmering gown of deep-blue silk, the moon and stars studded across its surface in braided gold. The material glistened like quicksilver as he folded his arms.

Small of build, neat, with sleek black hair graying around the edges and a close-cropped, tidy beard. He wore a scholar's cap and a smile that made Perani's seem genuine.

Lord Caswallon had come to parley with the king.

***

Roman Parrantios stormed through the passageway, the servants diving for cover. They knew better than to try stop the king's champion. He reached the far room and banged on the door. A woman's voice answered.

"Open it," Roman barked. A moment later the latch sprung and the door swung wide. A young woman blinked sleepily at him.

"Princess awake?"

"She is now." The voice came from behind the girl and Roman almost forgot to bow, recognizing Princess Ariane resplendent in green and gold, a wry ghost of a smile hovering on her lips.

"I'm sorry, Your Highness—but I've only just heard." Roman bustled into the room without invitation. The woman swore at him, but the princess snapped her fingers and told her to go and make some tea.

"None for me," Roman said. "Though I'll take brandy if there's some available."

"Brandy." Ariane nodded as the girl stared at her. "Get some." The servant nodded and departed swiftly with a sharp sideways glance at Roman, standing there clad in sweat and leather.

"That lass seems a tad grumpy," Roman said, taking seat at a chair and groaning.

"She's new, still training," Ariane said. "Has no idea what a pain in the arse you can be."

Roman laughed. "I've missed you, girl." He stood up and she threw her arms around him.

"Where've you been, old hound?"

"Here and there." Roman shrugged. "Traveling, roaming—a touch of drinking and wenching." He winked at her and the princess cuffed his ear.

"You are a rogue," Ariane said. "And were you not my father's closest friend, I'd order you clad in iron chains and dropped down a well."

"I've suffered worse," he said. "Ah, thanks lass." He winked at the servant who stared back at him with disapproval.

"You can leave us, Tilly." Ariane hinted the door and the girl used it. The princess perched on the corner of her seat and sipped carefully at her tea.

Roman slurped the brandy and wiped sweat from his face. "At last—Kelwynian brandy. I'm a happy man."

"You've been gone for fucking months," Ariane said. Her language might've raised brows at court but Roman seldom noticed. He'd taught her the sword after all, and like the late Lord Staveport, had been almost an uncle to her for so long.

"I was growing stale in Wynais," Roman said. "A fighting man with bugger all to fight. Therefore, I took to traveling for a few months—to keep my wits and steel sharp."

"You've been absent nearly a year."

"I wasn't counting."

"I was," Ariane said. "Every single day. Where did you go?"

"Laregoza, Shen—distant places inhabited by strange people. You're better off not knowing, Princess. Remote lands far beyond the Ptarni Steppes."

"I've heard tell of Shen and Laregoza," Ariane said. "At the edge of the world they say."

"Not quite, but it felt like it at times." Roman sipped his brandy again. "I just arrived from Calprissa where the trader I'd booked passage on docked." His smile faded as he remembered why he'd raced up here from the barracks. "My first drink." Roman hinted his glass was empty again.

"So, you've heard the news." Princess Ariane passed the decanter over so he could help himself.

"Aye, Staveport's dead and some bastard tried for your father." Roman stooped and refilled his glass. He took a steady sip. "And now your father's ridden north like a damned fool right into Caswallon's lair."

"You are speaking of your king, Roman Parrantios." Ariane's expression hardened, and Roman thought how the girl had blossomed from scrawny tustler into a fine young woman. She wore authority with a confidence that reminded him of her father, and a grace that recalled the mother—a woman Roman had cause to remember more than most.

"King or not—I fear he's lost his mind, like his overlord up north. What possessed Nogel to ride to Kella City? Is he afflicted?"

"Father wants to confront Caswallon, believes that man responsible for Lord Rowan's murder and the attempt on his own person."

"That may well be—most probably is—but it's not sensible to shove your fingers down the weasel's throat."

"You know Father."

"I do," Roman said, slurping brandy again. "That's why I'm riding north to greet him."

Ariane shook her head. "He'll have reached Kella by now, the merchant Silon had people sent to Whitestone Bridge to stop him, but I doubt they could."

"The merchant who . . . ?"

"*Silon*. From Raleen. He's a good man."

"I didn't know there were any good merchants," Roman said between sips. "But what the fuck has Silon of Raleen got to do with our king?"

"He's a spy."

"Even better." Roman's irony was scarcely contained. He drained the glass and smiled at her frown. "A Raleenian spy—seriously, Ariane? Your father trusts this man?"

"He does. Silon's a good ally, and—more importantly—an enemy of Caswallon. He's both subtle and clever and highly dedicated to stopping that villain's antics."

"Some chance," Roman said with a sigh. "Leaking buckets won't stop a flood. Nice of Silon of Raleen to try though."

"I've missed your fucking sarcasm," Ariane said.

"And I've missed your gentle tongue, Princess." Roman wiped sweat from his face. "I'm worried, Ariane. Our king is vulnerable in Kelthaine."

"Obviously, but what can we do?"

"You cannot do anything—but I can ride to Kella City, or at least in that direction and hope to meet your father on the road. I doubt Caswallon would try anything in Kella itself, no matter how influential he's become in that shithole. The Tekara's resident power will stop him from trying."

"Perhaps," she said, "but Caswallon seems ready to do anything these days. Kelsalion III is a broken man, they say. You should not have left us for so long."

Roman shrugged away his guilt. "A year ago, Caswallon was not a problem, or if he was, no one realized it. I was bored and spoke with your father, who wanted to learn about those distant lands, perhaps trade there someday. A mistake, I realize now."

"Regrettable."

"Regrets are useless, Princess. Let me get my shit together and ride out this evening, I'll go alone after dusk, so not to draw any unwelcome notice."

"No."

"I'm . . . sorry?" Roman blinked. "What do you mean . . . no? I'm the Champion of Kelwyn. This land's foremost battle master."

"And I'm King Nogel's only heir," she said, her feet braced and jaw set firm. "*No* means I need you here in this city, Roman Parrantios. Our people need their champion here."

"I'm the king's champion too."

"Not lately." Roman felt his face flush with heat as she placed a hand on is arm. "I need your help, Roman. *Please.* Surely you're not arrogant enough to think that you can alter the king's fate simply by riding out alone?"

"That's a fair point—but I'd like to try."

"I'm not allowing it," she said, gripping his arm tighter. "With Father away, I'm the boss." She awarded him an impish grin. "Have another brandy and don't look so glum."

Roman stared hard at her for a minute and then burst out laughing. "By the gods you're a wonder, Princess Ariane. Your father should be proud of you. Your mother most likely would be horrified."

Her eyes narrowed when he mentioned Queen Cailine. She let go of his arm and Roman cursed himself for mentioning her mother. "Tell me the real reason you left Wynais," Ariane said, reaching over and pouring more brandy into his glass. "Did it concern the queen?"

Roman avoided her gaze, his casual confidence replaced by a deep, shameful look. "I loved her, Ariane—*always*. Your father knew. It drove a wedge between us."

"Did you and Mother . . . ?"

"No, err . . . yes." He wiped sweat from his face. "*Not really*, not in that sense anyway. But we were close before the end. Nogel never forgave me, and rightly so."

"Did you sleep with my mother?"

"I did not." Roman shook his head. "Though I always wanted to—I loved her, Ariane."

The princess slapped his cheek with sudden violence. "Thank you for your candor," she said briskly. "I need some time alone." He nodded and stood up, dusting down his travelworn clothes.

"I'll take my leave then," he said. "You've grown into a fine young woman, Ariane." She ignored him until she heard the door close gently. Then she stared at it and felt the tears race down her face.

Oh, Mother . . . why did you leave us that cold day?

Chapter 17 | Back on the Road

Corin knelt and studied the tracks. He could see that a big man had led his horse down through the trees. They followed the imprints for several minutes until they found a rudimentary camp, the ash and faggots still warm.

"Must have left at first light," Corin said, as the woman watched him. Stane had left them two days ago after further discussion. He'd ridden back to Wynais and would report to Silon. Corin hadn't wanted him to, but had been out voted. Now he missed his friend's cheerful company.

"Three long days to Calprissa," Corin said. "He'll have to change horses—that means a village or hamlet. No doubt he'll stop by and steal one."

"There are plenty of villages along that road," Yazrana said. "Our best plan is to make haste and forget following his tracks. We'll not catch Postin unless he stops soon, but we can get to Dooly first. Deal with the merchant who's paying him and then wait for Postin to come for his money."

"What do you know about this Dooly?"

"Carne Dooly. A well-known Calprissan merchant. Has a shady reputation, and I can vouch for that, as I've been unfortunate enough to have had dealings with him myself." Corin studied her face but she wouldn't expand. "He's shifty and slimy," Yazrana said. "And, I've cause to believe Dooly works for Caswallon."

"You're that well acquainted with him?"

"Oh, yes. He's a broker, a familiar face in the squalid side of town. Carne Dooly has a lot of secret clients in Calprissa, and further up the coast. I took out a loan from him, before I met Silon. He shined me on. Man's a fucking snake. Silon wanted me to fillet his guts when we first met. They're old enemies. I was happy to comply but Dooly is crafty and got wind. He spread the word that I was the notorious Crimson Lady and sent men after me so I had to leave town."

"You've had a busy time." Corin grinned at her. "You'll have to tell me all about it one day."

"Maybe," she said. "But first stop asking fucking questions and get back on that shaggy monster you call a horse."

"His name's Thunderhoof."

"Ride on, Corin an Fol," the woman said. "We've wasted time enough here."

***

Carne Dooly's hand wouldn't stop shaking. He dropped the parchment twice, and then picked it up again and shoved it in the fire. Caswallon had sent word that King Nogel was on his way up there, and that Postin the Hammer and Dooly's two men had failed.

Caswallon didn't like failure. His letter stated that *someone* would be visiting Dooly soon to receive a full account. The last time one of his spies had received a letter like that from Caswallon, they'd been found floating face-down in the city canal. Dooly's men were rumored dead and Caswallon wanted him to join them. He was no longer useful. *Time to shift loyalties and sever ties. You always have to have a way out.*

Dooly smiled. Even Caswallon wouldn't find him at Highreach Hall. The ruined wind-ravaged manor house high on the cliffs, just north of Calprissa overlooking the ocean. Nothing but seabirds and memories, and silent ghosts that hovered in hallways. He'd bought the place five years back. Got it for a snip with future plans to furnish and repair. Plans that never reached fruition.

Dooly packed some garments in a trunk. A few warm clothes, a short sword and dagger, and a crossbow with a pack of twenty bolts. He waited till nightfall, and when his attendants were excused, crept into the stable and saddled the best horse. He led it from the city in silence, using the postern that he'd known in his smuggling days. Calprissa was built on a cliff face with tunnels leading down to the harbor, hundreds of feet below. Some were known, others secret.

Carne Dooly chose the latter. He reached the harbor as a horned moon rose above silver waves. He glanced sideways and glimpsed a bird gliding past. A white owl, silent as the night. It settled on a gatepost and watched him. Dooly felt an icy shiver along his spine. Like a premonition of doom. The bird lifted and the sea breeze carried it off into the night.

Just a bird—get a grip.

Shaken, but determined, Dooly found his skiff moored on the outer rim of the harbor, the cove leading to open sea beyond, those waves black and churning out there. He set the small craft free, coiled the sheets, and took to oar—working hard as the waves mustered, as he guided the small vessel free of harborside and corkscrew cove.

Calprissa's harbor was almost landlocked and the current was against him. Half an hour later, Dooly was exhausted but he'd made the open sea. The rising waves buffeted his craft and saltwater splashed over him. Carne Dooly kept his nerve, set aside the oars and hurriedly hoisted the single sail.

After that, he shifted back on his bench and fiddled with his pockets, producing flint, stone, and tobacco. He lit the pipe and leaned back, the sail doing the work, the moon and stars studding the night sky above. He felt better. The hard work spent winning free of the cove had dispelled his earlier fright.

Carne Dooly was a canny sailor. He'd been a smuggler in his early days, before King Nogel came down heavy on the trade, mopping up and hanging folk from Reln to the Raleenian border.

Careful as always, Dooly had bought stock with his profits and settled in the city as a legitimate trader. He'd prospered, dealing with those sorts decent folk avoided. The type who always needed men like Carne Dooly. The newly legitimate merchant became rich. For almost a decade he thrived. Then Caswallon had found him.

Dooly sucked in the tobacco, calming his nerves. He'd make the hidden dock before sun up and tie off. There was rope and tackle for pulling goods up that cliff. He hoped the system was still working, and that sea and rust hadn't choked the pulleys or chafed the ropes. No point worrying about that out here.

Carne Dooly closed his eyes and rested as best he could, the ocean swelling and shifting below. He would survive—*always had.* He'd lay low in that ruin for as long as he could, living off fish and rabbits. Then, when Caswallon had forgotten him, Dooly would slip back into Calprissa, sell his shares quietly at a slight loss and move south. Permio or Golt, or maybe even Yamondo. It didn't matter—money always talked.

***

Postin stood over the corpse and watched the blood pooling and dripping through the floorboards. The fool had challenged him. He'd been stealing a horse and the man had seen him. *Mistake.* Then he'd come running into the stables, a sword in his hand. *Worse mistake.* Postin had split his head open with his mallet and watched the mess of blood and brains explode and spray the stable yard. The man should have stayed put, and Postin would have let him be. He only wanted the horse.

They'd most likely ignore a horse thief, but not a murderer. They'd send word to the town he'd passed yesterday and the district sheriff and his men would be set loose.

Postin chewed his knuckles and led the horse from the stable. Outside the wind was up, buffeting the tin roof above his head. He needn't worry about disturbing anyone else. The hamlet was dark and far from anywhere. Once clear of the last house, he mounted up and guided the beast back onto the road. A bigger horse than the last had been. That one had died earlier in the night. He'd risked a fire and ate as much of the animal as he could.

Postin rode briskly, allowing the horse to canter. Judging by its look, the beast was used to pulling plows and suffered his bulk without complaint. Postin liked the animal and hoped he wouldn't have to eat this one too. He didn't have many friends, and the horse seemed to like him. On a whim he named the beast—Challenger.

Challenger and Postin. They made an impressive pair should anyone happen by. Postin preferred they didn't. Unchallenged, horse and rider reached the walls of Calprissa three days later. Postin camped in a wood full of crows that swore at him relentlessly, until night settled their feathers.

He sat up that long night talking to Challenger, and sometimes weeping. Postin felt so alone in a world that had always hated him. He'd been a soldier once, and a good one. He had respected himself back then. Had *pride*. But that had been driven away by the murders he'd committed. The countless atrocities. *What I am . . .*

Postin knew he was a monster and loathed himself. But he hated Corin an Fol more, and Keel, and Carne Dooly the oily merchant who had set him up for a fall. Dooly would pay first—with coin and blood. Then he'd go after that whoreson longswordsman and his woman. *Keel . . . ?* Postin decided he might leave Keel alone. Best not push his luck too far.

After sun up, Postin the Hammer rode back down to the road, waited until the wagons and carts cranked up for the mid-morning market, and then mingled as best he could, the pole-axe covered in cloth and resembling just another scythe or staff carried by a laborer. The guards let him through and Postin found a tavern close to the wall. He stabled Challenger and decided to drink the daylight hours away. At dusk he slipped out, heading for the villa where Carne Dooly would be counting his silver. Postin kept to the shadows, feigning a limp. Some giant hobbling wretch leaning on his staff. Most likely an impoverished veteran of the Permian Wars. Sensible folk would stay clear. Postin reached Dooly's villa and kicked open the door.

***

Corin and Yazrana sat their horses as the dozen or so riders approached. Angry-looking men led by a portly balding individual on a dappled mare. He reined in just a few yards clear of them, his red face flustered and eyes hostile.

"State your business," the official said, as his soldiers closed the gap behind him. Corin assumed this was some local militia with their boss. Clearly these weren't a crack unit. He feigned a yawn.

"Our business is our own," Yazrana said.

The man bristled. Corin smiled at him, guessing he'd expected Corin to speak and was offended by being addressed by a foreign-looking woman.

"You ride through Yanag County and therefore are in the jurisdiction of Sheriff Doney."

"And who might he be?" Corin asked, wondering how long this would take.

"You're talking to him," a soldier said, and the fat man turned and swore at him. He shifted in his saddle and turned to face them again.

"I need to know who you are." Sherriff Doney blew out his cheeks. He'd noticed Clouter slung across Corin's back and looked uncomfortable.

"Relax," Corin said, smiling again. "We are husband and wife out for a country ride—tis all." Yazrana flashed him a startled look and then smirked. Their mirth was lost on the sheriff.

"There was a murder," the same soldier spoke from behind.

"Shut up, Norris," the sheriff said without turning this time. "Know anything about that, you pair?" He blew out his cheeks again.

"Why would we know anything about that?" Corin asked, but his mind was racing. Postin had been here. *Who else?* Nogel's realm was the safest in the Four Kingdoms, murder was almost unheard of these days, such unfortunate happenings driven to the fringes of King Nogel's domain, like Port Wind and its neighboring Woods between the Waters.

"You're strangers and I don't trust you," Sheriff Doney said.

"His skull was crushed to bloody pulp," the same soldier cut in again.

"Shut up, Norris!" The sheriff placed a gloved hand on his sword. He froze, seeing the knife flash into Yazrana's hands.

"Shall I kill him, Corin?" Both the sheriff and his men backed their horses out of knife range. They looked startled and nervous, and Corin almost felt sorry for them.

"We'll catch your villain, Sheriff," Corin said. "My name's Hagan and I'm after a seven-foot, yard-wide brute called Postin the Hammer who owes me money. Carries a bloody great pole-axe."

"Sounds like our man, Sheriff," Norris said, and some of the others nodded enthusiastically.

The sheriff seemed to chew that over. Yazrana urged her beast forward and tossed the knife into the air, catching it and spinning it across her brown fingers in a lightning motion. "I grow weary of your company," she said.

The sheriff nodded nervously and backed his mount again. "Postin, you say? Hammer. Hmm, clearly a bad fellow. Murdered the stable hand and stole a dray horse. Uses a pole-axe? Makes sense—awful mess we found."

"When?" Corin asked.

"This morning at first light, the report reached my office mid-morning."

It's now late afternoon. Corin looked at Yazrana who nodded. Time they got going. "Well . . . thanks for your diligence and keep up the good work." Corin flashed the sheriff another grin and urged Thunder forward. Yazrana spurred her own mount alongside. Sheriff and men parted to let them through. Some of the men gawped at Yazrana so she blew them a kiss.

"See that you catch him," Sheriff Doney called out when they'd past.

"I'll send you his head," Yazrana yelled back.

"You were cruel to that sheriff," Corin said. They'd camped for the night. Two days had passed and they were close to the walls of Calprissa.

"They were idiots," she replied. "I've no time for clowns."

"They have their place," Corin said. "I think that sheriff liked you." She cuffed his ear and then kissed him. He responded and they made love on the bracken as the horses chomped grass, a small fire cracking warmth out into the dark sky above.

Once they were done, Corin lay on his back and smiled at the void. "I can't believe you're back in my life."

"I can't believe I've forgiven you." Her dark eyes were close, huge and dilated, the kohl had almost worn off.

"Seems like a dream," Corin said. "Or, perhaps it's a nightmare." He laughed as she bit his finger. "Maybe you're a specter—a creature of the night."

"You shouldn't jest about such things," she said. "The spirits are always listening."

"What spirits?" Corin looked around, feeling suddenly strange. A beautiful night with a waxing moon spilling silver on rolling fields. He glimpsed motion and saw a flash of white beneath that moon. An owl gliding low over pastures. He took a deep breath as a sudden feeling of premonition swept over him.

"They are everywhere," Yazrana said. If she'd seen the owl she didn't comment. Her face was strange, her dark eyes both intense and distant. "Always watching," Yazrana said. "Some are kind, others cruel—most capriciously indifferent."

"You don't get out enough," Corin said, and she bit his ear again. "The only spirits I need are the type you pour down your throat. I could kill a good jug of ale right now."

"And I could use a smoke," she said, rolling close again so he could hold her. "Chilly tonight—and they call this summer."

"Summer in the north."

"I long for the desert." The woman sighed.

"Not going back there." Corin rolled and looked at her. "Too many bad memories." He sat up and stoked the tiny fire, feeling suddenly cold and blaming her talk of spirits. Corin seldom dwelt on such fancies. They reminded him of the dream woman *Vervandi* and the cloudiness inside his head. But something untoward transpired here. Corin felt uneasy, tired. "What's our plan?" he asked, changing the subject.

"Same as before." She rolled and gazed into his eyes. "Kill them both, or let Postin gut the weasel merchant and then stab him from behind."

"How many men does Carne Dooly have?"

"Not sure. A few certainly. But Strowd and Tolc were his main henchmen. Dooly keeps a low profile in the city. Not liked. I say we find a tavern to rest up and then visit his villa after dark."

"Sounds good," Corin said. "You sleepy?"

"Not really."

He rolled over and kissed her again, and they spent most of that night lying together, oblivious of the cold and damp, and the dew creeping close as the fire finally died. Corin woke once just before dawn and saw the shadow of a woman staring from the edge of a willow. *You've returned. I thought so.* The white owl glided low through the trees and settled on her shoulder. Her features faded like smoke, or else mist chased by morning sunlight over water.

Vervandi. Seeing her was like a bell tolling inside his head. *Something is wrong.*

Corin rolled to his feet and shook his lover awake. "We need to get moving," he said. The sky was lighter and a faint pink settled the fields, the dawn breeze tussling grasses, its ripple effect creating a gray-green swaying ocean.

They reached the gates and were allowed through after Corin reluctantly explained he worked for Silon of Port Sarfe and had vital news for the Garrison Commander concerning the king. The captain wanted to press him further, but Corin's tone and Yazrana's cold stare halted the words on his lips. They were allowed to pass, though Corin knew word of their passage would go out immediately. No matter. Calprissa was a big city with lots of places to hide. They'd made it here. Now for the interesting part.

***

The purse was heavy and coin jingled as it thudded on the table. Hagan weighed it in his fist. *Gold.* More than he'd ever been paid. Enough to keep him in comfort for weeks. The visitor watched him in silence. A lone lantern hung above their table in a dark corner of a forsaken tavern lost in the tangle of Reln's abandoned market square.

The hollow-eyed man smiled. A mirthless grin. It gave Hagan the creeps, but then so did most of the Sorcerer's people. That didn't matter. What did was the vast sum of money on the table just inches from his reach.

Hagan made to grab it but the man tapped the table with his cane. "First I need your assurance."

"I won't let your master down," Hagan said, eyeing the gold. "Just tell me what's required, who I need to kill."

The thin smile again. "I know you'll prove worthy," he said. He removed his wide-brimmed cap and placed it on the table. His face was pale and stretched like old parchment, and his expression cold. "Were you to disappoint, then we would find you, Morwellan. Lord C likes reliable staff. The last one let him down. A regrettable business."

"Who?"

"Carne Dooly, recently of Calprissa."

Hagan shook his head. "Don't know him."

"You don't have to know him." The thin man smiled. "You, Hagan Delmorier, just have kill him."

"Calprissa?"

"No." The smile again. "The rat's scurried off, thinks we don't know about his hideout. A decrepit former mansion away up the coast from that city. You'll find a crossroads forty miles south of Port Wind. Highreach Hall—write that down."

Hagan tapped his head. "No need, it's in here." The man looked at him and nodded.

"Kill Dooly and cut off any beringed fingers—I know his seal and will want proof."

"That's it?" Hagan reached for the gold.

"No." The nameless man rapped the table again with his cane. Hagan didn't care for this character, but there was something menacing about him. Enough to stop him prying further. And an unsavory odor lingered about his person. *Let's get this done with and find a whore house.* There were plenty of those in this city.

"What else?"

"A man and a woman. Mercenaries. We don't know who the man is, but have cause to believe he works for the conniver Silon of Raleen, a longswordsman. The woman is a known pirate wanted for atrocities committed along this coast. Kill them both. Cut off the woman's head and bring it to me."

"That's unfortunate," Hagan said. *Corin an Fol—what have you been up to?*

"Is there a problem?"

"No." Hagan feigned a smile. "Where will I find them?"

"Same place, I suspect, together with your former ally Postin the Hammer."

"What's this about?" Hagan was having doubts and for good cause.

"Beyond your pay grade," the thin man said.

"At least tell me who the woman is."

"A Permian spy," the nameless man said. "And a former privateer. A scourge. The High King demands her head on a spike outside the palace walls."

"Very nice," Hagan said, reaching for the gold again. This time the man let him grab it. He weighed it in his hands. "I'll leave tomorrow."

"You'll leave now," the man said. He placed his hat on his head and stood leaning over Hagan and the table. He was very tall as well as skinny, Hagan noticed for the first time. He leaned closer and smiled.

"Don't fail us, Hagan Delmorier." The man's breath stank like sewers after sunset. Hagan choked back a cough at that reek. "Ride south immediately and wait for the other men to join you. They're former Tigers on loan from General Perani. Good fighters, but they lack your guile. Succeed, and you'll have a long, profitable career ahead." The man clapped Hagan's shoulder and turned away without further word.

Hagan stowed the purse in his waist belt and left the shabby inn. Outside, cold rain drenched the dirty streets of Reln, his home these last few weeks. A cheap grubby room above the tavern, the place where Caswallon's contact had found him.

Hagan wasn't happy about killing Corin but *business was business*. Theirs had been a fragile relationship, and that longswordsman had left him for dead in the desert. Payback. Gold was what mattered in this life. He could always buy new friends.

Shame though, and a woman too. Hagan whistled as he led the horse out onto the highway, the city gates closing behind him. It was going to be an interesting few days.

Chapter 18 | The Deceiver

Caswallon smiled and spread his arms in welcome as the King of Wynais burst into the palace courtyard amidst a cluster of servants and retainers. Birds chattered in bushes and fountains chimed in corners, and the infuriating glare cast by the residing crystal near blinded him. But he smiled amiably, and as the burley ruler paced toward him, held out his hand in greeting.

King Nogel stared at the offered hand as though it were a snake. "Where is Kelsalion?" the king demanded, very rudely in Caswallon's opinion.

"Your Highness, you do us great honor."

"I asked a fucking question, meddler."

Caswallon shook his head and struggled to retain composure. The man was an oaf and a bore, and he wished Keel had done the job when first he had the chance, and not prevaricated.

"He is sleeping, Highness."

"Then wake him up."

"I'd sooner not—the High King needs a lot of rest these days. Regrettably, our beloved monarch's very troubled and not the sage ruler you remember. You haven't been in Kella for a while now. There have been some changes." Caswallon hinted a table and chairs with his hand. "Please, be seated." The king glared at him for a moment and then took a chair.

"I want to speak with Kelsalion," King Nogel said. "I won't be leaving until I do."

Caswallon smiled again, masking his inner rage. Such a waste of his precious time. Again, he blamed Keel. He'd hoped to avoid this confrontation, which was pointless. "My retainers will bring refreshment while you wait, Highness. It might be a long one."

Perani hovered close and Caswallon turned to the general. "A word in your ear, General," he said, and Perani nodded. "Please excuse us, Highness—our civic duties have doubled of late."

"Don't linger on my account," King Nogel said. Caswallon left him in the courtyard, with the chirping birds and glimmering glare. The Crown Room was halfway across the palace but the crystal always seemed brightest in the gardens. Caswallon detested that silver light. He would snuff it out in due course. Soon if things went to plan.

He stopped in a narrow cloister shaded by heavy palms. Servants parted like reeds and made themselves scarce. Perani loomed up behind him. "Keep your distance," Caswallon said. The Lord High Councilor couldn't abide his personal space being invaded. Perani took a step back. *Another stupid soldier.* But at least this *loyal* puppet had uses. "Where is the assassin?"

"He's here in Kella," Perani said. "I'm not sure where exactly."

"I thought you always knew where everyone was?"

"That one's hard to pin down." Perani avoided his gaze. Caswallon liked that. Perani was a hard man but still just a tool. A blunt instrument. *A slave.*

"Well, then send soldiers to find him and command his presence. I need to finish this nonsense before we can move on. Oh—and tell that whelp Tarin to wake his father. I don't want that southern king loitering around all day."

Perani left him with a curt salute, and Caswallon wandered back through the royal rooms. Tired and irritable, his head throbbing, he kept to the shadows and avoided the Tekara's radiance whenever he could. He needed to prepare the way for those who would come. The sorcerers he'd called on to help with his task. *A summoning.*

Caswallon trembled with excitement at the thought of that ancient power. The dark knowledge those beings retained. The old enemy. *The Urgolais.* He'd made preliminary contact up in the tower, a sacrifice too—they'd appreciated that. It's the little things that make all the difference.

The initial communication had taken time but he'd got through with his offer, and yes—they were interested. And so they should be, as they stood to gain much. Now he needed to act swiftly and decisively while he had their fully focused attention. The Urgolais were tricky folk. Caswallon needed to prove that he was fully committed, and on their side—those ancient, cunning enemies of the Crystal Crown and everything it stood for.

Caswallon smiled as he reached a quiet corner. All was in hand. This kingly affair was but a stone in his shoe. Kings were pawns like other men. His rise to power and fortune had only just begun. Careful planning first, then swift precise action. Timing was everything. Caswallon waited until he heard voices in the garden outside and then breezed back through the gilded doors to watch on.

***

King Nogel had wanted to swat the smiling councilor like the cockroach he was. Immaculately garbed in his smoky blue silk, the cloak of shimmering moons and stars a statement of what he'd become. A bold enchanter who was no longer hiding his nighttime pursuits. Enchanter was too kind. The knave was a sorcerer—worse, a necromancer were all the rumors true, and they most likely were. Gods alone knew what villainy occurred way up there in that dreadful tower.

Nogel was offered wine and ample food. He ignored both. Eventually the pale young Prince Tarin emerged like a scolded cur from the gardens.

"My father is coming," the boy said, taking a seat at the far end of the table. Nogel stared at the lad until he nervously shifted his gaze to the bushes.

"How fares the High King?" Nogel asked. Tarin just shrugged. *Suit yourself, child.* Nogel looked up as a cluster of white-clad servants emerged amid fuss and fiddle, and Caswallon reappeared with his oily smile. Staged, thought Nogel. The bastard's been hovering to see what I said. Then he looked past the sorcerer and saw a man hobbling behind him, supported by shaven-headed priests. The High King had come after all.

Kelsalion III had been tall. He wasn't now. Neither was he the handsome, confident ruler King Nogel remembered. The man staggering to stay upright before him was a disheveled, pale ghost of a man, hardly anything remained of the old High King. The noble, if reclusive ruler of all Four Kingdoms. What had happened to the Tekara? How could the crown's potent energy for good allow this to happen? A thousand years and then the sap runs dry? Didn't make sense. Caswallon must have found a way to tap into its source, drain the potency.

There was poison in this city. And the rot was deepest right here in the palace, despite that silver glow. Nogel stood as they helped the High King to his chair. He was dribbling, Nogel noticed, his blue eyes flicking about. Agitated, the High King waved the servants away like so many noisome blowflies.

"Stop fussing me," he said, voice reedy and thin. "Go away." They faded back, all save Caswallon who stood his ground, arms neatly folded into the pocket of his crimson gown, the customary half-smile masking his face.

"Cousin—why have you come?" Kelsalion III stared at Nogel without much interest. "Haven't you a little kingdom to rule down there?"

Nogel chewed his moustache and remained standing. "I have, my lord. But I also have concerns."

"*Concerns . . .?*"

"About your health and the state of this realm."

"We are old—*tis all.*"

"You're but seven years my senior, Lord. That's hardly *old.*"

"Well I am sickly then. *What of it?*"

"I fear you are corrupted by this man in the wizard's gown who calls himself your 'councilor,' but secretly plots against you." Nogel noticed the open shock on Prince Tarin's face, as though he'd been found out. *So, you're part of it too, weasel.*

"You're inferring that Lord Caswallon is a traitor? My sole comforter and greatest friend? Have a care, sir!" The High King's face looked flustered, outraged. He coughed for a moment and then held up his hands, the rings loose and slipping. "I suggest you return to Wynais, Cousin Nogel—lest we become vexed."

"You need to know the truth, Kelsalion," Nogel said.

"You'll address me as your overlord!"

"Lord . . . Exalted Highness," Caswallon stepped forward and placed his hands on the table, his cool dark eyes watching Nogel carefully. "The King of Kelwyn is a strong and honest man. We all admire him. But, forgive me Highness"—that smile again— "your younger cousin's misguided and has listened to lies spun by traitors who would work against you."

"The only traitor here is you." Nogel glared at Caswallon and noticed the brief flicker of rage in those coaly eyes, swiftly covered by that easy half-smile. *Have a care,* Nogel told himself. *Hold your temper.*

"It saddens me that you believe such follies," Caswallon said glibly. He turned to address the High King. "Your Exalted Majesty, please allow your premier servant to smooth this ruffled carpet. The King of Kelwyn has traveled far, and is clearly weary—*as are you*. Let's adjourn until everyone is properly rested."

"It's true, we are weary," Kelsalion said. He glared at Nogel. "You, cousin, have upset us with your foolish accusations. We are vexed by your disloyalty. We will return to our room immediately." Caswallon nodded approval, snapped his fingers, and the shaven-headed servants appeared from hidden corners. They helped the High King to his feet, and all King Nogel could do was watch as they half-dragged the emaciated ruler from the courtyard.

Pitiful, and a fruitless trip. Nogel should have known better than to come here, but he'd hoped the High King was reachable. Instead, Kelsalion III was beyond any help and Kelwyn had best look to its defenses. He stared at Caswallon's back until the man turned and surveyed him with those calculating eyes. *You knew I was watching you.* It was true what they said. This man gets inside your head if you let him. Nogel could feel the self-doubt jabbing him. Probing for weakness. *Why did I come here? How dare I accuse this man?*

Caswallon took seat at the table and neatly rested his hands on its surface. Nogel noticed Prince Tarin's eyes flickering his way like a frightened bird. Like his father, the boy was a puppet controlled by this consummate schemer.

"Sorcery is back in fashion, I see." Nogel took to his chair and accepted a glass of wine from a servant. He knew he'd lost here, but wasn't leaving without a fight.

Caswallon raised a dark brow. "Highness, I cannot grasp your meaning. Are you speaking of the Tekara, the Crystal Crown?"

"You know exactly what I mean."

"Ah, you are accusing me *personally*." Caswallon waved a hand. "I'm an astrologer and astronomer, my lord king. I study the stars in the tower above. For the good of these Four Kingdoms, I chart the skies so that we may steer free of obstacles. A hard and thankless business."

"Call it what you will, Caswallon. You cannot hoodwink me like Kelsalion or this foolish boy." Tarin glared at him with his mouth open, and Caswallon's eyes flashed angrily again.

"King Nogel, I find it regrettable indeed that you've such a low opinion of us. But I would advise you have a care. By all means, speak poorly of myself—I'm but a civil servant. But this young man is the High King's heir. He will inherit the throne one day, wear the Crystal Crown—the thirty-third of Kell's mighty line."

And suddenly Nogel saw it. Clear as the ice coating Lake Wynais on a bright sharp winter's day. *You're going to murder Kelsalion and place this boy on the throne.* Nogel stood up, spilling wine. His work was done here. Best he and his men return at speed to Wynais.

"I've nothing further to say to you, Councilor."

"Well, enjoy the city while you stay." Caswallon rose with him. "May I suggest a guided tour of the Crystal Palace to soothe your weary nerves? The Tekara's aura will soon banish your worries."

"Nay—they are too deep." Nogel turned briskly and left the courtyard, the servants fussing and following behind. Perani escorted him to the barracks where his men were idling the hours away.

"We ride out," Nogel said. "We never should have come here." His troops were ready within minutes, and an hour later they had left the city far behind.

***

"You can come out now." Caswallon strolled the gardens and stopped by a fountain. Beside him, a bush shivered slightly and a gloved hand appeared, parting fronds and followed by a body. A smallish, neatly clad individual with sharp, clever eyes the color of polished jade.

Keel smiled as he joined Caswallon in the gardens. Tarin had gone to see how his father fared, and the servants had made themselves scarce again. That left the two plotters time to stroll the gardens at ease.

"Why did he come here?" Keel asked, his green eyes fascinated by a blackbird scratching for grubs under a bush. "Stupid—even for him."

"To challenge me and see if he could get through to Kelsalion." Caswallon shrugged. "The arrogance of kings never fails to amaze me. If you'd have done your work last month, we could have avoided this nuisance." Caswallon glared at Keel but there was no give in those eyes. This was one individual he couldn't probe, though he had tried on several occasions. Keel's soul was veiled. This assassin wasn't like other men. An intricate killer, complex and twisted. *Useful, yet capricious and tricky to handle.* He summoned patience yet again.

"What do you wish me to do—follow them and . . .?" Keel's eyes were still watching the bird, much like a lazy cat on a hot summer's afternoon.

"Not right away," Caswallon said. "Let blustering Nogel go back to Kelwyn and rant about his visit. Once he's cleared the air, that fool will take to hunting again—that's when you come in, Keel. Just you this time. I'm not wasting anymore men, *clear?*"

Keel nodded indifferently. "How shall I do it?"

"I will provide an opportunity." Caswallon smiled. "Open a door so that you can slip away unnoticed. I have powerful allies who need proof of my loyalty to their cause. Do this, and we can move on to the next, considerably more important task. We will receive help with that—I'm assured of their assistance."

"Sorcerers?" Keel looked uncomfortable.

"You don't need to know anything else," Caswallon told him. "Do your job and no games, killer. Ride out at your leisure and get lodging close to the border, or in Kelwyn if you prefer. Await my signal." He waved a brief hand. "I'll bid you good day, Assassin."

Caswallon turned his back on Keel and walked through the gardens. *It has started.* Tonight, he would summon the Old Ones again and speak of his plans. He turned once to see if Keel still lingered, but there was no sign of the man. The Royal Gardens were quiet, the only sound was the persistent blackbird under that bush.

***

Ariane sat bolt upright in bed, the sweat streaming down her face. She was shaken badly and dressed quickly, yelling at her maids to get her tea. Once she had had a few sips of the hot liquid, the princess felt strong enough to walk out on the balcony, the star-studded void and shimmer of Lake Wynais seemed to float all around her. She felt giddy, almost sick.

A dream like no other. A vision—*but what had it meant?* She sipped her tea and ate a light breakfast, her swift busy mind processing the dream. She needed help with this one and decided to seek out the High Priest in the temple.

She wasted no time walking at speed to the temple. Once there, Ariane slipped inside unannounced. She saw several priests busy either with prayer or hard at study. Eventually she found him. Lord Dazaleon. He was lighting candles over by the altar, the Goddess's statue looming above, her sightless eyes seemed to watch Ariane's approach.

Ariane made the sacred sign and pulled the hood back from her face. If Dazaleon was surprised by this unannounced visit, he didn't show it. He smiled kindly, bid her kneel before the Goddess on a velvet cushion. He joined her in prayer for a moment and then gently shook her shoulder.

Ariane opened her eyes to see his calm blue gaze upon her. "Come child—we'll speak of this in private." He led her to a covered cloister, an alcove framed with green velvet, and a heavy oak door that closed with a soft thud behind them.

"You had the *Dreaming*," Dazaleon said, before she could speak. Ariane nodded. She still felt slightly sick, weakened by those powerful images that continued to hover and drone like so many busy bees inside her head.

"The *Royal Dreaming*." The High Priest smiled. "Your mother had it, grandmother too."

"I was frightened," Ariane said. "The visions were lucid and shocking . . . I . . . *fell*."

"Tell me, and fear nothing. The Goddess watches over us here."

She shook slightly, wished there was tea available. Eventually she spoke. "I was falling for a long time, into darkness. A horrible emptiness that sucked and smothered my person . . . down."

"The Void," Dazaleon said. "Where the dark things are."

"It pulled me down and down, and I felt as if I was choking. Then I saw a light far below. Tiny at first, but it grew. The light was calling me and I fought my way toward it. The dark tried to trap me, but the light grew so strong it won through, chasing back the shadows and I was free."

"But then the light vanished entirely—a candle snuffed by invisible fingers. I fell again, but this time settled in cool damp earth. I looked up. A circle of stones surrounded me. They started spinning, slowly at first then faster and faster. I felt sick—I still do." She shuddered slightly.

"Go on, child," the High Priest smiled reassuringly.

"They stopped—the stones. They were so tall, leaning over me. I fell on my face, Dazaleon—felt the damp cold touch again. I heard a voice calling out from far away, then an explosion and shards of light tore at my garments and cut my flesh."

"I saw a crown of light falling through blackness," she said as tears welled at the corner of her eyes. "Heard it crash and explode into fragments. Someone laughed cruelly and then I woke." She looked hard at his calm strong face. "I dreamed of the Tekara, didn't I?"

Dazaleon nodded slowly. He stood up and felt the door handle as though concerned someone listened from outside. He looked worried, concerned for her yet also frightened. A look she'd never seen before.

"I feared this," Dazaleon said. "A warning."

"The Tekara?"

"...Is vulnerable for the first time in a thousand years—at the mercy of an ancient evil."

Ariane looked at him puzzled. "The Void was calling you, Princess. Or rather those creatures within it. They sensed your latent . . . *talent*. Know you for their enemy."

"Who are they?"

"The Old Ones. *The Urgolais*. Someone has woken them from their long sleep," Dazaleon said.

"Caswallon," Ariane said. "He means to destroy the Tekara by using sorcery, shatter the hold it has on our realms?"

"I suspect so, but there is more. You dreamed of the Oracle. The sacred glade where stand those stones. It's where our Goddess holds court among her secret people—the Fain. One of the few places in *Ansu* where she can appear in person."

"The Goddess was summoning me?" Ariane was shocked, scared.

"It seems so," Dazaleon said. "We must make plans, my child. Plans for you to visit the Forest of Dreams."

"That's where the Oracle lies? Where is it?"

"Deep inside Kelthaine—what I now fear is enemy country."

"Do I go there alone?"

"No, child." He smiled at her courage. "Let us think on this—wait until your father returns."

"I don't want him to know."

"But he's the king, Ariane."

"I know—but I'd sooner keep this between the two of us, at least until I can get my head straight."

Dazaleon nodded slightly. "Go back to the palace. Sleep, or rest and drink tea. We'll move on this later today. Discounting your father, is there anyone else you would share counsel, trust?"

"Silon of Raleen, and Roman Parrantios—he's back you know."

"Not before time, and yes—the king's champion should be made aware. Silon is sound. Anyone else?"

"Galed my scribe, and my cousin Tamersane." Dazaleon frowned hearing those last names.

"Galed is hardly a stalwart, Princess. And your cousin Tamersane is an idle sloth, a pest to every lady at court. A wastrel and dreamer."

"He's a sunny heart I'll grant you," she said. "But Tam has a sharp mind, and a hunch tells me we will need him."

Dazaleon stared at her for a long moment and then nodded. "Summon them to the temple this evening. After prayers—the later the better. We need utter discretion. I'm saddened to add that I cannot trust all my priests. I fear Caswallon's arm has reached us even in here. Go, Princess—we will speak more on this later."

Ariane nodded and thanked him. She replaced the hood covering her features and returned briskly to the palace. She was exhausted and worried and slept for several hours, awakening to the news that her father had returned to the city in a rare foul mood.

Chapter 19 | Wind and Ruins

"The king's back." Stane leaned out the window and watched the throng mustering close to the gates. "A hero's welcome—the people love Nogel."

"Warriors are always popular with the masses," Silon said, looking up from his parchment. "They're also thickheaded and stubborn."

Stane assumed he was speaking of Corin an Fol, and not the king. Maybe both.

"Don't fall." Silon glared at him. "I'm short staffed currently. People keep dying or running off."

Stane moved back and shut the window. "What's your plan?" he asked the merchant. Silon made an exasperated gesture and stood up, rubbing his eyes.

"I was working on that but your constant chattering renders me numb. Go see what's going on out there, what the king is saying . . . *anything*. Find out what you can." Stane flashed him a grin and left via the side door. Silon watched him leave and then sighed.

Stane was a good man, reliable and thoughtful. Such folk were on short supply. He'd gotten back yesterday with news of the events at the bridge. Curse Nogel for a damn fool, and Corin an Fol for a bigger one. And Yazrana—he'd expected better from her. That woman should have more sense. Both of them off on some personal vendetta against the brute Postin. Ignoring what mattered most. *The fool king's protection.*

Whatever game Keel was playing, he would strike soon. Call it a hunch, but Silon knew this game was playing out. Why the assassin hadn't already acted, Silon couldn't hazard a guess. But he knew Keel was as crafty as he was deadly. Playing his own game, and doubtless wrenching more coin from that conniver up north.

But Keel was already rich, so why the delay? He'd had many opportunities due to Nogel's obtuse stubbornness, putting his life and—more importantly—his realm in danger time after time. And what was Caswallon up to? Silon felt frustrated and irritable. He needed facts and they were slow in coming. And he needed Corin an Fol.

Silon went to pour himself a drink, and then stopped as Stane reappeared, looking red-faced and puffing, having just sprinted up the stairs.

"What . . . ?"

"You're summoned to the temple . . . this evening. No one is to know."

"What are you talking about?"

"This." Stane produced a roll of parchment and passed it across. Silon snapped it open.

"You broke the seal?"

"Wasn't one," Stane said. "A priest was waiting outside, shoved it in my hand and told me to give it to you."

"And you've read it." Silon glared at him for a moment and then unrolled the scroll. A letter from Princess Ariane. Short and to the point.

> *Silon.*
>
> *Caswallon means to usurp the throne. We are on the brink of war.*
>
> *I need you to attend a secret council this eve.*
>
> *Come to Elanion's Temple after dusk.*

The priest will let you in.

Ariane of Kelwyn.

"What do you think?" Silon asked Stane after a moment. *War?* He knew it was coming but why did she seem so certain? And how could she know what he didn't? Silon liked to be ahead of the facts. That wasn't happening today.

"Can't involve the king as he's only just returned," Stane said.

"She must have heard something."

"You *think?*" Silon cursed at his own sarcasm. "Look, Stane—I'm grateful you're here and that you had the sense to report back to me, and not run off with that idiot longswordsman. But please go and find out what you can about what the fuck is going on."

"I'm on it," Stane said, leaving him alone a second time. Silon retired to his chair. He had a few hours before dusk, so he'd spend that time in deep contemplation. He needed to be sharp tonight. If they were entering a new stage in this struggle, he wanted to be at the front.

***

Postin crashed through the door, kicking splinters and then lurched forward, his hammer held ready. "Dooly!" Shadows danced, cast by lanterns flickering. He saw movement and jumped after it. Just a cat, it vanished under tables. Clutter everywhere. Postin wiped his mouth. He was sweating, his belly full of ale and head light. *Dooly?*

The trader should be here, and so should Postin's gold. He searched around, passing from room to room and becoming increasingly angry when he found nothing. The candles had burnt down low. Carne Dooly had gone. *Escaped.* Postin swung his hammer in rage and stuck a heavy wooden desk, smashing it in two. He swung again, this time taking out a large chunk of wall.

He saw movement. The cat? Bigger. He raised the hammer again and heard a sob. "Come out," Postin said, staring at a tall cupboard in the corner of the room.

A whimper, and then the shuffle of feet. A girl stood there. A servant, perhaps sixteen. Her teeth looked bad and her mousey hair covered her face. "Look at me," Postin said, then added, "I won't hurt you—it's Dooly I want. Owes me money."

"Gone," the girl said, brushing her tangles away with a finger. She was comely enough in Postin's opinion. He felt sorry for her, left all alone in here. He took a step forward, meaning to placate, but she jumped back in horror, her shoulders thudding against the wall and knocking off more plaster.

Postin leaned the pole-axe against the broken wall and folded his massive arms. "Listen lovely, I'm half drunk and mad as hornets with your master. I need to know where he is. Dooly owes me gold. *Gold*, girl—can you imagine? Lots of it. I'm to be wealthy. I could help you." He smiled and the girl shrunk back again. "I'm not as bad as I look," Postin said quietly, feeling hurt by the horror in her eyes. He could feel the tears welling in his own. Why did he always get so melancholy after drink?

The girl looked at him as though he'd lost his mind. Postin grinned at her. That didn't help. He reached for his pole-axe. "I'll leave," he said. "Sorry about the mess. When your master comes back, tell him Postin the Hammer wants to talk to him. *Goodbye*." Postin turned away, the tears streaming down his cheeks.

"He's gone to Highreach Hall," the girl whispered, and Postin turned.

"Where's that?"

"It's a ruined castle, just off the coast road."

"Which way?"

"North. There's a crossroads and a sign. Last time I passed by, it was faded bad."

"You've been there?"

"Been past it with my father. He pointed the sign out to me and told me our master had just purchased it. Said it was a very bad place . . ."

"How far?"

"Twenty miles. Why are you crying?"

"I'm misunderstood." The girl looked at him askance and Postin risked another smile. "You've been very helpful," he said. "I'll come back."

"Please don't," the girl said, wiping hair from her face again. He left her standing there and departed the house without further fuss. Once back in the inn, Postin woke the patron and settled his debt. The man was half asleep but seemed relieved to be rid of him. Postin went outside to saddle Challenger.

He reached the crossroads at dawn and saw the faded sign. *Highreach Hall.*

A narrow track led down through woods and bracken. He could smell salt in the air and heard a roaring, the ocean somewhere below. Postin smiled as he thought of the gold he'd get after he'd shattered Dooly's weasel face. The man shouldn't have crossed him. First Carne Dooly, then that lanky longsword. After that he'd change his ways, become respectable. Perhaps the townsfolk would like Postin the Hammer more when he had money to spend.

***

"I think he might have left in a hurry." Corin looked at the broken door and plaster and splinters strewn everywhere. "Hammer work—I'd say. Not overly subtle." Yazrana nodded. "Postin must have got here first."

"I'll go see," the woman said. She passed him her horse's reins and made for the door.

"Wait," Corin said. "Someone's inside. I saw movement. Let me go in instead."

"I don't need a fucking nursemaid," she told him and vanished inside the door. Minutes later she reappeared with a nervous girl alongside.

"This is Clarna," Yazrana said. "Works for Carne Dooly. Poor girl's terrified. Said an eight-foot monster broke the door down and dribbled over her."

"He was crying," the girl said. They looked at her. "Seemed sad."

"He will be when I catch up with him," Corin said.

"Tell him what you told me, Clarna." Yazrana smiled at the girl.

"The monster said my master owed him gold. He also said he wasn't as bad as he looked, and nobody understood him."

"The other bit," Yazrana said, when Corin scratched his head.

"He's away north to the haunted mansion." Corin looked at Yazrana, who shrugged. "Highreach Hall," she added, as though that explained everything.

"Why would he go there?" Corin asked.

"The master bought it a while back. An investment—what my father says. It's abandoned and ruined and hard to find. Spect he went up there to hide from the monster."

"Spect so," Corin nodded. "Where is this place?" After she'd told them, Yazrana put a large silver coin in Clarna's fist.

"For you and your father," she said. "Go work for someone honest." The girl stared at the coin, and they left her and the merchant's house behind.

"Back to the coast road," Corin said as they guided their horses through the city gates. "Almost nostalgic." Yazrana didn't respond, but her face looked sad.

"What's wrong, Yaz?" But she wouldn't tell him so he let her be. It was mid-morning when they reached the faded sign that pointed left, where a track vanished into gorse and bracken. Corin smelled the sea and smiled.

Get this done and I'm going home . . .

A mile ahead, he saw stone peeping through the gaps in gorse. A tumbledown of broken pillars and the caved-in roof of what must have been an expansive residence. They stopped by a clump of low thorns. "Best tie our horses here," Yazrana said. Corin nodded and together they dismounted, the sound of waves crashing somewhere far below. A sound that made Corin think of his lost home.

"Be good—we'll be back soon," Corin told Thunderhoof as the horse looked at him mournfully.

"Do you always speak to that horse?" Yazrana asked him.

"He understands me," Corin said and she rolled her eyes.

"We've work to do, boy," she told him, and started making her way through the brush, the path having narrowed to almost invisible. Yazrana had a sword in one hand and small throwing knife clutched in the other. Corin slid Clouter from his shoulder and followed close behind.

The ruins revealed themselves as they got nearer. There were still walls in places, a large gable end, and some sections of roof intact. Corin saw a single light hinting someone was here. The place was huge and as they got nearer, he saw that a large part of it had fallen away, torn from its lofty perch and swallowed by the dark waters far below—a dark blue shimmer barely visible through the bushes, sketched over by the tiny darting shapes of seabirds. A long way down.

As the scrub withdrew to tussled grasses, Corin saw tall stacks parading the coastline away north and ahead. These rugged towers looked like sentinels, countless birds circling among them, the tiny waves breaking white on their craggy base. "I wonder who built this place and why?" Corin said.

Yazrana looked at him. "Who cares," she said. Corin noticed how she seemed unsettled, edgy. Unusual for her.

"Something amiss?"

"I don't like it here," she said, crouching low and watching for movement.

"It's just ruins," Corin said. "A good spot for Dooly to hide out with his gold, and now Postin too, I suspect."

"There's something else here." The woman shook her head. She looked at him with a strange, sad expression. "We need to get this done before our allotted time runs out."

Puzzled by her words and expression, Corin just nodded. "Let's go see if there's a back way in," he said. She nodded, her face troubled, lost in thought.

They skirted the tumbled expanse of stone, taking care to keep low and well hidden. Aside that one faint light, there was no sign of life. Corin halted once when a raven settled on a spur of clifftop and eyed him evilly. Corin felt a shiver creep up his spine. Maybe Yaz was right.

There is something uncanny here.

The raven lifted and was gone. Corin saw others high above and still more hopping about on the cliffs. *Just birds.* But they stopped suddenly as a gust of wind whistled through the ruins and set Corin's teeth on edge. A cold blast that made him think of winter on this summer's day. He turned to a corner of the ruins and stopped abruptly again.

A woman stood there watching him in silence. Dressed in ragged green, her copper hair disheveled, streaming across her face so he couldn't see it. He didn't need to. *Vervandi.* The dream woman had come to warn them. Corin turned to shake Yazrana's shoulder and alert her, but felt nothing.

He turned. Yazrana had gone. *Vanished*, and the copper-haired woman seemed to float across to him from those broken walls. She called out, but Corin heard no voice. Then a ragged scream from somewhere inside the broken walls jolted his attention back to where the lone lantern flickered.

Yazrana . . .

Corin saw Vervandi fade like gusty smoke from the corner of his eye. He ran for the buildings, passed broken outhouses and then spotted an arched doorway, the wood long rotten and a passage opening within. As Corin approached, a shadow filled that entrance. Postin the Hammer grinned at him.

He strode out onto the grass, the cold wind billowing his tattered tunic. "Time to die, Longsword." The pole-axe swung towards him and Corin jumped for cover.

***

Yazrana felt the icy touch behind her. *It's time* . . . The woman's familiar voice echoing inside her head. *The bargain we made* . . . Her husky tone trailed off, blending with the wind that had risen so suddenly, and battered her face, watering her eyes. Her memory so mercifully erased returned to full terrible clarity. The bargain she had made with the dream woman, back there in the desert.

A life for a life.

Corin . . . She reached out for him, but the chill wind separated them and Yazrana could hear other voices surrounding the woman's, shouting, screaming—or was it the birds? So many black birds circling above, and settling like dry flaky leaves on the wind-blown ruffled grass.

"I'm not ready!" Yazrana yelled at the woman and ran for the ruins as fast as she could. Anything to drive the voices away. She caught a glimpse of the woman smiling at her, saw Corin fading from view. He was in *her* power now. *The red-haired witch.*

Yazrana heard him call out to her but the shout sounded so distant, like a lost lover calling up from deep beyond the grave. A garbled murmur struggling to break free of the violent whispers reaching out for her. The birds lined the roofs, the walls. An eager host. They were everywhere, their cruel black eyes following her.

Yazrana entered the ruins at the main archway where the doors had once stood. The lone lantern flickered somewhere ahead. She gripped her sword and knife harder, took a deep breath and willed herself forward. The voices faded back as an icy stillness claimed Highreach Hall. Yazrana stalked from room to room seeking that remote light, but the lantern glow seemed to move away whenever she got near.

She heard a scream. A man dying—easy to recognize by the horror in that tone. She looked up, the roof was badly damaged above her head and exposed timbers hinted a sky gone dark. Up there were mustering storm clouds moving swiftly like vanquished armies fleeing from the wind. The fell voices were out there too; she saw several crows settle on the rafters.

You are not taking me yet.

Yazrana entered another room and silence closed around her. Ahead was a door still intact. She forced it open and strode inside, her sword probing for any sign of movement. The lantern flickered in a corner, casting dim light of the body lying there.

A man with his head stoved in, his scrawny fingers clutching a bag of gold, the flagstone floor glittering with the coins that had spilled loose. The man's dead eyes glazed up at her. A voice spoke then.

"Too late for him." Yazrana spun around, her sword cutting through air, and her knife ready to fly, gripped by the blade in her fingers. A man rose from the shadows, tough looking, lean and lanky, scarred face, a broadsword gripped in his hands.

"Who the fuck are you?" Yazrana tossed the knife but he ducked and the blade struck the wall and quivered slightly.

"They call me Hagan," the lean face smiled. "I'm here to kill you, lady."

"Did you do that?" She hinted Carne Dooly's smashed skull.

"Does it look like a sword wound?"

"So where is Postin?"

"Outside—I told him you and Corin would be here. He was excited about that and wanted to greet The Longsword himself. *Shame*, I'm going to miss Corin. Tis but business, my dear." The man Hagan leaped at her with lightning speed, lunging fast and hard with the broadsword.

Yazrana's sword knocked the blade away and she followed with a side cut which he parried. "You're quick," Hagan said. "The Crimson Lady's final stand."

"You know nothing about me!" She stepped forward cutting left and down, fast and hard, but he parried, and then slammed his elbow into her shoulder, knocking her backwards.

Hagan swung again, but Yazrana kicked out and caught him in the groin. He lurched forward and she jabbed her fingers in his face. She swung close with her blade but Hagan gripped the steel, allowing it to bite into his hands as he pulled it towards him.

She fell on top of him and jabbed down with her free hand. Hagan spat in her eye and kneed her crutch, knocking her off. "We could be lovers," he cussed, hand dripping blood, rising to his feet and readying another swing with his sword.

She waited for that stroke then rolled aside, lashing out with another kick, this one sweeping Hagan off his feet. She leaped to her feet, kicked him in the head and he slumped unconscious. Yazrana left him lying there. Her only thoughts on Corin and if he yet lived.

She screamed in rage, ignoring the pain and ran outside. A shadow blocked her path. Yazrana blinked once as the hammer thudded into her chest . . .

***

Corin felt the blood streaming down his face. That last swing had caught his cheek, ripping flesh and sending him spinning. Postin had roared and leveled his weapon, but then Yazrana had emerged from somewhere inside, screaming like a harridan.

Postin had seen her as she looked for Corin and struck out with the hammer. Corin saw her fall.

No!

He staggered to his feet, stretched out a hand for Clouter, gripped it by the tip and swung it hard across Postin's back, the crosspiece knocking the big man forward so he lost balance.

Postin forgot the prone woman and turned to face Corin again. "Need a woman to save you—*hey?*" Postin swung the hammer again and Corin stepped out to meet him.

Corin made a wild grab, catching Clouter's hilt in both hands, turning on his toes and swiping hard at Postin's face. The steel cut deep, taking an eye. Postin staggered backwards, one hand covering his face, the pole-axe jabbing outwards with the other.

Corin braced his feet and leveled Clouter to finish the job, but something hard struck him in the face and he fell backwards, crashing into the soil.

Corin saw a man looming over him.

Hagan . . . ?

"That bitch could fight," the Morwellan mercenary said. "*Shame she's gone* . . . Just you and me now, Corin an Fol."

He tried to rise, but Hagan's steel-tipped boot pinned him by the chest. "Why?" Corin spat blood and tried to focus.

"Gold," Hagan said. "I work for Caswallon now. Good payer—you should have come with me when you had the chance. Too bloody loyal, Corin. That's your problem."

"Fuck you."

"Time's up, old mate." Hagan raised his sword. Corin knocked the Morwellan's boot away with an elbow and rolled to his left as the steel cut deep into the turf. Hagan swung again and Corin rolled the other way.

"You won't get far on your belly." Hagan laughed, readying to swing a third time. Then Corin heard Yazrana scream as she rammed her body into Hagan's back, knocking him off balance.

Corin only just got back on his feet when Postin emerged, yelling, the blood streaming down his face, and the pole-axe swinging wide. That blow caught Yazrana's side, knocking her away. The giant stepped forward and thrust the weapon's base at Hagan, causing him to double over in pain.

Postin ignored man and woman as he stepped over Hagan and swung hard at Corin, the hammer clipping Corin's thigh and knocking him off his feet. Corin reached for Biter, pulled the saex free and sliced hard into Postin's calf as the giant stood over him. Postin hardly noticed. He raised the hammer again and then jolted forward as Yazrana pitched headlong into his back.

The pair stood rocking for a moment as a piece of cliff tore off under their feet. Then they were gone.

"Yazrana!" Corin screamed as she vanished from sight. To his right he glimpsed Hagan staggering to his feet and lurching off into the bushes. *Yazrana . . .*

She was gone. Corin saw birds circling ahead and felt the earth spinning below him as he leaned forward and spewed blood. *Yazrana—I cannot lose you again . . .* He fell to his knees, his vision blurring. Glancing up, he saw Vervandi standing there, faint and hard to define.

She knew the price. The woman's sultry tones echoed through his head. *Was happy to pay.* The vision faded and Corin heard the soft sound of harp music floating out from the ruins of the house. Then he slumped forward on his face and the world went black.

***

"You saved him yet again—you should be proud." The red-haired witch was smiling at her. Strangely, she saw no cruelty in that gaze. Only sorrow, and irony.

"I love him," Yazrana said. "Always have."

The woman smiled again. "Me too, in my own way. What is it about him, do you think? I cannot grasp it. A lost soul perhaps." She seemed to drift over to the rocks where the sea was lashing and booming. Postin's broken body tossed back and forth in the froth, the white stained pinkish red. "I should thank you, Yazrana."

"It was the bargain we made." Yazrana stared up at the woman. She felt no pain and a kind of peace settled on her. "I wasn't ready back then. Now . . . I think I am."

"You've taught me much, sharing your body—your earthly passions and moods. To spend time as a mortal is not what I'd imagined—the life I gave you and took into myself."

The woman drifted and faded as the waves rose high. Soon they would carry Yazrana's broken body far away.

"You will look after him for me . . .? You have the power."

"I shall do my best, I promise you. Corin's is a very dark path, and his greatest challenge only just beginning. I bid you farewell, brave Yazrana," the woman said. "May we meet again in time . . ."

The woman vanished behind the rising water, and as the peaceful weariness rose up engulfing her, Yazrana's last sight was of a silent white owl lifting over those dark waters and gliding far out to where skyline met uncharted horizons.

***

It was a choke that woke him. Jolted him to move. Corin rolled to his knees and blinked back tears. *Yazrana.* She was gone. Forever this time. He knew that now.

Corin found Clouter lying in the grass and reached down for the hilt. He stuck the longsword point first in the soil and leaned against it, taking deep breaths while resting his battered body. He was alone on that crag, the remnants of Highreach Hall fading into gloom as last light filled the sky.

A whisper of breeze ruffled his locks. "I know you're there." Corin turned, and saw Vervandi glide and shimmer into view. "Why did you take her from me again?"

"You give me too much credit, Corin." The woman smiled sadly. "I did as she requested, and for a time the trade worked well for both of us."

Corin felt his head swim as he tried to stay upright. The woman blurred in and out of his vision. "I don't understand . . ."

"I gave Yazrana life in the desert—she was trying so hard, I pitied her so saved her from that choking death. But I wanted something too. We traded roles for a time."

Vervandi's smile turned whimsical. "Yazrana got an extension of life, whereas I, a Fate, sampled a first taste of it. The air, the excitement, fear, sadness, joy and despair—at last I know what it is to be human! To laugh and weep, to love . . . *to hate.* I shared her experiences and rode beside you for that time, Corin an Fol. Felt your hot urgency within my body. You have no idea how it feels—to live and breathe, and not be a creature of the ether, tasked by the gods to watch and wait . . ."

Her words faded in and out and their meaning was lost. Corin felt himself falling, his head settled on damp grass. "Why do you haunt my dreams, my nightmares?" he felt the words trickle like blood from his mouth.

"I have a mandate and you are my charge." Her voice was fainter. "Your destiny is linked to that of this world. A finely tuned connection leading to the great event—the Final Dance. Your part in that game is key, Corin an Fol. I am tasked to ensure you follow that right path."

"Your words mean nothing." Corin's head was heavy with sleep, his eyes closing, but he could still see her shadow flicker in the falling dusk. Vervandi became an owl, white as snow settling on a winter field. She rose above him and was gone. He closed his eyes.

I am one of three sisters—you will see us all in time. You must be strong; the greatest challenge is yet to come.

The voice buffeted his head like the wind. Perhaps it was the wind. He closed his eyes, allowed the silent darkness to claim him.

When Corin came to, it was nighttime and the wind had slowed to a cool breeze. He rose shakily, stood swaying on that cliff edge, the dark waters churning so far below. His mind was numb. He couldn't recall what had happened here.

Dazed, Corin wandered back through the ruins of the manse, Clouter slung over his shoulder, head throbbing. He found Thunderhoof cropping grass. *Her* steed was gone. Corin clambered up into Thunder's saddle and urged the big horse back to the highway, his body slumping as though he were still asleep.

Corin stopped by the faded sign, no longer sure which way to go. Back to his old home in Finnehalle, to try to drive away the fragments of memory slipping through his mind? Or else return to Raleen, to Silon and renew his life as a mercenary? It felt as though he'd lost something tangible he couldn't grasp, and a great emptiness had opened inside him. Her dark eyes flashed before him.

Yazrana—had that all been a dream?

Corin felt shaken, exhausted and his mind wandering. He sat hunched in the saddle scarcely keeping awake, his head throbbing as he tried—in vain—to remember what had passed. Somewhere close an owl called out three times. A signal. He still had work to do. Corin chose the southern route. He needed answers and knew exactly who to ask. Mind made up, Corine rode hard throughout the rest of that night.

Chapter 20 | The King's Quarry

"You had a secret meeting in the Goddess's temple?" King Nogel stared hard at his champion. "Without consulting me?"

"You were absent, Highness." Roman kept his eyes on the road, the woods and fields, the hawk winging low ahead—anything rather than focus on his king. Nogel's mood was ugly this morning.

"On whose authority?"

"Your daughter, Princess Ariane."

"I know who my daughter is," Nogel snapped at him, then held out his arm and the hawk sailed back down, alighting with precision on his heavy glove. Roman watched it preen its feathers. At least the bird was happy today. They were out on a hunt: the king, his champion, and some of the younger nobles, Yail Tolranna and Tamersane included. These kept their distance, sensing Nogel's mood. Roman had nowhere to go.

Sit on your horse and take what's coming. "She was anxious about you, and she'd been having dreams." *That didn't help.*

"Dreams." Nogel let the hawk fly again, and Roman watched it dart into trees far off to their right. *Lucky bird.* "You held a clandestine gathering because of a fucking dream?"

"It's more than that, Highness—the *Royal Dreaming* . . . like the queen her mother."

"And of course, you would know all about that." King Nogel glared at him, and Roman dropped his gaze. Some wounds couldn't be stitched without seepage.

Despite the shame, he persisted. "She has it, Dazaleon interpreted the dream and it was full of portents and warnings. The High Priest agreed with your daughter that we needed to arrange a council. And quickly. Nobody knew when you'd get back."

"Or if I got back," Nogel said. He smiled slightly. "A rash decision of mine going north—I see that now." The king reined in his horse as he studied the road ahead. Half mile in the distance, Roman could see the riders with hounds and just make out the sound of yelps and laughter. How he wished he was with them.

But Nogel's face softened as he watched his hawk glide back into view. "Dorlas hunts well today," the king said, allowing the bird to settle on his glove again. "I was as much to blame in that affair as yourself. But I was angry, Roman—at all three of us, but mostly myself. I'm sorry that drove a wedge between us, old friend."

"Not as sorry as I am, Highness."

"Well, she's gone," Nogel said, after a moment. "I'm glad I have my champion back. Those young tossers down there haven't a clue." The shouts and baying were louder as they closed the gap. Roman saw hounds scampering about, then someone blew a horn.

"They must have seen something worth a royal chase," Roman said.

"I hope it's worth all that racket," the king added, as they rode close. "What was the result of the secret council?" the king asked him as they cantered down the lane toward the excited party. Roman told him what had been decided and the king just shrugged.

"I'll see my daughter when we're back," he said. "Enough for now—let's see what these young fools are so excited about."

"Highness, it's huge!" Lord Tamersane spurred his horse up the hill towards them, his handsome features flushed with excitement and his long fair hair flowing free in the breeze. The young noble reined in a few yards ahead and struggled to regain his composure.

"This is what I've had to deal with," the king said to Roman. "What's the fuss, man?" This to Tamersane.

"A white hart, Highness—a king's beast if ever I saw one. It's huge . . . beautiful."

"And very rare." The king looked at Roman. "Best go see."

"I don't like this," Roman muttered, but the king hadn't heard him, was already spurring his horse behind Tamersane's, down toward where the other nobles sat the beasts, the hounds scurrying around them and circling.

Roman eased his horse forward. *A white hart.* A mythical creature. There had been rumors of such a beast in the distant past. But that was up in the mountain folds and farther from the city. Roman had the nasty feeling that something was awry here. But he had scant choice but to be part of it.

Tamersane and his older brother hinted at a break through the trees, off to their right. The king rode through it with the two younger nobles flanking him. Nogel held Dorlas aloft and the bird took wing, his keen flight forgotten as the woods parted on a glade.

Roman, riding a few yards behind, saw the sun's glimmer on that level sward of grass, a stream running beyond, and the distant slopes of the High Wall framing the horizon. A beautiful clear morning, the dewy grass cropped low and gleaming like scattered emeralds.

In its midst stood a beast. A white hart, bigger than a horse, with antlers spanning four foot across. A magnificent creature. Roman reined in behind the king and his escorts. Nobody spoke. Then the king turned and winked at him.

"I feel my youth returning, Roman. Surely this is a kingly beast!" It was as if the animal heard him, for the moment Nogel spoke the beast turned and sped, arrow swiftly deep into the woods at the far end of the glade.

"My kill!" King Nogel shouted, urging his horse forward and spurring the beast to canter.

"Follow him," Roman said, wiping sweat from his face. Cold this morning, yet he was sweating. "Don't let the king out of your sight." But the brothers weren't listening, had already disappeared in the trees somewhere behind their king.

Roman waited until the rest filed close. "We follow slowly," he told them. "I fear that is no natural beast. Be on your guard—there is glamour here." The six riders gathered beside him looked nervous, but they nodded and Roman eased his mount forward, leading the animal into the dense thicket of hazel, briar, and willow. "Stay together," he said as they were swallowed by the canopy, the light dimming to false dusk.

**

King Nogel had heard the stories. His grandfather had spotted a white hart once high in the mountains. Had ridden for days tracking the beast but no sign was ever seen of it again. The animal became a legend in Wynais, a myth. His father claimed to have seen it once, but then admitted in his dotage that he'd imagined the sighting.

But there was no doubt here. Nogel grinned as he guided his horse along the switch, his head held low, avoiding branch and briar. The horse was struggling to find a way through. He could hear Dorlas somewhere high above the trees, invisible in that thicket.

The white hart stopped again on a slight rise, its noble head turned toward him, and those haunting eyes surveying the king with curiosity. "You are a wonder," Nogel said as he slid an arrow from his saddle pouch and nocked shaft to bowstring. He waited, pulled back and loosed, but the white hart sprang clear and faded deeper into the bushes.

King Nogel cursed and spurred his horse deeper into the murk. A plain shot—*how did I miss?* Ahead, through the thickening maze he glimpsed the beast. It had stopped again and watched his approach. *Damn the animal—is it mocking me?*

King Nogel guided his horse the best he could through the tangle, finally reaching a break where the trees parted in a wide-open track, which led down into folds of bracken, the odd pine studding the sky, like so many silent guards.

The white hart had reached a small hillock and stopped again. A clear bowshot. This time Nogel wouldn't miss. He reached for another arrow and then froze as a horn blast echoed somewhere back in the woods. *Curse those fools!* The creature had turned away and was trotting down the slope.

The horn sounded again, this time further away. He heard muffled shouts, a dog's bark, and then looking up spotted Dorlas soaring through blue. He held out his glove but the bird vanished behind the distant trees, ignoring its master's signal.

Nogel was angry now. He urged his horse to canter along the stony track for half a mile before he spotted the white hart again. Standing in the sunshine, crowned head held high. A long shot—but possible. Nogel was done chasing this beast.

He set nock to string again. Felt the breeze, forced himself to relax, taking long slow breaths. The creature hadn't moved. Nogel released the shaft and the arrow shot true, striking the white hart in its flank. He felt a rush of excitement as the animal staggered and then slumped prone. Nogel grinned, he rode along the track. They'd be singing about this tonight.

He didn't stop to wonder where his company had gone to. Nor did he dwell on the distance he'd traveled. The mountains were closer than before, as though he'd ridden for many hours. He could see the animal lying there as he approached, but clouds had stolen the sun and a sudden mist was rising in the fields surrounding him.

Strangely cold here. Nogel felt the tiny hairs prickle along the base of his neck. The mist descended and he could hardly see the dead animal. He rode faster, cantering down a slope. Then the mist fell away and bright sunshine revealed the spot where the white hard had lain. It had vanished. Instead, a man stood there with something in his hands.

A sack. Before Nogel could slow his horse, the man deftly untied the sack and cast something onto the track ahead. A serpent writhed and wriggled as Nogel's horse bore down on it. The beast reared and bucked, the sudden movement knocking his rider from saddle.

Nogel felt his body sail through the air and crash onto stone, the pain of impact jarring him badly. He tried to move but the pain tore into him. The man approached in silence, the snake in his hands. "It's always the little things in life that catch you out." The man slid nimble fingers up the snake, reaching its neck and twisting it hard, killing the creature.

He cast the dead snake aside and walked toward where Nogel lay, the pain tearing into him. The man smiled, revealing perfect teeth. His green eyes sparkled irony. "The death of kings," he said. "I bid you greeting from Caswallon."

"It's you . . ." Nogel barely whispered, before the green-eyed killer stepped forward and brought his boot down hard, snapping the king's neck.

***

Roman saw the horse first, standing mournful over a shape. He rode close and as his heart thudded in horror, saw what he had feared. The king lay dead, his neck broken from a fall. Roman slid from his horse. He knelt by King Nogel as the tears streamed down his face. The others found him there, their young faces stunned and stark. High above, the lone hawk Dorlas folded its wings, dropped silent from the sky and vanished in the trees.

***

Caswallon jolted backwards as the room spun around. He gripped the table and shuddered. The glamour had exhausted him. A legendary beast created from his mind's eye. He'd never tried this kind of magic before. A new power, a gift from the Old Ones. They had demanded a demonstration.

With his fargaze, Caswallon had seen his hunter lay the trap for the king. Keel had done his work well, but not before time. He was needed back here to finish the task. Caswallon stared into his mirror. He looked haggard, older than before. *The price of sorcery.* That didn't matter, because the power he possessed would seal his fate as the ruler of this corner of *Ansu*.

His destiny fulfilled at long last. Years of planning and scheming, with just one task remaining. He washed his face in the basin and tidied his desk. Then he took the long-spiraled descent down to the palace far below.

It was time to find Prince Tarin and prepare the boy for the final treachery. Caswallon smiled his secret smile. The long-awaited day had almost arrived.

***

Princess Ariane dropped her cup, the tea spilling over her lap, and the object crashing noisily on the floor at her feet. She lurched to her feet shaking, her head spinning and stomach cramped. For the briefest instant she'd seen her father's face, white and ghostly. Then the vision passed, and turning she saw Roman Parrantios standing there, the doors to her balcony thrust wide. The champion was disheveled, his clothes torn and face red with emotion.

"He's dead—isn't he?" Ariane felt the tears muster at the corner of her eyes. The High Priest appeared behind Roman, others too. She hardly noticed them.

Dazaleon stepped forward and placed a heavy hand on her shoulder. "Goddess, bless you—Queen Ariane." He dropped to a knee, as did Roman beside him, and the blur of faces behind.

***

Silon stepped out of the carriage and walked through the doors of his beloved home. Vioyamis sparkled in sun and Nalissa ran into his arms. He smiled at her, kissing her cheeks, the strain of the last few days washed away—at least for this brief moment—by the joy he felt seeing his daughter.

"You were away so long," she said, much later while they took their ease strolling through the gardens. "I was getting worried, as was Uncle Rubaan."

"A grim business." Silon accepted a glass of wine from a servant as he took a chair on the veranda, the girl slipping into one beside him. "Now it's time to watch and wait."

"Will there be war, Father?" He'd told her about King Nogel's sorry demise two weeks prior, and how he suspected Caswallon's involvement. And that the fiery young Queen Ariane and her champion were planning revenge.

"Eventually," he said. "There has to be—though I fear Caswallon may prove unstoppable. Come beloved, let's discuss lighter issues." She nodded, and together father and daughter watched the sun slip from view beyond the vineyards, the distant walls of Port Sarfe glowed gold for brief moments then vanished from sight.

A ruffle in the bushes turned their heads. Corin an Fol stood there, his face hidden by shadow and the longsword slung across his shoulder.

"Thought I'd find you pair here," Corin said, as Nalissa jumped to her feet and threw her arms around him.

***

"We leave in the morning," Queen Ariane said, as Roman Parrantios and the others sat with her to watch dusk settle like a veil of mist over distant Lake Wynais. Lord Dazaleon was here, as were the brothers Yail Tolranna and Tamersane. Her scribe Galed was seated in the corner, his face worried and sickly.

Yail Tolranna stood up and began pacing the room. "Highness, please allow me to accompany you and not stay stranded in this city."

Ariane shook her head. "You are Captain of Guard, Tolranna. Your principal duty is here, protecting this city. Besides, I have Roman and your brother—two of the finest swordsmen I know. And Galed is here to help me think straight and log our journey."

"Galed is hardly suitable—"

"—That's for me to judge," Ariane said. "You forget yourself, sir." Tolranna subsided but Roman stood up.

"The four of us against Caswallon. I like the odds." Roman's irony was lost on the queen, who'd had three more visceral dreams since her father's fatal accident. Each one had been more vivid. Those dreams and a hasty coronation had left her humor fractured. The full weight of their vulnerability sat squarely on her shoulders alone. At twenty-two winters, it was almost more than she could bear.

"We go in secret, *so yes*—that's the whole point. Two warriors, Galed to record everything and archive, and myself to seek the Goddess in that distant wood."

"Hope you can cook?" Roman said to Galed, who hadn't ventured a comment yet and seemed entirely out of place. Ariane shot Roman an austere glance and he shrugged.

"Dawn, gentlemen," Ariane said, dismissing them. "I suggest you go get ready and then rest up." They took the hint, left to peruse the city. All save Dazaleon who stood watching like the tall sentinel he was.

"A rash venture." She smiled at the High Priest. "And I criticized my father for such impetuousness."

"This is different, My Queen. The Goddess has summoned you to Her Oracle, Elanion will ensure the way is clear. I've spoken to the others in our council. Silon of Raleen will send somebody efficient to aid you. A guide who knows that region—says he has someone perfect for the task."

"What chance do we have of countering Caswallon's malice?" Ariane asked. "Kelwyn is no match for the might of her northern neighbor."

"Let us hope it doesn't come to that," Dazaleon said. "I will scry this evening. Use my third inner eye and find that knave, see what he's up to."

"Risky."

"Very," he said. "But we are in too deep now, Ariane. And, like you, I believe your father's death no accident. But hold to hope, Queen! The Goddess has summoned you for a reason. I sense this game is just beginning." He touched her shoulder again and left Ariane watching over her city. Far away she saw eagles circle—tiny distant shapes fading in the half light. Ariane envied them their freedom.

***

Night fell deep and hushed over Kella City, a blanket of cloud smothering moon and stars. The single pale light of the Astrologers' Roost glittered like a baleful eye winking down on the streets far below. The palace was shrouded in gloom. Guards stood motionless and anxious. A dark mood had filled this city of late.

A shadow emerged from the gardens. A lithe graceful figure, it became a man flitting from cover to cover, then climbing up, hand over hand until reaching a window.

Keel shattered glass with his cloak-covered elbow, wriggled the latch free and then slid inside. He paced through the sleeping palace like a hungry, restless hound. He knew these rooms from childhood, a distant memory.

He found the great corridor, sensed the throbbing brightness of the Crystal Crown somewhere far below. That made him shiver slightly, almost pause in his actions. But Keel had been planning this day for years. And now he was part of something bigger—another reason to destroy utterly the family that had forsaken him.

Keel entered the room, saw the figure asleep on the bed. The High King's face was peaceful. Keel shoved a rough hand over Kelsalion's mouth. The High King opened his eyes. They widened in horror when he recognized who had come.

"Did you miss me, Father?" Keel said, as he struck down with his dagger and opened the High King's throat. He stabbed again and again, until the sheets and bed were drenched in blood. Finally Keel stopped and gazed down, his memory flashing back to that terrible day when his mother had drowned. They had abandoned him that day. Left to drown. And Kelsalion III soon forgot the spiteful son he'd never loved, weeping only for the mother, his queen, and their new born baby lost the same day.

***

Two days later, Caswallon was approached by an aide. "There is a man requesting your presence, Lord. He calls himself The Assassin."

Moments later Keel walked into the throne room and Caswallon smiled. "I've put word out that it was Permian infiltrators. That should work."

Keel said nothing but took his ease in a chair. "We will need to trust each other, *Prince*." Caswallon said.

Keel shrugged. "That depends on you, *Sorcerer.*"

"That shipwreck was an accident, so why the hatred? You must have stabbed Kelsalion twenty times. Excessive, even for you."

Keel shrugged. "You, meddler, wouldn't understand. What's next then—the Crown?"

"Prince Tarin is working with me on that. Once that idle youth has served his purpose, he's all yours, Assassin. Stay local, Prince of Crenna—I'll be in touch."

Epilogue

"You missed him," Nalissa said as Stane enquired after his friend. "Corin quarreled with father—over me. A misunderstanding. I don't know where he's gone."

"Home I expect," Stane said. "Back to rainy Fol and the sheep. Your father said he had work for me?"

"He's in his study," the girl said and drifted off to admire the roses.

***

Hagan stood fidgeting as the stony-eyed councilor studied him. He didn't like being here. The palace was like a morgue and Kella City stank of death. Worse, there were rumors of untoward happenings, dark summoning and incantations in the black of night.

"Keel suggested I employ your skills," Caswallon said.

"I'm honored, my lord."

"Good, I've an urgent matter for you to attend. Get this task done and you'll be swimming in gold, Hagan of Morwella."

"What of Keel?"

"What of him?"

"You know who he really is?"

"*Of course.* Rael Hakkenon the Pirate Prince of Crenna has always been known to me."

***

Corin an Fol reined in at the edge of a cliff. Far to the west as the sun sank crimson below water, he could just make out the twinkling lights of Finnehalle, his long-lost home. He'd be there tomorrow, his chaffed hands locked around a tankard. Corin smiled as he led Thunderhoof toward that distant glow. *This time I'm staying for good.*

Would you trade your soul to save your life?

The Crimson Lady knows that's the only way to find the man she wants to kill. The mercenary known as Corin an Fol.

If you enjoyed Gray Wolf, you will love this new tale The Crimson Lady. It's available free for newsletter members only. Don't miss out. Join our fun newsletter, the JW Webb VIP Lounge. Subscribe and pick up The Crimson Lady to delve deeper into this exciting series today.

jwwebbauthor.com/

Enjoy this book? You can make a big difference.

Reviews are the most powerful tools in my arsenal when it comes to getting attention for my books. Much as I'd like to, I don't have the financial muscle of a New York publisher. I can't take out full page ads in the newspaper or put posters on the subway.

(Not yet, anyway.)

But I do have something much more powerful and effective than that, and it's something that those publishers would kill to get their hands on:

A committed and loyal bunch of readers.

Honest reviews of my books help bring them to the attention of other readers.

If you have enjoyed this book, I would be grateful if you could spend just five minutes leaving a review (it can be as short as you like) on the book's Amazon page. You can jump right to the page by using the links below.

UK & US

Thank you very much!

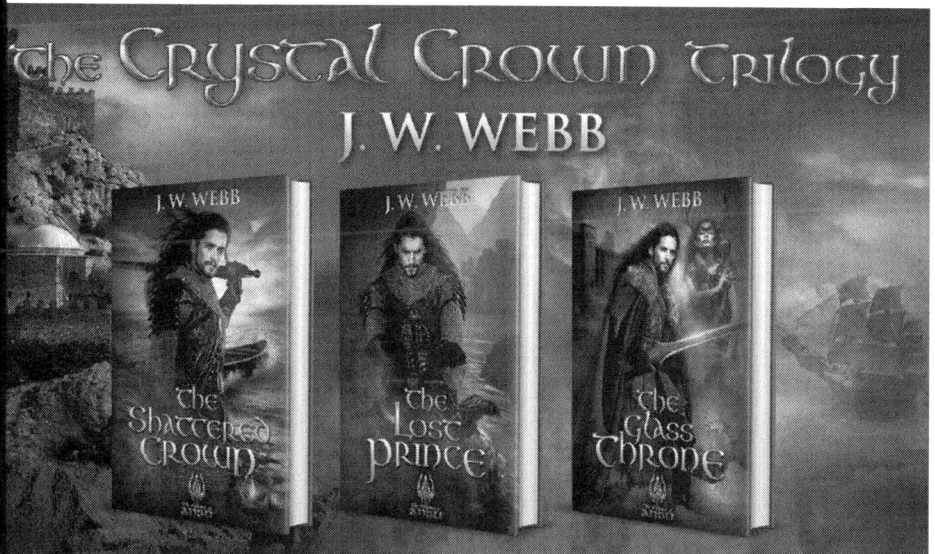

Now that you've read Corin's mercenary adventures, why not delve deeper?

The Shattered Crown, the first novel in the Crystal Crown Trilogy puts Corin an Fol, Queen Ariane, and some new desperados head to head against the conniving sorcerer Caswallon. The stakes are higher than ever in this adrenaline-rushed, fast-paced battle for survival. Click this link to view the books on the author's Amazon Page: http://bit.ly/AuthorWebb

Read this sample to capture the mood…

Chapter 1 | The Smithy

Corin an Fol, recently redundant longswordsman, determined cynic, and downtrodden wretch, was not having one of his better moments. His head hurt, his feet were soaked (leaky boots did nothing for morale), and it hadn't stopped bloody-well raining for three days—and worse—three nights.

He was wet through, his hands frozen and his nose running, and now Thunderhoof, his very expensive foreign warhorse, had chosen to start limping. It was all an act, of course. Thunder did this kind of thing when he'd had enough tromping about the countryside.

Corin wiped the snot from his nose and blinked through the rain. Fog and moor, moor and fog—he remembered why he'd left this place.

"It isn't my fault you were born in the south," Corin told his horse. Thunderhoof had been a generous gift from his former employer, Silon of Raleen, back in the days when they were getting on. It seldom rained down there in Raleen, it being half desert, and Thunder, worthy beast though he was, had scant appreciation for this damp northern climate.

"Besides," continued Corin, "we've only a few miles to go. You can stew in a nice warm, dry stable, and I can get soused." Thunder didn't respond, nor did he pick up his sluggish pace.

A mile marker loomed out of the murk: *Finnehalle Seven Miles*. The words were barely visible.

"See, look you!" Corin, excited, patted the horse's soggy back. "We're almost there, boy." But if Thunder had been impressed by the milestone, he didn't show it, which wasn't that surprising considering he couldn't read.

A lane entrance yawned off to their right, just past a stubby clump of hedgerow. Above that, a battered sign dripped and creaked on a rusty pole: *Polin's Smithy One Mile*.

An arrow pointed down the track. Corin reined in as he took in the sign. Down in the wooded dip he could see smoke rising crooked from the smith's cottage and forge. Polin was a stout soul. He'd been a good friend to Corin, back then.

I suppose we could always . . .

Moments passed. Rider sat thinking whilst horse looked mournful and did something peculiar with his right foreleg.

"Oh, sod it then. Have it your way." Corin dismounted onto the lane with a squishy thud and then hauled hard at Thunder's reins, urging the snorting beast to follow him down the side track and on toward the smithy. The horse gave him that superior look—an expression not dissimilar to the one Silon used to visit upon him when he'd just said something obtuse (which happened now and then).

"Horse, I hope for your sake Polin's ale barrel is full," complained Corin. He'd had his heart set on spending a night or two in the Last Ship, the inn he'd frequented a lot—back then. Still, Polin used to keep a decent keg and it would be good to catch up. It had been fourteen years after all, and Finnehalle would still be there in the morning.

Halfway down the lane, the rain stopped and a wan sun pierced the grey. Corin smiled as sunlight danced and sparkled in the puddles ahead. This was more like it. But the grin fled from his face when a woman's shriek of rage sent rooks croaking skyward.

What's this?

Corin reached the outer fence to the smithy's lands, tied Thunder's reins to a stump, and then, hand reaching back across his shoulder, slid Clouter, his heavy longsword, free of its scabbard.

"Stay here!" Corin hissed at the horse. Thunder blinked at him but obliged with indifference. Corin left him and approached the gate. He turned the latch and carefully stole inside the stockade, his wet clothes and cold feet forgotten.

Trouble. It was something Corin an Fol understood, it having been his constant companion for over fourteen years.

The woman screamed again—more anger than terror betrayed by her tone. Corin cursed and broke into a run, Clouter gripped between calloused palms and his grey-blue eyes steely hard. It had been two long weeks since he'd last had a scrap. Corin was more than ready.

***

Ulf laughed when the woman threatened him with her rusty knife. His twin, Starki, had already done for her husband, whilst the boy, Cale, had slipped inside the cottage to collect any spoils. That pimply bag of bones had his uses—sometimes.

They hadn't killed the smith yet, just brained him half senseless. The big fellow crouched spewing and moaning in the dirt just outside the stables. Ulf had forgotten him already, having eyes only for the blacksmith's wife.

She was comely, in a spitting, shrieking, red-haired, freckled kind of way. But it wouldn't have mattered if she were ugly. Ulf had never been the fussy kind.

He turned slightly at a noise to his left—Cale returning, his grubby fingers full of silver coin and his bright blue bug-eyes gawping at the scene. Ulf ignored him. Instead he goaded the girl with mock kisses and obscene hints.

Starki, lacking the finer qualities possessed by his twin, grabbed greedily for the girl. She stepped backwards, hissed, and flashed the tiny blade at his blood-shot eyes.

Starki laughed and winked at Ulf. "While you're trying to prick me with that I'm going to prick you with this." He cupped his groin with a hand and made a lewd thrusting gesture with his hips.

"Get that out and I'll slice it off!" The woman spat in his eye.

"Feisty mare, eh, Starki," observed Ulf. "Mayhap we should draw lots." Behind him the gawky Cale watched in fascinated silence.

"I'm having her first!" Starki grabbed again, but the woman knew what she was doing with her knife. She sliced hard, took a finger.

"Bitch!" Starki's meaty left fist hammered into her face, knocking her prone. He stood over her then, panting, swearing, and flicking the blood from his dripping right hand so that it splattered her linen gown.

She rolled over and tried to get up, but Ulf's studded boot thudded down onto her back, sending her sprawling again. Starki, his eyes lit with murderous rage, freed his dagger and crouched low over the woman.

He froze when the sharp kiss of steel pricked lightly at the nape of his neck.

"Play time's over, ugly," a voice said.

Starki rolled free of the stranger's blade, but only just. He looked up wild-eyed. Where had this bastard come from? A tall, nasty-looking bugger clad in dun-leather tunic over a rusty mail shirt. Lean-faced—a white scar crooked up from right brow to hairline—with shaggy brown hair and scary eyes of smoky blue-grey. In his hands he clutched a bloody great sword, perhaps five-and-a-half feet long.

But Starki was no craven. In a grunting blur he'd freed his axe and swung out hard and across, aiming to split this lanky impostor in two. To his right, his twin watched slack-jawed as Starki's broad swipe cut through air alone.

Clouter did better.

Ulf swore as his brother slunk to his knees, Starki's fingers trying in vain to staunch the great rift opened in his belly. He wept as his guts spilled free, shuddered for a miserable moment, and then lay prone.

Ulf had his sword out, a wickedly curved blade, half sax, half broadsword. He leveled it, roared, and waded in, but the steely-eyed stranger's longsword held him at bay.

Meanwhile, the boy, forgotten by everyone, sidled slowly toward the rear of the stable, believing it prudent to vacate the premises. Trouble was, the woman saw Cale out of the corner of her eye. Worse, she was blocking his escape route.

"Stay put, yer little shite," she said. Cale wasn't about to argue with a madwoman armed with rusty knife, however small. She stomped over, grabbed his wrist, and yanked hard. Cale yelped and the stolen coins spilled and sparkled to vanish in the dirt. "I've a rope just perfect for your scrawny neck," she told him. Cale gulped.

Ulf slipped a dagger into his left hand. He circled Corin, the two blades gleaming in the sunshine. Corin smiled at him. Ulf studied the stranger's nasty-looking blade. Barely, he kept a lid on his fury, hearing his twin's dying shudders behind him. Then the stranger's smoky eyes flicked across to where that idiot Cale was succumbing wimperingly to the smith's wife. He seemed half amused at the boy's antics. Ulf seized his moment, tossed his dagger hard and fast. Corin grinned, having expected that. His heavy blade sent the knife spinning away with a blaze of sparks.

But Ulf didn't waste any time. He shouldered into Corin with both hands on his curved blade, seeking to hack hard into his enemy's side. Instead, Corin's counterstroke clanged into the twin's blade, knocking him off balance.

Still grinning, Corin leaped at Ulf. Reversing Clouter, he rammed the wolf's-head pommel hard into Ulf's chin, breaking the big man's jaw and launching him backward. Ulf groaned once and then lay still.

Corin knelt and wiped Clouter clean on Ulf's woolly coat. He gave its steely length a critical eye before slinging the longsword back in its scabbard, hanging lateral across his back. Corin turned to the woman who had the spitting youth in a headlock.

"You get some rope, girl," he said, "and I'll hoist this fat bastard from that tree out there." He motioned toward Ulf's prone fur-clad lump and then pointed to the large ash shading the far end of the stockade.

"What about this streak of piss?" The woman yanked Cale's left earlobe and he squawked enthusiastically.

"We'll hang him too," replied Corin, grinning evilly. "By the ears," he added. "Over hot coals. Slowly." Corin winked at Cale, who for his part looked wan and sad.

"Aw . . . you wouldn't," the boy said as the woman left him to source the rope. Corin ignored him. Instead he went to the well across the yard, hoisted a bucket, and spilled the contents over his head.

"I'm hungry," he said to the boy then. Cale didn't reply. He was looking past Corin at someone's looming approach.

"I'm Tommo," said a gruff voice. The smith was big and fresh faced, though blood matted his sandy hair and rouged his stubbled cheeks. "We are in your debt, stranger," he said.

"Where is Polin?" Corin asked. He didn't like being called 'stranger.' The smithy was only seven miles from where he'd been born. Still, he didn't know these people, so why should they know him?

"Father died last winter," the girl answered, returning. She threw a heavy coil of rope on the ground and then stood with feet braced and arms crossed to study Corin.

"I know you." She smiled impishly, which made her look younger, perhaps twenty-five. "You're Corin an Fol," she said, and he nodded. "I used to quite fancy you back then, but you buggered off to foreign parts. I'm Kyssa. Remember me?"

Corin recalled a freckled twelve-year-old girl with wild red hair and a mischievous grin. He nodded. "Aye, I do so, yes." Corin was awkwardly aware of Tommo's lowering brow and somber expression. "I'm sorry to hear of your father's death. He was a good man, Kyssa."

She shrugged. "Everyone dies."

Half hour later, big Tommo helped Corin hoist the kicking, fully conscious Ulf skyward while Kyssa clapped and Cale soiled his pants, this day not going as he'd planned it.

"Well," said Corin, awarding the boy a steely stare. "What have you got to say for yourself, shithead?"

"I've done nothing! I don't deserve . . . that." Cale's bulging eyes glanced up to where Ulf quivered and kicked.

"We will see." Corin turned and winked at Tommo, but the smith didn't look the forgiving type.

"He's a thief," said Tommo. "Thieves hang, it's the law."

"Bugger the law," said Corin. "How old are you, boy?" Corin asked Cale.

"Almost fourteen winters," Cale replied, and sensing he might have a chance, stuck his chin out. "What's it to you?" Cale was in awe of this stranger and his massive sword but determined not to show it. This bastard had easily bested the two toughest men he had ever known. They might not have been house trained, but they had been his only companions.

Cale had wanted to do for them both when they were taunting the woman, but that was different. Cale didn't like that sort of thing, having his own sense of honor. Not that the wench didn't deserve it, the way she'd treated him.

Master Cale had his pride and wasn't about to forgive this weirdo stranger's executions of Ulf and Starki. For three profitable years, Cale had accompanied the brutal twins, learning much as they robbed and murdered their way across the wilderness of Kelthaine and Fol.

"Thirteen and three quarters to be exact," he answered eventually.

"Well, be grateful you're not yet fourteen. If you were, I'd slit you open like an overripe melon!" Corin held the boy's defiant gaze for a moment longer, then turned away to spit on Starki's mangled, fly-clustered corpse.

Slowly his anger faded, replaced by fatigue and sorrow. Corin remembered what had occurred on his own fourteenth birthday. The memory of that day would never fade; it was branded into his skull like the sword scar on his forehead. That had been the day of the raid on Finnehalle by Crenise pirates, culminating with the death of his father and brothers, and later the loss of his mother and sister too.

"Where are you from?" Corin glared at the boy.

"It don't matter where he's from," Tommo cut in, but Corin motioned him to silence. Beside her husband, Kyssa fingered her knife fondly and smiled at Cale. He pretended not to notice.

"Kelthara," Cale muttered then, staring sulkily at the field outside. His quick mind was calculating a way out of this unpleasant situation. He heard footsteps, and turning back he paled—it was apparent Tommo's patience had finally dissolved. The ominous hulk of the blacksmith loomed over him, massive hands bunching in fury.

"Leave him be." Corin's voice halted the big man's fist. Tommo turned, glowering at the longswordsman.

"Why?"

Corin shrugged. "There's been enough retribution today," he said. Kyssa shook her head. She looked disappointed.

Ignored for the minute, Cale seized his chance. With practiced ease he scooped from the dirt the coins he'd stolen. "I'll be taking my leave now, masters," the boy announced as he spun on his heels and fled the yard. "I don't suppose we'll meet again." As Tommo and Corin gave chase, Cale turned and hurled a dagger he'd kept stowed up his left sleeve. Tommo dived and Corin ducked as the blade whooshed over their heads. Corin was angry again. His fast legs soon carried him ahead of the laboring smith, his longsword swinging behind him as he vaulted the wall with athletic ease.

To no avail. Cale was a city lad, well used to being pursued by vengeful adults down the labyrinthine lanes of old Kelthara town. He'd soon vanished into the thorny knot of woodland enclosing the western end of Polin's Smithy.

Corin yelled out to him. "If I come across you again it will go bad for you boy! Remember the name Corin an Fol!"

His only answer was the wind in the trees.

Shaking his head in disgust, Corin returned to the stockade. Before he reached the gate, the strange sound of laughter made him stop and glance up at a nearby oak. There, scarce ten feet away, beautifully balanced on the stout limb of a level branch, sat a girl. Her face was pale perfection dominated by two huge tawny eyes. These watched him with mocking humor. There was something decidedly odd about this child. Corin felt uneasy under her gaze.

"You did well today," she giggled, her bare legs swinging high above his head. It seemed odd how the chilly breeze didn't bother her, despite her only garment being a pale blue dress hemmed well above her knees and elbows. Long golden braids cascaded down her back, and she wore shoes of softest red leather. The girl grinned down at Corin with impish delight.

"We are watching you with interest," the strange girl said. Then her lips twisted into a cat's feral grin. Suddenly she looked cruel, spiteful. "Be careful in the woods. *He* is stalking you."

"Who are you, child?" Corin managed before Tommo's heavy footsteps distracted him. He squinted through the afternoon sun to see the blacksmith approach.

"What are you looking at?" Tommo enquired. He awarded the tree a quizzical glance. Corin pointed above, then swore under his breath. The branch was bare.

"I . . . nothing," Corin struggled, doubting his senses. "The boy's gone," he said, stating the obvious just to change the subject. Corin wondered whether those field mushrooms he'd found yesterday were having an unwholesome effect on him. It wasn't a good sign seeing strange girls in trees.

Tommo shrugged. "I wouldn't have hung him," he said eventually, "just wanted to scare the little shite." Corin nodded. "Why not stay and sup some ale with us," Tommo offered then. "Kyssa's got a three-day stew on the stove—turnips, coney, broth and all."

"I thank you, but no," responded Corin. He'd changed his mind after the fight. He desired solitude: time to think on his own. "I wish to watch the sun set on the ocean this very evening, take my leave in the taverns of Finnehalle. It's seven miles away if I read that last marker correctly, though my memory makes the distance shorter." Corin had a sudden notion. "There is a service you can do for me, Tommo, if you will," Corin added.

"Name it."

"My horse, Thunderhoof, is lame, or pretending to be. He's covered many leagues over the last week and isn't happy, doesn't like the wet. Could you stable him and see to his needs? He's a good old boy but gets a bit stiff sometimes."

"Gladly," responded Tommo, insisting once more Corin stay for some respite at least. "Finnehalle *is* only seven miles away, yes, and I've other steeds to lend you. Those rogues left shaggy mounts tied outside the north gate. They'll not be using them again, nor do I expect that young cutpurse will return to reclaim his pony."

Corin could not be persuaded. He made his excuses to the blacksmith and his wife, who joined them, insisting he wanted to walk the last few miles. It would clear his head, Corin told them. Tommo was nonplussed, but Kyssa gazed at him askance.

"You are a strange one, Corin." She yielded a shrug. Corin, feeling awkward, didn't respond. Instead he went to get the horse.

They waited in silence, both worn out by this troublesome day. Eventually Corin returned with Thunderhoof clomping noisily behind him. Then, just a few minutes later, the longswordsman bade farewell to the blacksmith, his wife, and Thunder. Heart heavy, Corin took his leave from Polin's smithy. He vowed to return after a few days' hard drinking. Thunderhoof didn't notice Corin's departure. He was already at his oats. Corin left lane and smithy behind. Time to go home. He wondered if Holly was still in town. He'd liked Holly—back then.

mybook.to/CrownUK | viewbook.at/Myths

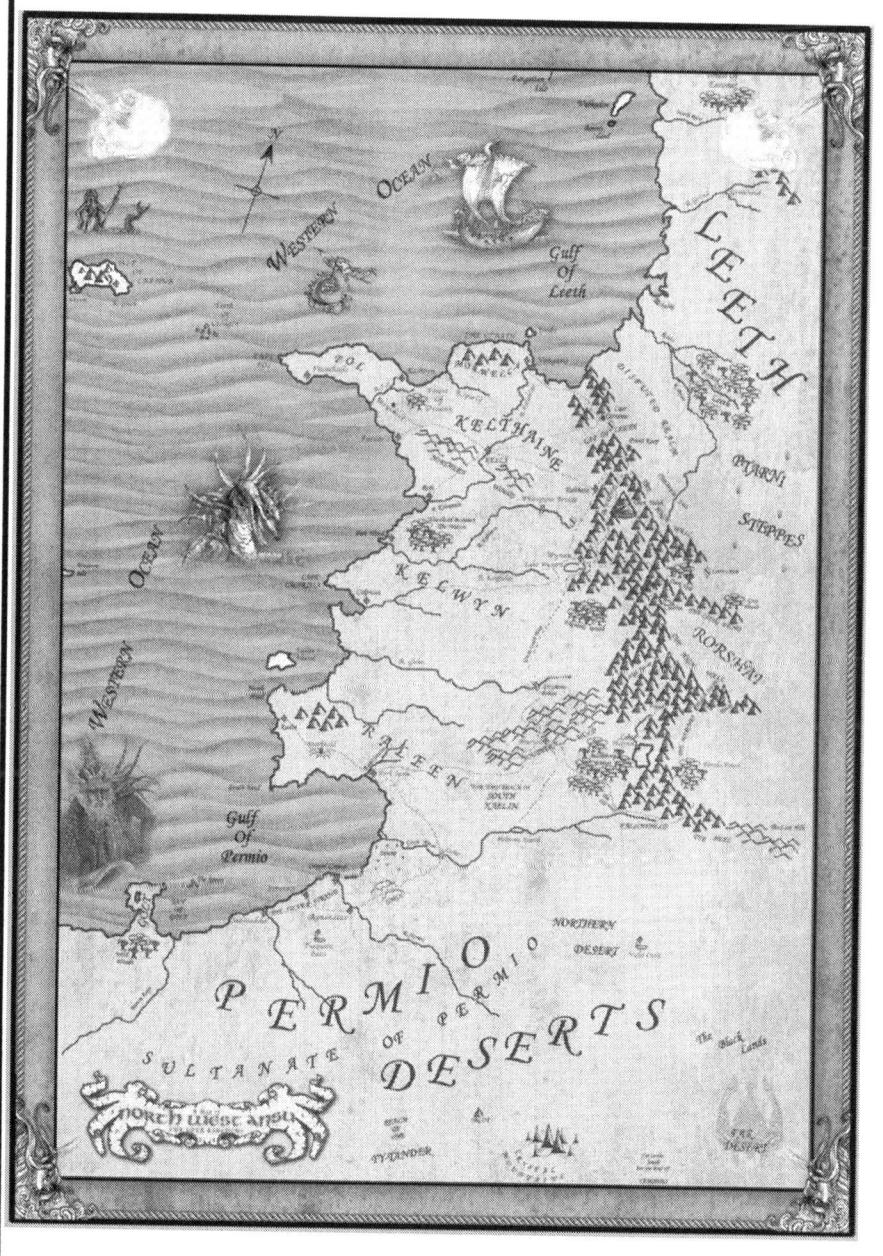

A Map of Western Ansu showing the
Four Kingdoms and Permian Desert

Made in the USA
Las Vegas, NV
05 February 2022